# SIX BULLETS

## MARK COLT

# ACKNOWLEDGMENTS

This book is dedicated to the memory of Jerry Harden, Deputy Sheriff of Marshall County, Tennessee. You always knew how to make me smile.

A special thank you to my family and friends for all of their support and encouragement over these past five years.

# 1

BEN STEVENS SLOWLY began to regain consciousness. He tried to open his eyes, but the left eye was swollen shut. He looked around the room with his right eye and noticed that his two captors had disappeared and left him for dead or so they believed.

*What should I do?* Ben thought to himself as he tried to sit up on the dirty bloodstained floor. He found his hands bound with barbed wire behind his back and he felt as if he had been struck by an eighteen-wheeler. A solitary light dangled from the ceiling. Moths danced around it, playing with the light, tempting the light to burn their delicate wings. He heard music coming from the next room, low and muffled, full of bass. It sounded like that psychedelic rock song that went on forever and ever. The shiplap walls were stained with blood. Was it his blood? He couldn't remember. The air was musty and heavy in the room while the odor of stale cigarettes and cheap perfume hung in the air like an invisible cloud. He groaned under his breath. Beneath his knees, his legs had deep gashes and he understood why as he glanced at the broken beer bottle on the floor. He sat there in his own blood and sweat for what seemed like an eternity before he realized he had time to escape.

Ben struggled to get on his feet. Every move he made was like sticking his finger in a live socket. He thought his ribs must be broken. He felt the barbed wire cutting into his wrists, tearing his flesh, warm blood dripping free from his body. He shivered as he glanced around the dank room that kept him prisoner and saw a desk to one side, a bed behind him and an old broken chair that lay abandoned as if it had forgotten where it needed to be. A fan sitting on the desk blew air on his face. He shivered again. The fan made a constant low humming noise. He looked at the bed anew. It was covered with a bloodstained sheet. Something was hiding under the sheet, making a basketball-sized lump. Then his eyes jumped to another lump in the shape of a cylinder. He stared at the lumps on the bed for a minute and remembered there had been a second man who had been captured. Ben tried to recall more, but couldn't. All he wanted to do was get out of there. He scrambled to the door, pressed his back against it and twisted the doorknob. It was sticky but unlocked. Ben pushed his way through only to find himself in a larger room. He looked around and saw no one. A ceiling fan sliced through the air, the spinning blades casting shadows around him. The fireplace crackled in the corner. Directly in front of him, he saw a desk under the window with a radio still playing that song on a low volume setting. The front door was next to the window.

Ben believed his captors would return soon given how everything was left running. He looked out the window. It was raining heavily. His time was running out. He stumbled through the room to the front door, turned his back and twisted the doorknob in the same manner as before. The door opened and Ben lost his balance as his bruised and bloodied legs buckled. He fell backwards onto the cabin front porch. He screamed silently in pain. The barbed wire had cut deeper into his wrists and he bled profusely on the wood planks. Ben mustered all his strength and stammered almost drunkenly as he rose once again to his feet.

He quickly looked around and staggered towards the tree line. Through the forest Ben ran and ran, but he was losing blood fast. The rain drenched his tattered clothes. He tripped on a rock and fell hard on his front. He cried out in agony. He stopped to listen. His heart was beating faster and faster. He listened again. He was sure he heard the sound of cars driving on wet asphalt. He realized the road was nearby. If he could only reach it. With difficulty, Ben rose to his feet one final time. He was covered in mud. The barbed wire continued to gnaw at his wrists as he tried to stand straight. Ben reeled forward, focusing on what he thought was the road ahead of him. He ripped his bloodstained white shirt on a tree branch, but kept going until he finally emerged from the brush. His head began to spin wildly. Suddenly, a flash of light seared his retinas. His body hit the ground, his face confronted the dark sky and he lost consciousness one last time near the roadside.

**2**

It was Friday evening at the Miller Hill Mine where Dylan Sanders worked. Soon, he and his friends would gather at the Rusty Mule, something Dylan always looked forward to.

He stood next to his '69 Camaro and attempted to light a cigarette in the rain with no luck. He opened the car door, sat down and put his foot on the gas. Spinning his tires in the mud, he sprayed muck all over the side of the shack. Hearing the mud splattering on the wall, his boss, Doug Ramsey, jumped out of his chair, almost tearing the rickety old door off its hinges, and yelled as loud as he could: "DYLAN! You jackass! Get back here!" Dylan snickered to himself as he took off like a bolt, leaving Doug stomping mad in the Tennessee mud.

Dylan was off to pick up his friend, Scott Rogers, who worked at the River View Mine. The two young men had an enduring friendship from childhood. Dylan had been Scott's commanding officer in Vietnam and Scott looked up to Dylan like an older brother. The two friends were glad to be alive and home from the war after serving two tours of duty.

Dylan arrived at Scott's place and waited in the car. Scott came out of his parents' home and ran across the front yard in his cowboy boots.

"Dang boy, you're wetter than ol' Charlie's rusty mule," Dylan joked as Scott climbed into the Camaro.

"Let's go before the girls kill us for bein' late!"

Dylan put the car in gear and tore off into the night, with sounds of hard rock music roaring over the radio.

Dylan and Scott were five miles from the bar. The rain danced with the wipers on the windshield of Dylan's Camaro. The windows began to fog. Dylan turned the ventilation on full, while Scott rolled down the passenger window a crack. The air whisked into the vehicle and began to clear away the fog. It was hard enough to see anything that night. The sky was as black as the asphalt. The car lights were as dim as two candles in a graveyard. Dylan made a turn onto Coleman Road, when he and Scott, both saw it. The wind was picking up something, tossing it about, back and forth, something white along the roadside.

"Did you see that? Turn around. Let's go back," Scott shouted at Dylan over the music on the radio.

Dylan looked at his watch. "Dang, we're already late, man. Oh, what the heck." He pulled onto the shoulder of the road, stopped, flung the gear in reverse and backed up.

"Grab the flashlight," Scott exclaimed over the music.

Dylan reached across into the glove compartment and seized the flashlight. The two friends exited the vehicle and stepped into the driving rain.

"What do you think that was, Scotty?"

"I'm not sure. This storm is making it darker than usual."

"Well, maybe we'll have a good story for the girls, huh!" Dylan said jokingly.

They approached the spot and quickly realized there was a body lying on its side in the mud. The white cloth they had seen was a torn shirt now covering the face of the body. Dylan glanced worryingly at Scott and bent down. He peeled the shirt back and shown the flashlight on the face. "It's Ben Stevens from Earl Hopper Mine. He's been beaten pretty bad and his hands are bound with barbed wire. It's hard to make out anything else with all this water and muck around him," Dylan said.

"Ah shit, what the heck happened to him?" Scott asked in a sad tone.

"Who knows? Come on, let's get to the bar and call the sheriff."

The two looked down at the body one last time. They walked back to the car and drove off heading in the direction of the Rusty Mule.

Dylan pulled into the bar parking lot, but the lot was full of vehicles. People had parked everywhere, but Dylan managed to find a parking space in back.

Dylan and Scott got out of the car and raced to the entrance of the bar. The girls saw their boyfriends through the windows and scampered towards the doors to greet them.

"What's wrong darlin'?" Sue-Ellen asked as she gazed into Dylan's eyes.

"Ah, I'm sorry, honey. We came across somethin' on our way here and I need to call the sheriff right away," Dylan replied.

Sara noticed the same concern in Scott's eyes.

The four friends walked over to the pay phones. Dylan placed a dime into the slot and dialed the sheriff's office.

The Reeves County police station stood in the downtown square of Lancaster Falls, on the ground floor of a hundred-year-old red brick building. The station had several small offices, one for each of the deputies and a big office for the sheriff. There were three large jail cells in back and a pay phone hung on the far wall. A staircase behind the wall led to the basement where case files and evidence were stored. The floors were made of old, worn hardwood and two big ceiling fans spun the air around the main room. There was a coat rack near the front entrance and the windows were shielded with Venetian blinds. When you came inside, you were greeted by Beth McCormick at her front desk. Everyone affectionately referred to her as the gatekeeper because she never let anyone see the sheriff.

Sheriff Robert Yates opened his desk drawer and took out a lockbox of mementos. He opened it and removed a black and white photo of himself and his lifelong friend, Sean Finley, standing next to a F-86 Saber jet plane. Both Yates and Finley had served with the United States Air Force during the Korean war. The picture was a reminder of a war that everyone had forgotten but him. Now at forty-eight years of age and separated from his wife, Yates pondered the future and what it had in store for him. He struck a match and lit a cigar. He ran his fingers through his iron-grey hair and stared at the photo. A few more grizzled lines on his face, and still carrying the moustache after all those years. A knock came at the office door. "Come in," he said in a rich baritone voice.

Beth and Deputy Bonnie James walked into the sheriff's office. "Robert, I have one of the mine workers on the phone. His name is Dylan Sanders. He says he found a body," Beth stated.

Standing at six feet, muscular and lean, Yates rose from his chair and grabbed the phone receiver: "Sheriff Yates speaking."

"Sheriff, sir, Dylan Sanders here. Scott Rogers and I were driving on Coleman Road and found a body in the ditch."

"Did you recognize who it was?"

"Yes, sir, it was Ben Stevens, the manager at Earl Hopper Mine."

"Where exactly on Coleman Road did you find him?"

"His body was lying in the ditch, heading west, around five minutes before reaching town. His hands were bound with barbed wire and it looked like he had been beaten pretty bad, but it was hard to tell in the rain," Dylan replied in a sad tone.

Sheriff Yates looked at Bonnie and Beth standing at the door. "Okay, we're leaving now," he said and placed the phone receiver down. "Grab your jacket, Bonnie. We've got a body out on Coleman Road. And Beth, tell Peter to meet us there."

"I'll call him at home," Beth said as she turned around and headed back to her desk.

Sheriff Yates and Bonnie arrived at the crime scene. Yates pulled onto the shoulder of the road. Bonnie got out of the sheriff's car first with police tape in hand and proceeded to tape off the area. Yates took a pull on his cigar, grabbed his camera, headed over to the body and began documenting the crime scene. Deputy Peter Thomas pulled up behind the sheriff's car. He exited his vehicle and walked towards Yates. Peter sipped a coffee as he stood beside Yates in the rain and watched him examine the body. "Hey, I know him. That's

Ben Stevens. He works for my pa at one of the mines. I think he's a low-level manager or something, over at Earl Hopper Mine," Peter said.

Yates looked up at Peter and said: "Radio Beth and tell her to get ahold of the medical examiner."

"Yes, sir." Peter returned to his car.

Yates clicked one last photo and noticed a piece of glass next to the body as the camera flashed a beam of light. He removed a plastic bag from his coat pocket and grabbed the mud-covered glass shard.

"What's that?" Bonnie asked.

"Piece of glass," Yates replied as he looked at the glass shard inside the bag. "I'm done here for now. We should cover the body while we wait."

Yates and Bonnie retrieved a plastic cover from the sheriff's cruiser and went back to the body to cover it.

"Not much more we can do with this bad storm tonight. We'll come back first thing in the morning and get a better look at the area in the light," Yates said.

"Hopefully, that storm will've passed," Bonnie said.

Yates agreed.

The two officers walked back to the squad car, met Peter and the three climbed into the sheriff's cruiser to get out of the rain while they waited for the medical examiner.

# 3

AROUND SINCE THE turn of the century, the Rusty Mule was the busiest and oldest bar in town. It was the place where all the mine workers went to unwind, especially on the weekends. Charlie Rhodes, when he moved to Lancaster Falls from Florida, bought the place from the previous owner. It was a western themed bar, large enough to accommodate one hundred people or more. It had a dancing area, a stage for live entertainment, a bucking bronco ride that the patrons loved to use when they were drunk, and several pool tables tucked away in a corner. The bar itself measured a good length from end to end, was made of oakwood and ornamented with brass footrails and red bar stools secured to the floor. The place had a few large ceiling fans that kept the air flowing, seeing how most people liked to smoke. Charlie even had two longhorn cattle skulls mounted on the walls. The front entrance doors were made of oakwood and were adorned with brass latches. There were glass windows all around covered with Venetian blinds and a red neon open sign hung in one of the front windows. A large mule statue was on top of the roof, if you can believe it. It's how the place got its name. The mule looked like a bucking bronco, only smaller, and was rusted from years of neglect. The joke around town was what came first, the rusted-out mule statue or the bar. Charlie was proud of the place and felt at home with the western theme. He had a good chef and staff to prepare and serve the food and drinks. It was the perfect place to unwind.

All the regulars were there that night. From the garage down the road, Jack Thicket was there every night and always left drunk. Bryan Long and Ted Tillman from the filing station were there too. They were good friends and ran the gas station together. Bryan was the brains while Ted was the brawn. The rest were all locals from around the area or employees of the mining company wanting to let off steam on that stormy night.

Sue-Ellen and Sara comforted their boyfriends as they all drank beer together.

"One last beer, and then you're going home with me Scotty. I'll help you to relax," Sara squealed. Scott sat there half drunk and confused. He gulped down the remaining beer in his mug while Sara managed to coax him with a kiss. "We can leave the last pitcher of beer for Dylan and Sue-Ellen. I'll drive you home," she said. Scott and Sara got up from their seats, said their goodbyes and left holding hands.

Dylan and Sue-Ellen finished off the pitcher of beer, and chatted into the night. Sue-Ellen grabbed her empty glass, looked at Dylan through the bottom and asked: "Do you think the sheriff will find out anything about what happened to Ben, honey?"

Dylan polished off the beer, lit a cigarette and replied: "I hope so. I just can't figure out who would want to kill

Ben. He always kept to himself and never bugged a tick on a hound dog."

Sue-Ellen set her empty glass down on the table and let out a sigh, "I know, but no more frowns tonight. Let's enjoy the rest of the evening together."

Most of the patrons had already gone home as the night lingered on and there were only a few stragglers left behind. Dylan and Sue-Ellen rose from their seats, approached the bar, sat down on the bar stools a few seats up from Jack Thicket and ordered two more drinks. "Hey Charlie, give me and my sweetie pie a couple of Tequila Sunrises'!" Dylan hollered.

"You got it!" Charlie bellowed out.

With a whiskey glass in one hand and a cigarette dangling in the other, Jack rose from his bar stool and sat down beside the couple. He took a drag from his cigarette and asked: "How y'all doin' tonight?"

"Good," Dylan replied.

Sue-Ellen lit a cigarette of her own.

"It's not like you to smoke Miss Sue-Ellen," Jack said.

"Well, it's been one of those nights," Sue-Ellen replied in a sad tone.

"Wanna tell me about it?" Jack asked curiously.

"Ben Stevens is dead. Scotty and I found his body badly beaten in a ditch," Dylan replied.

Jack, mostly drunk, nearly fell off his bar stool. "That's bullshit! Y'all are pullin' ol' Jack's leg?!"

"I wish I was," Dylan said.

Jack polished off his whiskey, rose to his feet and almost tipped over, but grabbed the bar counter in time.

"Dang it, Jack, stop actin' like a horse's arse!" Sue-Ellen said in an irritated voice.

Jack rose from his bar stool once more, lost his balance yet again, grabbed Dylan's arm this time, and almost pulled him off his bar stool in the process, but it did not help as Jack fell to the floor on his backside. In the commotion, Dylan accidently dropped his drink and cigarette on Jack. "Fire! Fire! I'm on fire, dang it!" Jack yelled in a drunken panic as he flopped on the floor like a fish out of water. Charlie came over and threw his bar apron on top of Jack and pretended to smother a fire that wasn't really there.

"Jack, you're so drunk, you couldn't hit the floor with your hat!" Sue-Ellen commented.

The remaining patrons scrambled to see what was going on. An old bearded man approached Jack and nudged him: "He's not dead, is he?"

Sue-Ellen looked at the old man and blinked twice in disbelief at what he said. "Uh, no. He's passed out!"

Dylan looked at Charlie. "So, who's gonna take the big lug home this time?"

Charlie did not know whether to laugh or cry. "I've got a small cot in the stockroom. I can put him there for the night, and he can stay 'til morning. Not much else we can do with him."

The three picked Jack up off the floor and carried him to the stockroom. Jack kept talking nonsense the entire way. "You guys are so ugly," Jack slurred out loud, "but Charlie, you're uglier than a sack full of turds… and Sue… Suuuuee-Ellen… you're just a lil'…"

Sue-Ellen did not want to hear what was about to come out of Jack's mouth and slugged him to shut him up. Dylan looked at her. "What? Someone had to shut his piehole," she said as Dylan and Charlie dumped Jack on the cot, turned off the lights and shut the stockroom door. They walked back into the main bar area, and the couple said their farewells to Charlie. Sue-Ellen and Dylan headed for the entrance doors with the last remaining patrons and the couple left in Dylan's Camaro.

Charlie walked back into the kitchen and observed the staff as they gathered their belongings and left out the backdoor. Charlie locked the door and went to the cash register to add up the receipts for the night. He brought the money to his office and put the cash in the safe hidden behind a painting of a horse. He put the receipts in a daily report folder and placed it in his cabinet. Then he turned off the lights and locked the office door. He checked on Jack one last time and made sure the stockroom door was locked. Charlie did not want Jack getting out and wandering about the tavern in the middle of the night. Charlie left the bar through the front entrance doors like he always did, turning off the neon sign on his way out.

Early in the morning, after a few hours had passed and before dawn broke, Jack slowly rose from his cot. He slipped off his boots and snuck over to the light switch next to the door in his socked feet. He turned on the light and tugged at the door, but it was locked. "Shit, I guess Charlie's gonna make this tough on me," Jack muttered to himself. He searched the stockroom to see what he could use to open the door. He went over to a desk near the wall and found a sturdy paperclip, and then he went to the shelf units and grabbed a small tension wrench and a flashlight. He returned to the locked door with his tools and began picking the lock. After a few attempts, he succeeded. He put his tools in his pocket, opened the door a crack and peered into the hall. All the lights were off inside the bar and he saw the place was closed for the night. He turned off the stockroom light and slipped out into the hallway. He went straight to Charlie's office and yanked at the office door, but it too was locked. "Going to be one of those nights, huh Charlie," Jack said under his breath. He took the tools out of his pocket, held the flashlight in his teeth and picked his way into Charlie's office.

Jack knew a thing or two about Charlie, one of which was that Charlie was a creature of habit. Jack heard that Charlie kept cash in a safe in his office at all times and rumor had it that there was a lot of money. Jack also knew that Charlie did his banking once a week like clockwork, keeping all the receipts and cash on hand until that time, but bar receipts wasn't what Jack was looking for. He was after something else.

Jack looked at the light switch on the wall and thought about turning the lights on, but decided against it when he noticed a window at the far end of the room. "If I were a safe, where would I be?" he said to himself. He approached a cabinet against the wall, next to a couch on the right side of the office. He opened the cabinet, shone the flashlight and pawed through all four shelves and found bar receipts, but nothing else of interest. Next, Jack approached the gun cabinet against the wall. He looked at it, felt around it and stepped away from it. "Dang it, Charlie!" he said. Next, he shone the flashlight on the floor and kicked back the rug half expecting to find a secret door, but again there was nothing. "Come on now boy, where'd y'all put the safe!" he cried out loud. He shone the flashlight at the walls looking around the room. He noticed a painting of a horse on the wall and approached it. He felt around it and found a latch under the frame of the canvas. "Bingo!" He pulled the latch, the painting swung open on one side like a door and there was the safe starring back at him. "Jackpot!" he said aloud and let out a whistle.

Jack inspected the safe and wondered how long it would take him to crack it open. He took a few steps back, turned his head around and looked out the office window. It was still dark as ink which meant he had plenty of time to deal with the combination lock. He returned to the safe, placed the flashlight down and patiently began to work. Jack was a man of many talents, one of which was being a locksmith a decade ago in middle Tennessee. Jack cracked his knuckles and fingers, stretched his neck and arms and began turning the lock wheel. After a few attempts and some patience success finally came to him. The door of the safe opened and he grabbed the flashlight to look inside. "Well, well, let's see what we've got here," Jack said to himself.

Jack saw quite a few stacks of cash, a Rolex watch, an old revolver, a few old documents and a map detailing the mines and rock quarries in the area. First, he grabbed the Rolex watch and let out a whistle. "Now, where'd you suppose Charlie got the cash for this lil' trinket?" Jack wondered aloud as he admired the watch, and even tried it on his wrist before placing it back in the safe. He took the stacks of bills next and began counting the money. "Ten thousand bucks. That's a lotta dough. I wonder," he said to himself as he set the cash back in the safe. Next, Jack grasped the old revolver and looked it over. "Smith & Wesson .45 Schofield," he said to himself as he spun the cylinder and placed it back where he found it. Lastly, Jack removed the documents and map out of curiosity, brought them over to the desk, sat down and began to examine the papers one by one. "What do we have here? Charlie, you ol' dog, you! You've been holdin' out on me," Jack said under his breath. The old documents detailed a bank robbery dating back to 1901 that Charlie's grandfather had been involved in. According to the document, the money had been buried in one of the mines outside of Lancaster Falls. Jack's eyes widened as he remembered Ben Stevens and wondered if his grizzly death had anything to do with the loot. Another document detailed how much money was stolen. Approximately one million dollars was hiding in a mine somewhere in the county. Jack leaned back in the chair and looked at the map of the area. Charlie had marked each mine with an x or a check mark. Jack assumed the check marks meant that those mines had been searched and nothing was found, and the x meant those mines hadn't been searched. Jack deduced that Charlie had not found anything as of yet, but also had to be working with someone else because there was no way Charlie could gain access to the mines on his own. Jack scribbled down as much information as he could and placed the documents and map back into the safe. Everything looked like it was in its original positions, or so he thought as he locked the safe, swung the painting back and closed the latch. He left the office, locking the door behind him and returned to the stockroom. He put the flashlight and tools back on the shelves, and lay down on the cot. He stared at the ceiling in the dark with a smile, mulling over in his head what he had found, and how he would get his hands on the score of a lifetime.

**4**

THE THREE OFFICERS arrived at the hospital on the outskirts of Lancaster Falls early in the morning. Built in 1965, the hospital was of mid-century modern architectural design and replaced the old clinic. The new hospital was large in comparison and was constructed to accommodate a growing community and county. Paul Langford, the medical examiner for Reeves County was smoking a cigarette and holding a clipboard in one hand when the sheriff and two deputies entered the room.

Yates walked over to the crystal ashtray on the counter near the sink while Bonnie and Peter approached the desk. "What were you able to find out for us?" Yates asked.

"Over here," Paul said.

The three officers followed the doctor to the center of the room where three autopsy tables stood. Two of the tables were empty. The body of Ben Stevens lay on the center table. The doctor pulled the cover back midway and began to summarize his findings. "Ben Stevens was strangled as you can see the bruising around his trachea, but that's not what killed him." Paul took a drag from his cigarette and continued: "Here, his midsection, you can see evidence of severe bruising on his ribs and stomach. If you look here, you can also see bruising around the eyes and a broken nose. The one interesting thing that I did find was this on his jaw." Paul grabbed a magnifying glass, "Look here, Sheriff. Tell me what you see."

Yates leaned over and looked through the magnifying glass at the bruise around the jaw. "It looks like an indentation in the skin," he said.

"Yes, I removed a few tiny pieces of red crystal from his jaw and examined them. It had me stumped at first, but I examined the indentation again and arrived at the conclusion that it came from a shattered ring when the assailant struck Ben," Paul said.

"You'd have to hit someone pretty hard to shatter part of your ring," Yates said.

"Yes, I'd agree with that," Paul said. "And did you notice the shape it made?"

Yates looked again. "It looks like a partial imprint of a skull."

"Yes, that's what I saw too," Paul said.

Yates handed the magnifying glass to Bonnie. Bonnie bent down and peered through the lens. "That's crazy. I've never seen anything like that before," she said as she handed the magnifying glass to Peter.

Peter looked and handed the lens back to Paul. "Now, we just have to find a guy with a shattered red crystal skull ring," Peter said.

"It won't be that easy," Yates remarked.

"It never is," Paul said.

Paul placed the magnifying glass in his pocket and continued with the analysis. "On Ben's wrists, you can see where they were bound with barbed wire. He was severely beaten and somehow managed to escape only to bleed out from the deep cuts the barbed wire made in his wrists. He died where you found him somewhere between nine and ten p.m. last night."

"That jives with when the phone call came in," Yates said.

"I'd hazard to guess he was mixed up in something bigger than he could handle," Paul said.

"The assailant must've left Ben alone thinking he was unconscious, dead or dying from the beating and the barbed wire around his wrists would have been the insurance policy," Yates said.

"But the killer underestimated Ben's will," Paul said. "And when the killer left, Ben made his escape. Yes, I'd agree with that. Poor fellow, he probably didn't even realize he was bleeding from the barbed wire around his wrists until it was too late."

"What about the piece of glass I found in the mud next to his body?" Yates asked.

"I'm glad you brought that up," Paul said.

The doctor lifted the sheet covering Ben's legs and pointed at the lacerations. "I found tiny fragments of glass still embedded in Ben's legs that match that one piece you found. You can tell by the specific color of brown glass that it was probably a beer bottle."

"Between the barbed wire on his wrists, the lacerations on his legs and the beating he took, it's a wonder Ben managed to escape and get as far as he did," Yates said.

"There is one final thing, Sheriff. It may be nothing, but

tell me what you see," the doctor said as he picked up Ben's tattered white shirt and pointed to a spot around the collar. The three officers looked at the shirt.

"Is it blood?" Peter asked.

Yates crossed his arms. "No, it's not blood. So, what is it?" he asked.

"One of the nurses who came in earlier to bring me some paperwork recognized it right away. It's called Scarlett Cherry Red lipstick. She told me it's all the rage with the youth," Paul replied.

"Lipstick?" Yates asked curiously.

"Yes, here Bonnie, take a look," Paul said.

"That's Scarlett Cherry Red alright. I have a tube myself," Bonnie said.

"So, you're looking for a male assailant with a shattered red crystal skull ring and a mysterious female who wears Scarlett Cherry Red lipstick."

"Maybe, it's a guy in drag?" Bonnie said. "You know, like those two actors in that movie *Some Like It Hot.*"

Yates started coughing on his cigar smoke.

Paul patted Yates on the back. "Marylin Monroe. Oh, I'm a fan of all of her movies!"

"Swell," Yates said. "Peter, did Ben have a girlfriend or was he seeing anyone?"

"He didn't have a girlfriend and wasn't seeing anyone that I know of, unless he recently started seeing someone," Peter said.

"Well, that's pretty much all I can tell you for now, Sheriff," Paul said as he placed the shirt down on the table.

"Thank you, Paul. Call the office if you have anything else," Yates said.

The three officers exited the room and headed down the hallway. They walked back outside to their cars and left for the crime scene on Coleman Road.

# 5

SHERIFF YATES TOOK a camera from the trunk of the squad car, put on his gloves and walked past the yellow police tape to the ditch where the body had been found. He knelt down and began to examine the area, taking pictures of the surroundings. He noticed the trampled brush leading to the tree line and saw broken branches where Ben had possibly come through. It appeared as though the victim had come to the road, collapsed and died just as the medical examiner had speculated. Yates peered into the forest and saw more broken branches. "Over here Peter," Yates called out.

Peter approached. "You called, sir?"

"I want you to look around here for anything out of the ordinary, while Bonnie and I take a hike to see where these tracks lead."

"Yes sir," Peter replied.

Bonnie approached Yates and looked at him, then at the bushes and trees, then back to Yates again. "I'm not goin' in there with all those bugs skitterin' around!"

Yates smiled, grabbed Bonnie by her coat and took her

away with him into the bush. They walked off together following the trail of broken branches and crushed weeds.

Yates and Bonnie kept following the path further into the trees when they heard a branch snap behind them. The two officers crouched down and took out their handguns. More cracks were heard, but they sounded as if they were heading away. Yates looked around and spotted a piece of white cloth on a broken tree limb. He pointed the cloth out to Bonnie and the two officers quietly moved towards it. An animal suddenly jumped out from behind a tree near the cloth and startled the officers for a brief moment before scurrying away. The officers both let out a sigh. Yates took a plastic bag from his pocket and grabbed the torn cloth from the tree limb. "Piece of Ben's shirt?"

"Fits the bill," Bonnie said.

The officers commenced there hike again, carefully making their way through the trees until they reached a clearing with an old abandoned cabin in the center. They stopped and crouched down in the brush.

"Wonder if anyone's home?" Bonnie said

Yates slowly stood up straight, looked around, and motioned to Bonnie to follow him. They dashed across the open clearing to the cabin and stood up against the front wall, near the entrance door.

"The door is open," Bonnie whispered.

"Check around back, while I look inside," Yates said quietly. He pushed the door open with his foot. The door slowly moved and made a long creaking sound. Yates peered inside, but saw that no one was there.

Bonnie circled the cabin and met Yates at the front door. "I didn't see anyone and the backdoor is locked," she said.

"No one appears to be inside either," Yates said.

Bonnie looked down and pointed to the bloodstains on the wood planks near the door. Yates bent down, snapped a few pictures and rose to his feet.

The two officers carefully walked into the cabin with their guns ready. They looked around, but there wasn't much there aside from a desk, radio, a few chairs, a stained floor, and a brick fireplace in the corner with a poker beside it and scorch marks around it. The place had an eerie, uneasy feel to it that sent shivers up Bonnie's spine. She saw the trail of blood drops on the floor that led from the front door to another room and glanced at Yates. Yates nodded his head. Bonnie slowly approached the room, opened the old creaky door and immediately noticed a smell coming from inside. She quickly turned around and motioned to Yates to come over. Yates approached and entered the room. He looked around and saw an old bed with a stained sheet over it and a few lumps under the sheet. There was garbage and what looked like bloodstains on the floor and a desk in the corner with a broken chair and a fan.

"Do you think this is where Ben was beaten?" Bonnie said as her eyes continued to scan the room.

"The trail of blood leading from this room to outside would indicate that," Yates said. "Who's on the bed?"

The two officers went over to the bed. Bonnie looked squeamishly at the bloodstained sheet and lumps. Yates reached over and pulled the sheet back. Underneath, they found a severed head and a partial arm. Bonnie covered her mouth and gasped, "Who is it?" Using the barrel of his handgun, Yates rolled the head over face up, and they both saw who it was. It was Foreman Raymond Moore from the Reeves County Mine.

"Go get Peter on the radio. Let him know what we found, but be careful. I'll keep looking around," Yates said.

Bonnie nodded, went into the main room and walked outside with her gun drawn, ready for anything that she might find. She took her walky-talky and held it to her mouth: "Peter, Peter, do you read me?" Static. Bonnie scanned the area and tried again. "Peter, Peter, where are you at?" More static, and finally, Peter's voice came through.

"I hear you, Bonnie. What's going on? Did you find anything?" Peter inquired.

"We found a cabin with body parts, about a five-minute hike straight ahead of where we went in. Grab a bag in the trunk of the squad car and bring it here."

"Body parts? Anyone we..." More static and then suddenly, a loud crack and the radio went silent. Peter had been assaulted from behind at the roadside by a mysterious person who had been watching him from the brush. Peter lay motionless on the ground. The stranger ran back across the road, hopped onto a dirt bike and drove away.

"Peter! Peter! Shit!" Bonnie yelled frantically into the radio. She ran back into the cabin and found Yates rifling through the desk drawer. "Robert! It's Peter. I think someone attacked him while we were talking!"

Yates grabbed the papers he found and stuffed them into his pocket. The two officers quickly exited the cabin and ran into the clearing and through the trees. The birds flew off into the sky, and the shrubs cracked under the weight of their boots as the officers continued their way back as fast as they could.

The officers found Peter lying on his stomach on the ground. Bonnie knelt beside him and turned him over. His eyes were closed, and he was unresponsive. She put her fingers on his neck to see if his heart was still pumping blood, and it was. She checked if he was breathing, and he was.

"Don't move him anymore. I'll radio for help," Yates said as he ran to the police cruiser. He opened the car door, took the radio in his hand and looked around before he talked, but saw no one. "Beth, Peter's been hurt. We need an ambulance."

"Oh my, I'll call right away! How is he?"

"Unconscious."

Yates put the radio back into the cruiser, walked over to Bonnie and Peter, and knelt down.

"If I catch who did this to our Peter," Bonnie began.

"I know, I know. I feel the same way," Yates replied. He rose to his feet. "I'm going to look around while we wait."

Bonnie looked at Yates with concern in her eyes. "Don't go off too far."

Yates drew his handgun and started to look around while they waited for the ambulance. Suddenly, Peter began to stir and regained consciousness. He looked up at Bonnie and asked, "What happened? I remember talking to you."

"Easy, Peter. Robert called the ambulance. They should be here soon to take you to the hospital," Bonnie said.

It wasn't long before the ambulance arrived.

Yates walked back shaking his head. "I found evidence of dirt bike tracks across the road in the trees," he said. "Someone was watching and now they're gone. I don't like it."

The paramedics approached the officers. "How is he?" the first paramedic asked.

Peter looked up and tried to stand as Yates and Bonnie helped him to his feet. "He got hit on the head," Yates replied.

"Easy now, come with us. You'll be alright," the second paramedic said. "Sheriff, you two wanna follow along behind us?"

"Go with him, Bonnie. I'll stay and head back to the cabin in case our mystery stalker returns. Bring Paul back here when you're done with Peter," Yates said.

Bonnie nodded and joined Peter in the back of the ambulance. The ambulance sped off. Yates turned around and walked back into the brush, gun drawn, fully expecting more trouble.

Yates emerged from the tree line and saw the abandoned cabin once more. The cabin stood there silent, holding onto its secrets. He approached the front door, carefully opened it and stepped inside. He bent down, looked at what appeared to be fresh shoe marks on the floor and touched them. He wiped his fingers on his pants and rose to his feet. He smelled the faint odor of cigarettes lingering in the air as he turned his head and faced the next room. Yates entered the room where he had found the body parts and noticed right away that the sheet on the bed was no longer there and neither was the severed head and arm. "Shit," he said under his breath. He looked around the room and walked over to the bed. He moved the bed aside revealing the bloodstained floor underneath and a few broken beer bottles. Yates bent down, took a cloth and bag from his coat pocket and scooped up the glass pieces. He made out a partial brand name. He rose to his feet and approached the desk, shoved it out of the way and saw barbed wire and a pair of wire cutters on the floor.

He bent down and picked up the items when suddenly he heard a noise and then smelled smoke. Someone had lit two fires, one inside the cabin, and a second outside, next to the back door, near the propane tank. The arsonist circled to the front of the cabin where a second person was waiting, hiding amongst the trees with the body parts and bloody sheet in a garbage bag.

Yates exited the room and tried to reach the front door, when suddenly a shot rang out. Yates was now trapped between a shooter and a fire. He jumped back and looked around the room for something he could use as a distraction, but there was nothing and his time was running short. "Think, you've been in tighter spots then this," he said to himself. The room began to fill with smoke. Yates started coughing. He looked outside the window and saw two perpetrators hiding behind trees, but couldn't make out their faces. They were wearing ski masks over their heads. Another shot hit the side of the cabin. He was pinned down with only one way out. He entered the room where he had found the body parts originally and took the mattress from the bed and brought it with him into the main room. "I must be crazy," he said. He stepped back, built up a full head of steam and with the mattress protecting his body ran through the burning room and crashed through the flaming rear exit door. He looked back and saw how bad the fire had become. The propane tank was engulfed with flames. He quickly hit the dirt and ducked under the mattress for safety. Suddenly, the propane tank exploded and sent a ball of fire into the air. Pieces of burning wood and debris from the old cabin flew everywhere. Yates peered out from underneath the mattress, saw the fire raging and saw that the mattress he was hiding under had caught fire. He jumped out from under the mattress and drew his handgun. He went around the fire, saw the two perpetrators running away and pursued them.

Through the trees Yates ran, dodging bullets and jumping over rocks and tree limbs. Yates kept returning the shots and running until there was only silence. He stopped and listened. Suddenly, he heard the engine of a pickup truck and the motor of a dirt bike.

Out of the trees Yates flew and jumped over the ditch to the roadside. He saw the truck speeding away, and the dirt bike roaring into the trees on the other side of the road. He looked around, recognized where he was, and began to walk back down the road to where he had left the police cruiser.

Paul and Bonnie arrived in Paul's pickup truck as the sheriff was calling the fire department on his radio. "There he is," Paul said. Bonnie turned her head and waved at Yates.

Yates approached Bonnie and Paul.

"What happened? You look like you've been through a war zone," Paul said as he casually struck a match and lit a cigarette.

Yates shook his head. "I feel like it!" He began to tell them what had happened. "In the end, one got into a pickup truck and the other onto a dirt bike. One took off down the road and the other into the trees. One was driving a two-tone, blue and white Chevy K20 and the other an orange Honda dirt bike with a broken rear fender. Unfortunately, I didn't get either of the plate numbers."

"I guess you won't be needing my services then," Paul said. "I'll head back to the hospital. Look after him Bonnie." Paul got into his pickup truck and left.

The two officers waited for the fire department to arrive.

# 6

YATES AND BONNIE returned to the police station. Yates unlocked the door to his office and the two officers entered. Bonnie turned on the lights. Yates put his spent cigar in the crystal ashtray, removed the papers from his pockets and placed them on his desk. He sat down and examined the papers one by one. The first was a receipt for some tools bought at the Lancaster Falls hardware store ten months past. A second paper was very old, and most of the ink was faded. He tried to read what was written as Bonnie sat down in front of the sheriff's desk. The letter partially read:

> I know I wasn't much of a father to you growing up. But I'm trying my best to make it up to you. I'm sorry for how you grew up, always on the move. I miss your mother and love her with all my heart.
>
> This is the last heist we're doing. The heat is closing in on us and I don't know what I'm going to do about him. I don't trust him anymore.

Yates couldn't read any more of the letter and wondered

what it meant. The final paper he found was a map of Reeves County with the mines circled on it. Yates put the papers down, struck a match, lit a fresh cigar, took a deep pull and looked at Bonnie thoughtfully.

"What do these old papers have to do with the deaths of Stevens and Moore?" Bonnie asked.

Yates scratched his head, rose from his chair, walked to the window and opened it. He sat down on the leather couch under the window, put his boots up on the coffee table and said: "I think we got a real mystery on our hands. Ben Stevens is dead. Peter was knocked out by the roadside and then we find the head and limb of Foreman Raymond Moore from the Reeves County Mine, plus two unknown suspects and now an old letter, a receipt for tools bought at the hardware store ten months ago, which would indicate that what is going on has been going on since before I took office and lastly, a map of Reeves County with the mines circled on it."

Bonnie looked at the receipt. "Paid in cash. Doesn't say what was bought. Just the amount of twenty-four dollars and fifty cents," she said.

"That could be anything. The shopkeeper wouldn't even remember from ten months ago who it was sold to either. Let me look at that map again," Yates said as he rose from the couch, grabbed the map on his desk and looked at it. "What the heck is going on? That Chevy K20 and orange dirt bike with the busted fender I saw today need to be found. I know it's not much to go on."

"What about the smudge of lipstick on Ben's shirt?" Bonnie asked.

"Peter said earlier that Ben wasn't seeing anyone, which

would mean he may have picked up a girl. What happened after that, we can only guess. It may or may not have something to do with his death. I think for the time being, there isn't much we can do except to be aware of it," Yates said.

Bonnie got up from her chair. "I'll give Peter a call and let him know what's happened," she said.

"Before you go, send the papers, broken beer bottle, wire cutters and piece of barbed wire over to the boys at the lab. See if they can pull prints off 'em. And see if the glass from the beer bottle matches the glass that Paul took from Ben's legs," Yates said.

"We'll do," Bonnie said.

# 7

Jack Thicket's garage was called Hickory Creek Auto Body. It was located a few miles up the road from the Rusty Mule. The garage was old but in adequate condition. Jack had bought the place from the previous owner who had retired ten years earlier. The shop had two big garage bays for servicing vehicles and Jack kept the bays clean and organized despite the shoddy work he sometimes did. In the reception area there was a large front counter, chairs, magazines, a ceiling fan, and a coffee machine was located on the far-left side near the wall. In the back of the building, there was a stockroom and an office. Outside, there was a big neon sign by the roadside in the shape of Hickory Creek that was partially lit at night and stood on two rusty worn-out legs. The garage was painted blue, and the cracked concrete parking lot was baked white from age and sun. Sometimes weeds and grass would spring up from the cracks in the concrete and Jack would wage war, spraying chemicals until the weeds died out. "It's me or them," he'd say.

Dylan and Scott arrived with their girlfriends at the garage shortly after lunch. Dylan and Sue-Ellen sat in the reception area, while Scott and Sara approached the front desk. Scott rang the bell on the counter, but no one came. Scott took off his ball cap, scratched his head and tried to spot Jack through the window behind the counter that looked into the first service bay.

"Now where do you suppose ol' Jack could be?" Scott asked.

"Well, he's probably on the shitter," Dylan replied sarcastically.

Sue-Ellen smacked Dylan's leg and said, "Hush you! I'm sure he'll be here soon."

"Hey! What did y'all go smackin' me for?" Dylan snapped back.

"Why, to keep you in-line darlin'," Sue-Ellen replied in a soft voice as both she and Sara snickered.

"Now don't go encouragin' her," Dylan said.

"Oh, I won't," Sara replied devilishly.

Scott hit the counter bell again a few more times and made louder and faster chimes until Jack finally emerged from the stockroom. Jack walked behind the service counter and opened his work schedule book.

"Easy on the bell, Scott," Jack complained.

"Uh-huh, I got my pa's truck parked out front for you. Will it take long?" Scott asked.

"It'll take as long as it takes. Lucky yer pa called yesterday," Jack replied.

"Alright, then I'll stay and wait for you to swap the tires and give it a tune-up and such," Scott said.

Dylan and Sue-Ellen put their magazines down and rose from their chairs as Sara kissed Scott goodbye. "Okay, we'll talk later," she said.

The three friends walked out, jumped into Dylan's Camaro and drove off.

Scott tossed Jack the keys to the pickup truck. Jack caught the keys and walked out the front reception door. He climbed into the truck, drove it into the first service bay and began his work.

About a half-hour had passed, and Scott became restless in the waiting area. He had had one too many coffees and was walking around, in and out of the waiting room, back and forth, here and there.

Jack finished changing the tires on the pickup truck and started working under the hood when he noticed through the glass that Scott was outside pacing around the parking lot. He placed his tool down on the workbench next to him, cleaned his dirty hands on a rag and walked outside to see what Scott was up to. "Scott!" Jack yelled out. "Come on over here and give me a hand. Your pacin' around is makin' my ass itch."

Scott turned around and followed Jack into the garage. They walked over to the truck, and Jack grabbed the socket wrench. He began working under the hood while Scott leaned over the side of the truck handing Jack the tools and parts he needed.

"Did y'all hear anythin' more about Ben?" Jack asked. "Dylan told me what happened last night at the bar."

"Oh, the sheriff headed out there late last night. Haven't heard anythin' since," Scott replied.

Jack moved to the opposite side of the vehicle. "Scotty, can you grab me that box of spark plugs over there on the other bench?" Jack asked as he poked his head back under the hood again.

Scott approached the bench and grabbed the box of spark plugs. "These?"

"Yes, sir. Bring 'em over."

Scott walked back to Jack with the box of spark plugs and handed the box to him. Jack opened the box, began taking out the new spark plugs and laid them on the workbench beside him. "Tell me somethin'. Have you heard anythin' goin' on in the mines 'round here?" Jack asked.

"Nah, not much goes on. Why you askin'?"

"You and Dylan both work at different mines, right?"

"Yeah, we sure do."

"Good, it'll make the search quicker. Now, how'd you and Dylan like to go into business with ol' Jack here? Just us three, real hush, hush kinda deal. Make a lotta money," Jack said.

"What did y'all have in mind?" Scott asked curiously.

"Well," Jack began as he finished installing the spark plugs, placed the socket wrench down on the workbench and cleaned his hands on a rag, "Ol' Jack came across some information at Charlie's place. Information that our friend Charlie has been hidin'. You see, Charlie's grandpa was a bank robber back in 1901 and he stashed money from his heists in one of the mines 'round here. Charlie doesn't know which mine the money is in and he may be paying off the foremen to get information. Hell, he may even be workin' with the owner. The bottom line is, you two help me find the money before Charlie does and we'll split it three ways. Do it for Ben."

Scott stepped back, not believing what he had just heard, paused, thought for a moment and said, "Ben was a good friend. How much money are we talkin' about?"

"Well," Jack continued as he lay on his backside on the mechanic's creeper and slid under the truck, "From what I reckon, from the newspaper clippings I read, it was about one million dollars," Jack said from under the truck.

Scott let out a whistle, knelt down and stuck his head underneath the truck. "I'll talk to Dylan. We can both go to the library and see what else we can find out and then start poking around at work." Scott rose to his feet.

Jack rolled out from underneath the truck with a pan full of dirty oil. He handed Scott the oil pan and stood up straight. "Sounds good to me partner," Jack said as he wiped his hands on a rag. "Let's shake!" Jack went to shake Scott's hand. Scott reached out and forgot he had the oil pan in his hand and dropped it. The pan made a loud clank and the oil spilt all over the floor and started seeping into the drainage hole. Jack yelled out and took a step back: "Shit, Scott! Nah, it don't matter. I'll buy a new place with my share!" Jack started to dance as Scott slipped on the oil and fell on his backside. Jack howled with laughter: "Dang, Scott! Did you just do what I think you just did!"

Scott's jeans, shoes, and back were covered in oil as he lay on the floor laughing. "Yes, I did, but who cares! We're rich!"

They both roared with laughter. Scott rose to his feet and began to wipe himself off with Jack's clean rags.

"You look like hell," Jack said.

Scott looked at himself and took off his clothes. He stood in his underwear and rolled his oil-stained pants and shirt into a ball and wiped his hands clean.

Jack looked at Scott standing half naked and laughed again. "Well, don't that beat all," Jack said.

"I can't go gettin' pa's truck dirty."

Jack smiled. "I suppose not," he said as he took out a new can of oil from the cabinet and started pouring the new oil into the truck. He finished and closed the hood. Jack then took another rag from the workbench and began to clean himself. The two walked back into the reception area where Jack rang up the bill.

"I'll let you know what I find at the library," Scott said.

Jack nodded his head in approval. "Sounds good to me, partner!" he said as he tossed Scott his truck keys. Scott exited the reception area, climbed into the truck, honked the horn and waved goodbye to Jack. The pickup truck drove much better now and sounded great after the tune-up as Scott headed for home to put some clean clothes on and call Sara.

**8**

It was closing time for Charlie at the Rusty Mule. Everyone left for the night, and he was the last one out the door. He approached his pickup truck and left for the River View Mine.

Charlie drove onto a long dirt road, passed the open gate and parked next to the foreman's shack. The light was on inside as John Thomas, Peter's father who owned all of the mines and quarries in the county, was waiting for Charlie to arrive.

John Thomas was a local businessman who had become entangled with the mafia through Charlie Rhodes years ago while on vacation in Florida. John had gambled a large amount of money at the horse tracks, suffering extensive losses. He sought help and quickly gained the attention of the notorious Romano crime family whom Charlie worked for.

Charlie parked his truck near the office shack and exited his vehicle. He heard shouting coming from inside as Foreman Nathaniel Thompson and John Thomas were having a heated argument. Charlie opened the door and walked inside. There wasn't much to the office. It was a tight squeeze for three or more people. The foreman's shack had a single light dangling from the ceiling, a desk towards the back, some chairs along the side near the windows, two filing cabinets and a table with a coffee machine and some Styrofoam cups.

"You're finally here, Charlie," John said in an irritated voice.

Charlie seemed puzzled and wondered what was going on: "What's this all about, John?"

John spun Charlie around and the two walked out of the shack.

"He knows about our operation. We have to deal with him," John whispered to Charlie.

"First Raymond Moore, then Ben Stevens, now Nathaniel Thompson?" Charlie murmured.

The two re-entered the shack and faced Thompson. Thompson rose from his chair and started shouting: "You'd better let me go or…"

"Or what?!" John yelled out as he shoved Thompson back down on the chair, and slapped him hard across the face causing his nose to bleed.

Charlie approached Thompson, bent down to his eye level and let out a dastardly laugh. "What do you think you can do? Go to the sheriff? What do you think that stupid cowboy is going to tell you? He knows nothing and it's gonna stay that way."

Thompson spat on the floor, looked at Charlie and started laughing nervously. "If everyone only knew the real you!" he said.

Charlie stood straight and punched Thompson across

the jaw "You see this scar on my face! I'll do worse to you!" Charlie shouted.

Thompson spat blood on Charlie's shirt. Charlie lost his temper completely and was about to strike Thompson again when John said calmly: "I've got a better idea. Go get the rope in my truck."

Charlie was breathing heavily and was mad as hell at Thompson, but Charlie listened to John. A smile crept onto Charlie's face as he exited the shack.

John struck Thompson hard across the head, knocking him out.

Charlie quickly returned with the rope and the two men proceeded to bind Thompson's feet and hands to the chair. "Let's leave him alone for now," John said.

The two men left the foreman's shack and walked back to their trucks. They each lit a cigarette. "You go home and let me handle it, Charlie. I'll make sure Thompson pays before the night is done," John said.

"You'd better. I don't like this. Someone's been flappin' their gums," Charlie barked as he got into his truck and drove off.

John threw his partially smoked cigarette on the ground. He turned around and looked back at the foreman's shack. "Stupid old bastard," he muttered to himself.

John got into his truck and drove back in the direction of Lancaster Falls. He stopped at the first filling station he found, pulled in and parked near the side of the building, away from the gas pumps. He got out of his truck, walked into the pay phone booth and dialed the number of the man who did John's dirty work, a man named Cornelius Bennett. Cornelius was a lowlife criminal who worked for the

Romano crime family in Florida where he was wanted for extortion, money laundering, counterfeiting, drugs, prostitution and murder. John lit a cigarette as the phone rang.

"Who's this?" Cornelius demanded in a gravelly voice that sounded like he was talking through a box grater.

"It's me. I need you to do a job, right now," John replied.

Cornelius was watching a boxing match on TV and drinking a beer with his girlfriend. He mashed his spent cigarette in the ashtray on the coffee table in front of him and lit a fresh one. "When and where?"

John looked at his watch. "River View Mine. Thompson, the foreman. He should still be there when you arrive. We left him shaken and tied to a chair, about five minutes ago. See what you can find out before you ice him."

"Just have my payment in the morning," Cornelius said.

John hung up the phone, tossed his cigarette on the ground and left the filling station, heading for his estate outside of town.

Cornelius got off the couch as his girlfriend flashed him a dirty look. Shawna Ray was her name. She was a flirtatious blonde that Cornelius met at The Lucky Dollar, a strip club owned by the Romano crime family in San Martino, Florida.

"Where are you goin', suga'?" Shawna asked in an irritated nasal voice.

"I gotta a job to do. Don't wait up for me," Cornelius replied.

Shawna pouted and sulked to herself as she flipped through the channels on the TV "You and your boring jobs," she said.

Cornelius raised his hand in the air as if he was about

to strike her, but changed his mind. "Shut up, woman," he yelled out as he reached for his coat.

Shawna did not flinch at his gesture and glared at him from the couch. "Oh, big man. You're such a tough guy!"

Cornelius ignored her remark and walked out the front door of her home as he did not have any time to spare. He jumped into his truck, backed out of the driveway onto the main road and headed in the direction of the River View Mine.

Once he arrived, he parked his truck near the open gate. He loaded his handgun and put on his gloves. "Good, the ol' bastard is still here," Cornelius muttered to himself as he walked by Thompson's pickup truck.

Cornelius approached the foreman's shack and saw Thompson through the window. He had managed to untie the ropes on his hands and feet. "John can't you do anything right," Cornelius grumbled under his breath as he watched Thompson free himself from the chair. Thompson grabbed the phone receiver and began to dial the sheriff's office. Cornelius burst into the shack and quickly ripped the phone cord from the wall socket. The two men struggled hitting each other. Cornelius was the bigger, stronger and younger of the two and aggressively shoved Thompson out of the office shack and onto the dirt. Cornelius bent down and grabbed Thompson by the neck and picked him up. "Don't waste my time old man. How did you find out what was going on?" Cornelius demanded angrily.

"John sent his muscle, eh!"

"Don't be stupid!" Cornelius said as he threw Thompson back on the ground and kicked him in the gut. Thompson sat up and spat blood.

"You'll have to do better than that, Cornelius," Thompson shouted.

Cornelius glared as he heard his name being said and stepped maliciously on Thompson's hand grinding it into the dirt. You could hear the small bones cracking under Cornelius' boot as Thompson let out an awful howl.

Cornelius looked down at Thompson and slugged him across the chin, knocking him back in the dirt. Thompson lay unconscious on the ground. Cornelius walked towards the tool shed and flung open the rickety wooden door. He removed a hammer and walked back to Thompson just as he began to stir.

"I'm only going to ask you once more. Tell me how you found out about the operation," Cornelius demanded angrily as he started smacking the head of the hammer against the palm of his hand in a threating manner.

Thompson coughed up blood again and wiped his mouth with his shirt. He looked up with fear in his eyes and his legs began to tremble. "Alright, I found out from Moore and Stevens," he said.

"You're not tellin' me anything I don't already know! Try again!" Cornelius shouted.

"I guess it makes no difference now. You already killed Moore and Stevens."

"And you'll be next if you don't start talkin'."

Thompson knew he was dead no matter what he said: "Moore told me and Stevens about the heist money, about John, about Charlie, about you and about what's really going on at the Rusty Mule!"

"You figured out everything, eh!"

"And the sheriff will figure it out too!"

Cornelius shoved the hammer under his belt, took his handgun from his backside and shot Thompson as if he had a bullseye painted on his forehead. Cornelius grabbed Thompson's arm, dragged his corpse across the dirt to Cornelius' pickup truck, and threw Thompson's lifeless body onto the bed of the truck. Cornelius lit a cigarette, spat on the ground, and climbed into the cab. He started the engine and sped off into the stillness of the night to dispose of the body.

# 9

THE NEXT MORNING, John was sitting in his leather chair in his office at his estate home while talking on the phone with Charlie. The mining industry had made the Thomas family wealthy over the decades, and John showed it with his lavish mansion.

"Who do you have to replace Thompson?" Charlie asked over the phone.

"I got a guy we can trust. I'm going to talk to him tomorrow," John replied.

"Who?" Charlie asked.

"Joshua."

"Damn it, John. Of all the damned people, why him? You know he's plum drunk half the time," Charlie complained.

"Don't worry about it. He knows who's paying him to shut up."

"You'd better be right."

The phone call ended and John rose from his chair, headed down the hall and into the kitchen. He poked his head in the refrigerator and began looking for something to eat.

"Hey, pa," Peter said as he entered the kitchen.

John turned around and looked from the fridge. "Peter, my boy, how are you feeling today?" he asked.

Peter approached the kitchen counter, sat on a stool and pointed to the lump on his head. "Better, but my head still hurts," he complained.

"You'll be alright," John said with a chuckle.

John left the kitchen with biscuits on a plate and returned to his office. Peter got up from his stool and walked around the counter to the fridge. He poked his head in the refrigerator looking for something to feed his sore head when he heard a knock on the kitchen screen door. He let out a huff, closed the fridge door and went over to see who it was.

"Your pa around?" the stranger inquired.

"Who's asking?"

"Tell him it's Jeb."

"Alright, hold on."

Peter walked slowly back through the kitchen and down the hallway, before getting to his father's office. Peter knocked on the open office door and poked his head inside: "Pa, there's someone at the kitchen door to see you. Says his name is Jeb."

John rose from his office chair, left his biscuits on the plate and headed back to the kitchen with Peter slowly following behind. John reached the kitchen screen door and recognized right away that it was really Cornelius using an alias. John joined Cornelius outside, and the two walked together to where Cornelius had parked his girlfriend's car.

"Did you take care of things?" John inquired.

"Let's just say the matter is closed," Cornelius replied.

"Did you find out who the leak is?"

"No, he told me about Moore and Stevens. That's it."

"Stevens told you it was Moore and Moore told you it was Stevens and now Thompson told you it was Stevens and Moore. All they did was point the finger at each other."

"Yeah, and well, they're all fuckin' dead."

"Well, that's something at least," John said as he took an envelope full of money out of his pocket and slipped it to Cornelius discreetly.

"You know he said my name before I shot him and he knew that you had sent for me," Cornelius complained angrily as he slipped the envelope of money into his inside coat pocket.

"It's that leak. I'll handle it," John said.

"You and Charlie and that fuckin' heist money will jeopardize the entire operation."

"Look, from now on, you do the killing and I'll do the thinking," John said under his breath as he lit a cigarette.

"You'd better 'cause I don't think Fernando wants to hear how you've been fuckin' things up lately," Cornelius warned as he stepped into his girlfriend's car and left in a cloud of dust.

John was angry at what Cornelius had said. John returned to his house and found Peter eating a large meal.

"Is everything alright, pa?" Peter asked with a mouthful of food.

"Yeah, everything's fine, boy," John replied.

John returned to his office while Peter wondered what the meeting outside was all about and who Jeb was. Peter let out a yawn, finished his meal and took two painkillers. He felt groggy still and decided to go lie down for the rest of the day before going back to work tomorrow.

# 10

SHERIFF YATES ARRIVED home late at night. The sheriff lived by himself in a two-bedroom, mid-century modern bungalow on the outskirts of town. The home had a beautiful view of the sun, rising over the hills every morning and in the far-off distance he could make out the Great Smoky Mountains. He had put a down payment on the property when he moved from Montana.

Gnawing on beef jerky, Yates stepped into his home and was immediately greeted by his loyal German Sheppard, BJ. "Good to see you too, BJ," Yates said as he bent down, scratched BJ's ears and gave the dog a stick of beef jerky. Yates threw his hat and coat on the couch and walked into the kitchen. He grabbed a beer from the fridge, went to his desk in the living room and pulled out a box of cigars. He took a cigar, walked back outside with his beer in hand, and sat down on the front porch steps. BJ followed and sat beside Yates.

The moon was full that night and the stars shone brightly in the sky. The lightening bugs danced to the chirping of the crickets. The frogs croaked with applause. Yates sat there and enjoyed the night as he drank his beer, smoked his cigar and chewed beef jerky on the front steps of his home.

A car pulled into the laneway. Yates couldn't see who it was. The headlights were staring him in the face. BJ barked at the car. The engine shut off, the car lights turned off, and a short petite figure emerged from the driver's side. It was Bonnie, out of uniform and wearing bell-bottom blue jeans, a white t-shirt, and a jean jacket. Her auburn hair flowed down her back. She walked up the stone steps to the house and sat down beside Yates on the front porch. BJ barked again, rose and sat in front of Bonnie. Bonnie petted BJ and BJ licked her face. "He's a friendly sorta' fella'," she said.

"Yeah, I've had him since he was a pup. One of our station dogs back in Montana had a litter. I started giving the pups away to local families and kept one for myself. Melanie never liked pets," Yates said.

"No wonder you two separated," Bonnie said jokingly.

Yates laughed and offered Bonnie a stick of beef jerky.

"No, thank you, but I'll take one of those beers," she said.

"I have a few more inside," Yates replied with a smile as he rose from the front porch steps, walked back into his house and came out moments later with three more beers. He sat back down where he was before, put the beers on the steps and took a pull from his cigar.

Bonnie grabbed a beer and opened it. "Why three beers?" she asked.

"Because your one beer behind me," Yates grinned.

Bonnie smiled and began to drink her beer.

"What does BJ stand for?" Bonnie asked intriguingly.

"Beef jerky. It was my call sign in the Air Force," Yates replied. "But it wasn't as bad as Sean's call sign."

Bonnie took a gulp of beer. "Do I even want to know?" she asked.

"Hurl."

Bonnie laughed, "Hurl?"

"Yeah. He earned that one the hard way. One night, all of us went out to the bar and we dared him to drink as much as he could while eating raw eggs. Sean isn't one to back down from a dare and we all knew it. The booze didn't agree with the eggs and to make a long story short, he hurled onto the Captain's pants and shoes. From that moment on, his call sign was Hurl."

Bonnie began laughing. "Oh, my stars!"

Yates took a gulp of beer. "What brings you out my way tonight?" he asked curiously.

"I was in the neighborhood," Bonnie replied timidly.

Yates took a pull from his cigar, finished off his beer and opened another can. "Tell me, what did you do before law enforcement?" he asked.

"I was a waitress back in Texas where I grew up. One day I got sick and tired of having my ass pinched by truckers all day long, so I quit. My pa was in law enforcement, and my grandpa had been a Texas Ranger. I decided to do the same. My three older sisters thought I was crazy trying to become a cop in my late twenties. 'Go find yourself a husband,' they'd say to me. I showed them. I don't have any brothers, so It made my pa real happy when I told him," Bonnie replied with a smile as she finished her beer.

Yates took another pull from his cigar and pointed at the full moon. "Sometimes it's nice just to sit here in the moonlight, underneath the stars in the sky and listen to the music of the land," he said.

They stared together at the moon. Bonnie let out a sigh, grabbed another beer off the steps, opened it and took a drink. "What happened between you and your wife? You never did tell me."

Yates took a long pull from his cigar. "I came home one night from a failed bust and found her in bed with another man. Things had been rough between us for a few months prior. We were always fighting with each other over little things that never mattered before. In the end, I guess I found out the hard way."

"How come you two never had any kids?"

"We tried for years, but she could never get pregnant."

"Are you happier now?"

Yates smiled at Bonne and replied, "I reckon I am."

"Good, and thank you for being honest with me."

Yates shook his can but it was empty. He rose from the steps and said, "I think I have more beer in the fridge."

"No more for me, thanks," Bonnie said.

He disappeared into his home and came back. "Last one," he said as he sat back down on the front porch steps. Yates opened his beer can, took a gulp and a pull from his cigar. "How long have you been in Lancaster Falls?" he asked.

"It's been around five years," Bonnie replied.

"Do you like it here?"

"I think I do, yeah. Place has kinda grown on me. What about you. Do you like it here?"

"I think so," Yates said with a smile.

"Probably isn't as cold as what you're used to."

"It's warmer here for sure. Which is a nice change."

"How long have you been a cop, if you don't mind me askin'?"

Yates took another pull from his cigar. "I'm forty-eight. That would be twenty years. Started a year after I came home from the war in Korea," he said.

"Do you miss your family and friends back home?" Bonnie asked.

"My two older brothers died in the war. The oldest died in the Second World War and the other in Korea. All three of us were Air Force pilots. Parents passed away a while ago. There's some family on my father's side in Colorado and on my mother's side, there's family up north back in Montana, and then there's Sean. He usually finds a lady friend to mess around with. Sean may not be blood, but he's like a brother to me."

"From what I've heard, I think I'd like to meet Sean."

"Not unless you've had your shots first," Yates joked.

Bonnie laughed.

"My divorce paperwork should be in this week for me to sign," Yates said.

"What was the hold up?"

"Again, little things. She kept stalling. At least I got to keep BJ," Yates said and stroked BJ's head.

Bonnie smiled at Yates and the two sat on the front steps together, drinking beer and talking while BJ sat in front of them and watched, wagging his tail. Bonnie left for home after their talk was over and the beer ran out.

# 11

BACK AT THE Rusty Mule, the four friends met for drinks. Charlie had a local country music band playing, and everyone was having a good time. The male and female singers sang in harmony:

> *Left my heart in Tennessee.*
> *No other place I'd rather be.*
> *'Cause when I look into your eyes,*
> *and I catch you by surprise,*
> *whatever you say to me will be.*

Sue-Ellen held Dylan's hand. "Oh, I love this song," she said.

The male singer continued:

> *When I walked out to my girl,*
> *my heart raced halfway around the world.*
> *And when I took you in my arms,*
> *I was mesmerized by your sweet charms.*

The band played the chorus.

"I hear the singers are married," Sara said.

"They look so in love," Sue-Ellen added.

The female singer continued:

> *I've seen you smile a thousand times,*
> *and your kiss tastes like the sweetest wine.*
> *And every time I turn to go away,*
> *I'm drawn back to you, now here I am to stay.*

After four minutes the band finished their number and everyone stood up to applaud.

"Come on! Let's go freshen up," Sara said happily.

Sara and Sue-Ellen rose from their chairs and left to use the ladies' room.

"So, how did it go at the garage with Jack?" Dylan asked Scott as the band started a new number.

Scott moved his chair up to the table and motioned to Dylan to come closer. Dylan moved his chair nearer and leaned towards Scott. "Jack knows something about Charlie," Scott said.

"Oh, what?" Dylan asked curiously.

Scott looked around the bar for Charlie but did not see him anywhere. "Charlie's grandpa was a bank robber, and he stashed the loot in one of the mines around here, but no one knows which one. Jack found out the night he slept in the bar. He broke into Charlie's office and poked around. Jack said he'd cut us in if we help him find the money."

Dylan leaned back in his chair, took a drink from his beer mug and let out a whistle.

"I figure you can poke around at your work, and I'll poke around at my work. See what we can both come up with," Scott said.

Dylan took another drink of beer and lit a fresh ciga-rette. "Sounds good to me, partner!"

Scott extended his hand to Dylan and the two shook hands. "We should go look at the library. See if we can find anything else out," Scott added.

Dylan nodded in agreement. "How much cash are we talkin' 'bout?" he asked.

"One million dollars!"

Dylan let out another whistle and took a drag from his cigarette. "Dang, that's a whole lotta money for us poor people."

Sue-Ellen and Sara came walking back to the table, sat down with the boys and the four of them laughed and drank into the night.

It was starting to get late, and the four friends had just paid their bar bill and were getting ready to head home. Dylan smacked Sue-Ellen's bottom. "Come on girl, let's go home," he said with a smile.

"You don't have to ask me twice," Sue-Ellen exclaimed with a grin as she almost fell over.

Dylan laughed and said, "Drunk too, huh."

"Oh you, flattery will get you everywhere."

"We're all on a roll tonight," Sara said as she pinched Scott's behind.

Scott let out an "Ouch!" as they all headed out the door and went home for the night.


Later that night, after closing time, Charlie locked the doors to the bar and tallied the receipts. He packed the cash into a manila envelope, took the envelope into the back office and tossed it on his desk. He approached the horse painting on the wall, swung the canvas to one side, opened the wall safe and looked inside. "What the hell!?" he said out loud. Charlie saw that everything in the safe was just a little bit out of place. He immediately took out all of the cash for the week and counted the money using his money counter machine. The bills flipped through the gadget at a rapid pace and Charlie instantly thought of Jack who had stayed in the bar overnight and wondered if Jack had pretended to be drunk. Satisfied that nothing was missing, Charlie packed all of the cash into a leather case and placed it on his desk. He went back to the wall safe and looked inside again. "Jack, Jack, Jack, you're just a little too smart for your own good." Charlie closed the safe, swung the painting back and went over to his desk to grab his leather case. He left his office locking the door behind him. He walked out into the main bar area and headed for the front door to leave when he saw the headlights of a truck rolling into the parking lot.

The truck parked in front of the entrance of the bar and a large man stepped out. Charlie walked back towards the bar, put the leather case of cash under the bar counter and heard someone banging on the front door. Then Charlie heard a voice. "Hey Charlie, you in there, man?!"

It was Cornelius banging away at the door. Charlie approached the front door and unlocked it. He grabbed Cornelius by the arm and pulled him inside. "Fuck Cornelius, what the hell are you doing here?"

Cornelius was shaking like a leaf. "I need… need… another hit," he stammered aloud.

"What? Wait here."

Charlie turned around and walked back into his office. He went over to the gun cabinet mounted on the wall, opened the glass door and lifted a panel revealing a secret compartment. He grabbed a few small bags of white powder and closed the panel and door. He walked out of his office, locking the door behind him and returned to the bar. He approached Cornelius sitting at a table and threw the small bags of powder in front of him. "I got a job for you to do."

Cornelius looked at Charlie before opening a bag of white powder, and dumping it on the table. Cornelius snorted the powder and asked, "What? What kind of job? "

Charlie looked at Cornelius in disgust.

"What's the job, man?" Cornelius asked again.

Charlie pulled up a chair and sat down beside Cornelius. "I want you to take care of Jack Thicket."

"Who?"

"That wiry drunk from the garage."

"That wiry drunk from the garage?"

"Yeah, that's the one. I left him in the bar overnight 'cause I thought he was too drunk to drive home. He picked his way into my office and into my safe. The guy must be a locksmith or something 'cause he literally opened everything without any evidence of anything being fucked with. I want him dead. He knows too much. "

Cornelius stared at Charlie blankly and blinked twice. "That wasn't a smart move leaving him here alone, man."

"It's not the first-time people have been too drunk to drive home. That cot in back isn't for my beauty sleep you know. How the fuck was I supposed to know he could pick a fucking lock and open a damn safe," Charlie barked.

Cornelius grabbed the two remaining bags of powdered heroin, rose from the chair and angrily rubbed his nose.

"I'll do it this week," he said in an irritated voice. Cornelius turned around and left the bar.

Charlie stepped behind the bar counter, grabbed the leather case and exited by the front entrance door. He locked the bar, walked over to his pickup truck and headed for home in the dead of night.

# 12

THE SUN SHONE bright that morning through the tree tops and over the rolling hills. Scott pulled off the main road and drove onto the dirt road heading down to the River View Mine. The old pickup truck shook and rattled. He pulled into the entrance of the mine and turned into the parking lot. He climbed out of the truck and saw that a crowd had gathered by the foreman's shack. He scratched his head and wondered what the commotion was all about. Scott approached a group of workers and stood beside them. "What's going on?" he asked.

The worker looked at Scott somberly and replied, "It's the foreman, Nathaniel Thompson. He's missing. Looks like there was a struggle!"

"Did anyone call the sheriff or the mine owner?" Scott asked curiously.

"We called the sheriff and Mr. Thomas just before you got here."

Scott walked away from the group and took a seat at one of the many lunch picnic tables with a few other workers and lit a cigarette, not knowing what to do until help arrived.

It wasn't long before Scott saw the sheriff's cruiser roll in followed by the deputy's squad car, and John's pickup truck right behind. Sheriff Yates, Bonnie, and John all got out of their vehicles and walked over to the crowd of workers. Scott rose from his seat and headed towards Yates. John intercepted Scott. "I'll make an announcement. Get everyone together," John said.

"Yes, sir," Scott replied as he turned around and headed over to the rest of the workers calling out loud to everyone. "Listen up! Mr. Thomas is here to make an announcement. Follow me!"

The employees gathered around the picnic tables.

John approached the crowd, stepped on top of one of the picnic tables and started to clap his hands together to get everyone's attention. "I'm going to send everyone home until further notice to allow the officers time to do their jobs. I'll have someone from the office contact each of you when we're ready to resume work. In the meantime, allow the officers to take your statements, and if anyone knows anything about Thompson's whereabouts, please let the sheriff know." John climbed down from the picnic table and approached the officers as they began to interview the workers.

After being interviewed, Scott walked over to his pickup truck wondering what to do today now that he had free time on his hands. He unlocked the truck door, climbed inside and stared out the windshield blankly until an idea popped into his head. He decided that he would go to the library with Dylan who had Mondays off. Scott backed his truck out of the parking space and left.

Over at the picnic tables, Yates and Bonnie were taking the remaining statements of the last few workers. John glanced at the officers from across the grounds and decided to sneak over to the foreman's shack. He opened the shack door and stepped inside just as Bonnie turned her head to talk to another worker.

John looked around the room. Everything seemed to be as it was the previous night. He turned around to leave and spotted the rope that he had used to tie Thompson. John bent down, grabbed the rope off the floor and stuffed it into his coat pocket. He saw the phone cord had been yanked from the wall but did not touch it. He discreetly opened the office door, and exited the shack. He stood there for a moment and lit a cigarette. Bonnie saw him smile as she turned around to talk to another worker. However, John did not notice Bonnie. John returned to his vehicle and waved to the officers as he left.

After the workers had all gone home, Yates began taking pictures of the ground and shack. Bonnie nudged him and said, "I saw John leave the foreman's office while we were finishing the interviews. Then he lit a cigarette with a grin on his face. There's something wrong. I just have a funny feeling about it now. I don't like it one bit. "

"Grinning isn't a crime, but I know what you mean. Let's finish our investigation," Yates said.

Bonnie agreed and the two started looking around. Yates wasn't very happy as he scanned the ground. There were footprints everywhere from the workers who had contaminated the scene. You couldn't tell anymore if anything had happened and Yates became irritated by it. Bonnie noticed that he was upset and doubled her efforts in searching for clues when she stepped on a spent bullet casing in the dirt.

She bent down, slipped on her gloves and stuck her fingers into the ground. "I found something!" she yelled out.

Yates came over, bent down and looked at the bullet casing in her hand. "Good work. Keep searching," he said as he rose to his feet and headed for the tool shed. Yates saw that the door was wide open. He clicked a few pictures of the tool shed and looked around. There did not appear to be anything out of the ordinary. Everything looked normal. There was no way he could know that one hammer was missing.

Next, Yates entered the foreman's shack. Yates saw that the room was clean. He thought about fingerprints, but knew that every mine worker had been in and out of that office shack to pick up their pay checks or to lodge complaints or to use the phone. He turned around, and looked at the desk and chair. He bent down, spotted dried blood on the floor underneath the chair and took a sample. He rose to his feet and noticed that the phone cord had been yanked from the wall. He snapped a few pictures of the scene and thought about John smiling and what Bonnie had said. Yates exited the office and noted what appeared to be two lines in the dirt as if made by the heels of someone being dragged. The heel marks were then obscured by the shoe prints, but the marks reappeared near the entrance. Yates walked over to the entrance gate and looked back at the office shack. Yes, the heel drag marks were unmistakable.

"Do you see something?" Bonnie yelled out.

"Come over here," Yates replied as he motioned with his hand.

Bonnie rose from her location and approached Yates. Yates pointed at the ground and said, "I think your bad feeling is right, and Thompson might be dead. See those two lines that appear and disappear in the dirt, from the shack to the entrance gate? It looks like Thompson was dragged from the office shack to the gate. I don't think Thompson put up any kind of struggle either or those lines wouldn't be so straight. I'm speculating that Thompson was dragged from the office shack to a truck that was parked here by the gate and was taken away. I also found a couple of spots of dried blood on the office floor and the phone cord was yanked from the wall."

"Do you think John tampered with evidence or maybe even took something?" Bonnie asked.

Yates rubbed the dimple on his chin and lit a cigar. "Possible, but we have no proof and no way of knowing, only speculation. You have to keep in mind that we were the last two to look around. Between John and the employees, this entire area has been contaminated," Yates said.

"At least we came away with something," Bonnie said.

"Yes, I'm betting that a struggle took place in the office shack. The dried blood on the floor and the phone cord yanked from the wall could possibly indicate that. The bullet casing you found would suggest that Thompson was shot near the shack. Finally, the straight lines in the dirt would suggest he was dragged lifelessly and brought away in a vehicle," Yates said.

"I think you're right. Maybe we'll find suspicious fingerprints on the phone and cord, but I doubt it."

"I'll take a few more pictures and put out an APB on Thompson just in case we are wrong and he is just missing."

The two went about their work for a while longer until Yates was thoroughly satisfied there was no evidence left to be found.

# 13

Peter woke up from a good night's sleep. He rolled over in bed, opened his eyes and looked at the alarm clock. "Where did the dang time go," he said to himself in a sleepy voice as he got out of bed and walked over to the bathroom.

John decided to check in on Peter and knocked on his bedroom door, but no one answered. John heard the water running and assumed his son was taking a shower. John returned to his office, sat down at his desk, and decided to call the new foreman who would replace the now deceased Nathanial Thompson at the River View Mine.

Joshua Doyle was sitting outside on the weather-beaten porch of his dilapidated old home when he heard the phone ring. With a beer in one hand and a cigarette dangling from his mouth, he continued to sit as the phone rang. John grew impatient. Twenty rings went by before Joshua finally rose from his porch chair. He entered his old beaten down house, grabbed the phone receiver and took a drag from his cigarette.

"Finally, you picked up the damn phone," John said in an irritated voice. "Joshua, it's me. Charlie and I want… No, he's not here," John huffed under his breath. The two began to banter back and forth.

Meanwhile, Peter had come out of the shower and was now dressed. He decided to check in on his father. Peter walked down the hall, approached John's office, saw the door was ajar and heard him arguing on the phone.

"Joshua, shut your damn mouth and listen," John yelled in an angry voice. "Tomorrow, show up for work at the River View Mine. Remember our deal. You're taking over for Nathaniel Thompson… Yeah, you'll get your cut. Just show up for work or I'll send Charlie over to deal with you. You don't want trouble with Charlie, do you?"

Peter stood silently not believing what his ears had just heard. He very quietly walked away in his socked feet from his father's office. Peter headed for the front entrance door and stopped by the coat rack to gather his belongings for work. He slipped on his coat and boots when he suddenly heard his father's voice: "Peter, my boy, leaving without saying goodbye to your ol' man?"

"No sir, but I gotta go. Didn't realize how late in the morning it was," Peter replied nervously.

"How's your head anyway?"

"It's a little less sore. I'll take it easy though."

"Good. You do that. Well, off you go then."

Peter exited his home and headed for the garage. He hopped into his '65 Thunderbird and drove around aimlessly for a while thinking about what he had heard and asking himself if snitching on his father was the right thing to do. In the end, after wrestling with his emotions, Peter decided to tell the sheriff.

Peter arrived at work, jumped out of his vehicle, not

locking the door, and rushed up the sidewalk almost knocking over a few pedestrians. He opened the door to the station and bolted past Beth who was sitting at her front desk. "Slow down, Peter. Y'all got a trail of fire at your heels!"

Peter did not listen and ran straight to the sheriff's office throwing open the door. Sheriff Yates was sitting at his desk smoking his cigar and Bonnie was sitting on the sofa reading the newspaper.

"Easy does it, Peter. Have a seat," Yates said.

Peter was trying to catch his breath. He sat down on one of the chairs in front of the sheriff's desk and put his deputy's hat on the other. Bonnie put her newspaper down and went over to Peter. She picked his hat off the chair and sat down. "What's wrong, Peter?" she asked.

Peter caught his breath and yelled out. "It's my pa!"

"What about your father?" Yates asked.

Peter breathed a little slower. Bonnie put her hand on his shoulder to help calm his nerves. "I heard him on the phone talking to the new foreman at River View Mine. His name is Joshua Doyle. Pa has an arrangement going with Charlie!" Peter said.

Yates and Bonnie both looked at each other in surprise. "What in the hell is going on In this town?!" Yates shouted in exasperation as he threw his hands in the air.

"Wait, I think this makes sense. Remember, I said I saw John acting suspiciously. We need to figure out the connection," Bonnie said.

Yates leaned back in his chair, took another pull from his cigar and asked, "Peter, do you know this, Joshua Doyle? Has he worked for your father before?"

"Yes sir, I know who he is. He works odd jobs when

needed. He's a local. If I'm not mistaken, he has prior convictions. I'd have to check his file downstairs," Peter said.

"Let's go find out," Yates said.

Peter felt better after confiding to Yates. The three officers rose to their feet, exited the office and headed for the stairs. Yate's cigar left a trail of smoke as he descended into the basement with Bonnie and Peter following. Yates slapped the light switch at the bottom of the staircase. The officers walked past the shelves and searched the dusty filing cabinets looking for Joshua's file. In no time, Peter found the file and pulled it out. "Here it is Sheriff," Peter said as he handed the file to Yates.

Yates opened Joshua's file on top of the filling cabinet and began turning the pages. "He has multiple convictions for drunk driving," Yates said as he picked up a paper and began to read a note that the previous sheriff had written:

Mr. Joshua Doyle is prone to heavy drinking and possible drug use. Dangerous, approach with caution.

Yates finished examining the file and closed it. "Thank you, Peter, for the help today. Go home and get some rest," he said.

"It's been a bad couple of days," Peter replied as he nodded his head and thought about his father.

"Be careful and don't let on to your old man that you know anything. Just play it safe," Yates said.

The three officers returned upstairs. Peter gathered his belongings and left. Yates and Bonnie stepped into the sheriff's office. Yates sat at his desk and leafed through Joshua Doyle's file again.

Bonnie sat down on the couch. "What do you think this is about?"

"I'm not sure yet, and I don't care to speculate without more information," Yates replied.

"Oh, come on now, what do you think?" Bonnie insisted.

Yates leaned back in his leather chair and took a pull from his cigar. "After today, we're pretty sure that Peter's father is involved in something. What that is, we don't know yet. But it would have to involve the mines and not just one mine either, but all of them. What Charlie has to do with it intrigues me," Yates said.

"What should we do about Nathaniel Thompson being missing?"

"I'm pretty sure he's dead and his body will turn up soon."

"What about Raymond Moore? We don't know where his body went to either."

"We know he was butchered into pieces. We saw that with our own eyes. I'm not sure when and where his body parts will turn up, though."

"I'll send the bullet casing to the lab."

"Yeah, along with the dried blood sample."

"Do you think they're looking for diamonds or gold?"

"I don't think there are any in these parts," Yates said as he closed the file. "There's something going on and I think I know someone who just might shed some light on things."

"Oh, I know who you're thinking of."

"Yup, old man Callaghan," Yates said.

The two officers left the station for Lloyd Callaghan's house outside of town.

Lloyd Callaghan, the retired sheriff of Reeves County, was an older man in his late sixties He had a bad cough from a lifetime of tobacco use. He had retired to his farm with his wife and two grandkids, and was out back in the chicken coop when the two officers arrived.

"Callaghan!" Yates shouted.

Callaghan exited the chicken coop. "Over here, Robert!"

The three met and shook hands. Callaghan looked at Bonnie with a smile and said, "Bonnie, it's good to see you again. Has our friend from up north been treatin' you well?"

Bonnie looked at Yates with a twinkle in her eye and replied, "The cowboy's been treatin' us real good."

Callaghan smiled and said, "What do I owe the pleasure of your visit? Don't tell me you're stuck on a case?"

"As a matter of fact," Yates began.

"Come, follow me to the stables," Callaghan said.

The three walked together. "Tell me about Charlie Rhodes," Yates inquired.

"Charlie moved here a few years ago from Florida. He keeps to himself for the most part," Callaghan replied.

"Does he have any friends?" Bonnie asked.

"I never really noticed. Always saw him at the bar or at the bank in town."

"What about John Thomas?" Yates asked.

"Pete's pa? Now there's an interesting fellow. The Thomas family has been around these parts for generations. John's a bit of a loud mouth, but I never saw him do anything illegal. He does have a few questionable associates though. Joshua Doyle, to name one," Callaghan replied as the three entered the stables.

"Any others?" Bonnie asked.

"There was this one fellow, a large bald-headed man with tattoos, real mean son of a bitch with a Florida accent. Can't remember his name. Never arrested him for anything, but he just struck me as someone you didn't want to cross. He came here around the same time as Charlie," Callaghan replied as he grabbed a broom. "What's this all about anyway? You think Charlie and John are up to something?"

"Peter overheard his father on the phone talking to Joshua Doyle about something going on. Charlie is also involved," Yates replied.

"Well now, that is interesting. You don't know the story then?" Callaghan inquired.

Bonnie shrugged her shoulders. "What story?" she asked curiously.

"About John and Charlie's grandpas. The two were bank robbers in this state back around 1901. They were never arrested and no one knows what happened to them or the money they stole. They plum disappeared without a trace," Callaghan coughed and continued. "Later on, before the depression, the Thomas family got into the mining business. People used to say the son, John's pa, used the stolen money to finance the mining company, while others used to say that the money was still buried in the hills somewhere. There were all sorts of rumors flying around. To this day, everyone will tell you something different and no one knows the truth. Hell, I reckon not even John or Charlie know what happened to their grandpas or the money."

"Wait a minute. Before, did you not say that Charlie came here recently?" Yates asked.

"Yeah, it was just after John had returned from his vacation in Florida and I was announcing my retirement.

You think those two are up to their families' old tricks? That never entered my mind before," Callaghan said as he scratched his head.

"It's starting to sound more and more like that," Yates replied.

"If they are up to their families' old tricks, then you'd better watch them 'cause this town could be in for a shock," Callaghan said.

"Thank you, Lloyd. You've been real helpful," Yates said as the two shook hands.

"Anytime, Robert. Now, don't forget about me here. The wife might not like me going on adventures, but I miss the ol' days," Callaghan said. "You look after our friend here, Bonnie."

"Oh, I will Lloyd," Bonnie smiled.

Callaghan whistled for his hired hand to help him as the two officers walked out of the stables and left the farm heading back towards Lancaster Falls.

# 14

Dylan and Scott arrived at the local town library in search of information that would lead them to the lost heist money. Dylan pulled his Camaro into the parking lot and found a space under the cool shade of a Magnolia tree. The two friends got out of the car, strolled past the flower beds, walked up the steps of the large colonial building and entered through the heavy wooden front doors.

There were a few people sitting at tables reading and someone was looking through the card catalogue. Several university students from the big city were huddled together at a table in the corner, their backpacks sprawled over the carpeted floor. Everyone was quiet. The librarian's circulation desk, located in the middle of the library, was like an island in the middle of a vast ocean of books.

"Where should we start?" Scott wondered.

"Let's ask the librarian," Dylan replied as the boys approached the circulation desk. "Excuse me, Miss. Can you point us to where they keep old newspapers?" Dylan asked.

"Just a second, sweetie," the librarian replied. She finished her task and closed the desk drawer. "Now, what were you two handsome gentlemen lookin' for?"

"We're lookin' for old newspapers dating back to 1901. Maybe the Lancaster Falls Herald or the Daily from the big city?"

"Mostly for local news," Scott added.

The librarian rose from her chair, smiled and said, "Okay boys, follow me. I'll show you where we keep the microfiche." They walked over to a long desk with chairs and five microfiche machines. "Have either of you ever used this kind of machine before?" she asked.

"We did in high school, Miss." Scott replied.

"Great! The films are over here," she said as she opened the drawers for the year 1901. "Ah-ha, here we go. Over here sweeties, this should be what you're lookin' for. I'll leave you to your work. If you need me, just holla'. I'll be over at my desk or around helpin' other folks," she said with a smile.

Dylan and Scott nodded. They began looking through the drawers and took out the film they needed. Dylan turned to Scott and let out a huff. "Umm, I think this is gonna take some doin'."

"Just think of it as bein' back in school," Scott said.

Dylan smiled and said, "I don't remember our school havin' a librarian that looked like her."

Scott smiled.

The two friends sat down at the microfiche machines, placed the film under the glass and began to search for articles relating to the heist.

After an hour of searching through the microfiche, Scott rose to his feet, stretched his arms and said, "I need a smoke, man."

"Okay, make it quick," Dylan said as he continued to look.

While Scott was gone, Dylan inserted the next microfiche film into the machine and let out a huff in hopes that this film would be the one with the information. The first image appeared on the screen. This film was from June, 1901. He began glancing over the headlines, and there it was on the first page of the Lancaster Falls Herald. The article read:

The First National Bank was robbed at gunpoint by two armed bandits dressed in black and wearing masks. It was the fourth such robbery in the county and police believe that this robbery is connected to others across the state. Eyewitnesses saw the men back up a truck to the rear of the building. The two men entered the bank through the front door, shot a round into the air, tied up some employees and ordered the others at gunpoint to load the money from the vault into the truck.

Dylan finished reading the article when Scott returned.

"It's about time, man. Here, read this article I found. We need to find a few more stories like this. Make sure we got all the information," Dylan said.

Scott agreed. He read the article, removed the film and collected the other films they had viewed. He walked over to the microfiche drawers and returned the viewed microfiche films to their proper place. He took out more films from 1901 and returned to his seat.

"Now, I'm going for a smoke," Dylan said as he rose from his chair and walked off.

Scott sat back down and began to scroll through more films without any luck. He inserted the next film and began a new search just as Dylan returned. "One last film," Scott said.

"Good, 'cause I think I'm cooked for the day."

The first image came up on the screen. The two friends began scanning through the pages of the newspaper and found a story that caught their eye under the local section. The short article read:

> Police are baffled by a string of armed bank robberies throughout the state. The robberies appeared to have suddenly stopped and no one knows why or what happened to the money that was stolen. The names of the two suspects are Dwight Rhodes and James J. Thomas. If anyone knows the whereabouts of these two men, please contact your local sheriff's department. Do not approach the suspects. They are considered armed and dangerous.

Dylan and Scott stared at each other, astonished by what they had read.

"Don't tell me Charlie's and John's grandpas were working together?" Scott remarked.

"I think we got all we need for now. Let's talk to Jack tonight and let him know what we found," Dylan said.

Scott agreed, and the two turned off the microfiche machines and returned the remaining films to their drawers. They headed over to the librarian to thank her for her help.

"I hope to see y'all back here again soon. Reading is a wonderful thing," the librarian said with a smile. The boys smiled back and left the library heading for home.

# 15

THE RAIN BEGAN to fall heavily on the road. Dylan turned on the wipers and watched as the blades played with the water on the windshield. He lit a cigarette in the darkness. The match shone light on his face. He blew the flame out and strained his eyes to see the road ahead. The ventilation sent cool air on his brow. He wiped his forehead with his hand and rolled down the window. "Shit, here we go again. Hope it's not a bad storm."

"We're almost there. I can see the sign flickering ahead," Scott said

They approached Hickory Creek Auto Body and pulled into the parking lot in hopes that Jack was still there. Dylan parked his Camaro near the front reception door and turned the engine off. "I think he's in the first service bay. I can see the light shining through the window," Dylan said.

Dylan turned the car headlights off and honked his horn. The two friends saw a shadow through the glass moving around inside. They stepped out of the car into the rain and walked to the reception door. Dylan pulled the handle, but it was locked. Scott banged on the wet door until Jack came and unlocked it. "Dang boys, I wasn't expecting you after hours," he said.

Dripping wet from head to toe, the two friends entered the auto body shop. Scott proceeded straight to the coffee machine and poured himself a cup. "We did a lot of research today at the library, so we thought we'd drop by to fill you in," he said.

"Didn't you have to work today?" Jack asked.

"Nah, they shut the River View Mine down on account of foreman Nathanial Thompson, He's missing," Scott said.

"Do they know what happened to him?" Jack asked.

"Not yet," Dylan said as he got himself a coffee.

"Well, I'm still workin' on a job. Come on over to the first bay with me," Jack said.

Jack turned off the lights in the reception area, but forgot to relock the entrance door. The three walked into the first bay together. Jack took the tool that he had left on the workbench and approached the truck. He started tightening the valve and seal on the hose and looked up at the two friends. "What did y'all find out?" he asked.

"We searched through old newspapers on microfiche today. Apparently, there was a string of armed bank robberies throughout the state in 1901. Then, the robberies stopped and the robbers disappeared," Dylan said.

"The police couldn't find the money or the two bank robbers and get this: John Thomas' and Charlie Rhodes' grandpas were the robbers," Scott added.

Jack bumped his head on the hood of the truck with a thud. "Shit! I knew Charlie and John were up to somethin'!" he yelled out as he rubbed his head. He walked over to the table near the two friends, placed his tool down and started cleaning his hands with a rag.

While the three were talking inside the auto body shop, Cornelius rolled into the parking lot with his truck headlights off. He noticed a second car parked on the lot and assumed it had been left overnight for service. He parked his pickup truck near the side of the building so that you could not see the truck from the road. Cornelius bent over and took out his handgun from the glove compartment. A few cigarettes fell out of his pocket onto the floor of the truck as he brushed up against the steering wheel. He put on his black leather gloves and ball cap. He opened the door of the truck, stepped out into the rain and unknowingly kicked the loose cigarettes onto the ground. He put his handgun under the belt of his jeans and took one last drag from his cigarette before tossing it into a puddle. He quietly snuck along the side of the building, dodging the lights from the shop, until he reached the front entrance door to the reception area. It was raining even harder now as he tugged at the door handle and to his surprise, it was unlocked. He opened the door as silently as he could, while thinking to himself how easy Jack was making this for him. Cornelius entered the shop, snuck behind the front reception counter and stayed out of sight. The lights in the reception area were off, but the lights in the first bay were on. Cornelius stood up long enough to peer over the counter through the glass window that looked into the first work bay and saw three people. He did not know the two friends, but recognized Jack.

In the bay, Jack, Dylan and Scott were telling each other jokes. Jack poked his head under the hood again when he realized he had the wrong tool. "Shit!" he said.

"What's wrong?" Scott asked.

Jack poked his head back out from under the hood. "I took the wrong wrench. Can you bring me the one on the workbench?" he asked. Scott put his coffee down, rose from the stool, approached the workbench, and took the tool that Jack was asking for.

Cornelius was getting ready to take his first shot from inside the reception area. He took aim at Jack, but Scott was in the way. Cornelius figured he'd break the glass first and then shoot at Jack in the commotion. Cornelius grabbed a heavy metal stool behind the reception desk and threw it at the window looking into the service bay. Pieces of shattered glass flew into the bay as the stool fell to the concrete floor with a loud clank. Dylan, Scott and Jack were taken completely by surprise as shots rang out from Cornelius' handgun. The bullets missed both Jack and Dylan but a single bullet hit Scott. The bullet dug deep into Scott's shoulder and caused him to drop the wrench. The wrench fell to the floor with a loud clatter. The three ducked for cover behind the pickup truck. "Shit!" Dylan cried out.

Scott winced in pain.

"I've got a shotgun in the cabinet against the wall. I'll go fetch it," Jack said as he began to move towards the cabinet. More shots rang out, but Cornelius missed.

Dylan grabbed one of Jack's work rags from the floor and gave it to Scott. "Here, put this on your shoulder," Dylan said.

"Just like ol' times," Scott said as he nodded his head.

Jack made it to the cabinet. He opened the door and another bullet flew over his head. "Shit!" Jack yelled out. He quickly took his shotgun and a pack of ammunition from the cabinet shelf, while Cornelius was reloading his handgun. Jack moved back to the truck where the two boys were hiding. Another shot rang out. Cornelius was starting to get frustrated and fired yet another round into the bay. Jack stood up and let out a loud blast from his shotgun.

Thunder and lightning filled the sky. Suddenly, the power went out. One passerby saw flashes of light coming from inside the first work bay and pulled into the parking lot. It was Bryan Long from the filling station on his way to meet his friend Ted Tillman at the Rusty Mule. At first glance, he thought it was just a power surge from the rainstorm, but as he got closer with his sedan, he realized he had seen muzzle flashes. "Jiminy Christmas!" he said out loud to himself. He backed his car onto the road as quickly as he could and floored it.

Under the cover of darkness, Cornelius moved out from behind the reception area counter and slowly headed to the door that led into the work bay. Jack heard the door creak open, and let another blast out from his shotgun. The blast hit the door behind Cornelius. Cornelius stayed low and found a screwdriver lying on the floor. He picked it up, jammed it under the door to keep it open and moved behind a workbench to the right of the door inside the bay.

Jack crouched back down behind the truck and looked at Dylan and Scott.

"Before we all die in here, I don't reckon you have another gun or a flashlight lying around anywhere?" Dylan asked.

Jack looked at Dylan and pointed to the far wall. "In the other cabinet, top shelf. I'll lay down cover fire. Go when I shoot," Jack said. Dylan nodded. Jack rose to his feet and let two loud blasts out from his shotgun. Dylan snuck towards the wall as carefully as he could in the darkness. He opened the cabinet door, felt around the shelves and found a revolver and flashlight. He took them both as a shot whistled passed his chest. Dylan jumped out of the way, and Jack let another blast out towards Cornelius as Dylan made his way back behind the pickup truck.

Bryan arrived at the Rusty Mule and parked his car in the first empty space he found. Unlike Jack's garage, the bar had power to spare. Bryan got out and ran towards the bar entrance. He threw the doors open and scanned the bar hoping to find the sheriff. Bryan hurriedly walked around the bar, muttering to himself, until he spotted the sheriff with his female deputy sitting at a table in the corner. They were both off duty and out of uniform.

Bryan approached the sheriff, dripping wet with a wild look in his eyes. "Boy, am I glad I found you two! There's a gunfight over at Hickory Creek Auto Body!" Bryan said as he grabbed a nearby chair. "I saw muzzle flashes!"

Yates took a pull from his cigar, put his drink down unfinished, grabbed his coat and glanced at Bryan. "Don't worry, Bryan. We'll go investigate," Yates said.

Bryan let out a sigh of relief. "You gonna finish your beer?" he began to say as he turned around, but Yates and Bonnie had already left. Bryan grabbed the beer mug left behind and doused his excitement with alcohol.

Yates approached Hickory Creek Auto Body in the sheriff's cruiser with Bonnie by his side. He turned into the front parking lot and stopped on the west side of the building. The two officers got out and began to approach the bays in the rain. "I see muzzle flashes coming from inside. It looks like two, no three people? It's hard to tell in the dark with all this rain," Bonnie said.

"And that's Dylan's Camaro," Yates said. "He and Scott must be inside with Jack. There gotta be four of 'em?"

Cornelius saw a red light flashing from a car outside and rethought his position. He assumed it was the law and took no more chances. He retreated into the reception area while firing more rounds. The officers approached the entrance door to the reception area. Cornelius fumbled around in the dark and found a door. He quickly opened it and slipped into another room just before the officers opened the entrance door and stepped inside. Cornelius found himself in the stockroom of Jack's garage. He carefully made his way through the room, in the dark, until he found a rear exit door and silently stepped outside.

"Don't move! This is the police!" Yates called out.

"In here, Sherriff!" Jack yelled back.

Yates and Bonnie entered the bay as Jack and Dylan placed their guns on the floor and rose to their feet. Suddenly, they heard the engine of a pickup truck rumble through the storm. "I'll go after him. You stay here," Yates yelled. Yates ran out of the building only to see the assailant fire two rounds at the sheriff's cruiser, shooting the rear tire flat on the driver's side. Yates fired his revolver, shattering the back glass of the truck, and a rear tail light, but it did not slow Cornelius down. The truck roared off leaving Yates steaming mad in the Tennessee rain.

Jack yanked the service bay door open and shone his flashlight at Yates. "Did you get 'em?" he asked.

"No. The son of a bitch shot my tire flat and got away," Yates replied.

"Dang!" Jack said.

"Call the ambulance. Scott's been hit in the shoulder," Bonnie shouted from inside.

"You wanna replace my tire while we wait on the ambulance?" Yates asked.

"Will do, Sheriff. There's a phone in the reception area y'all can use," Jack said.

Yates entered the building, approached the counter and called the hospital. He returned to his car, took a flashlight out of the trunk and started to walk around the building. He reached the east side of the building where the truck had been parked. He shone the light around and bent down to pick up a few cigarettes lying on the ground. One was partially smoked floating in a puddle, the others lying in the mud. He placed them inside a small bag, rose to his feet and walked back into the bay. He saw Bonnie, Scott, Dylan and Jack standing together. "How are you feeling, Scott?" Yates asked.

Scott leaned up against the truck. "It hurts, but I'll feel better when I get to the hospital," he replied.

"Do any of you have any reason why someone would want to shoot you?" Yates asked.

All three men shook their heads.

"Scott and I just came here to bug Jack, and all hell broke loose," Dylan said.

"I was working on a customer's truck. I hope he's insured 'cause it's full of bullet holes now," Jack added.

Yates continued to interview the three men, taking their statements. When he finished, he turned around and walked away from the others towards the open bay door. He leaned up against the side of the wall and stared out into the rain, thinking to himself.

"I'll be right back. The ambulance should be here soon," Bonnie said as she walked towards Yates. "What's wrong?" she asked.

"That big Chevy K20, two-tone, pickup truck, was the same one I saw the other day where Peter was conked out," Yates whispered.

"You mean when I left you alone at the cabin?"

"Yup."

"That's good and bad. Wait, I know what you're thinking. No, those two boys couldn't possibly be involved."

Yates looked out into the rainstorm.

"It's not the boys," Yates replied. "I found a few unsmoked cigarettes in the mud."

Suddenly, the lights began to flicker as the power came back on. The rain finally stopped and the wind started to die down. Yates and Bonnie turned around, walked back inside and saw the full extent of the gunfight.

There were bullet holes and shotgun blasts everywhere. Yates noticed the broken glass window and the metal stool on the floor. He looked down and observed that the door connecting the bay to the reception area was propped open with a screwdriver. He walked into the reception area and determined that the assailant had thrown the metal stool through the glass window from behind the counter. Yates turned around and saw another door and walked over to it. He opened the door and turned on the lights. It was the stockroom. He walked through the room to the back door that had been left open a crack and pushed it with the toe of his boot. He looked outside and saw the back of the garage and deduced that the assailant had come in through the unlocked reception area door and escaped through the stockroom exit door. Yates returned to the bay and found Bonnie picking bullets out of the wall. "I found a back door that our assailant used to make his escape," Yates said.

"I'm finding .32 caliber bullets and casings here. The bullet casing I found at the River View Mine where Thompson disappeared was also a .32 caliber. We should check for prints," Bonnie said.

"You won't find any prints. Our man was wearing gloves. I saw when he shot my tire flat. Keep looking though," Yates replied as the ambulance arrived.

The ambulance came to a stop at the open bay door and two paramedics came out. "Where's the patient?" the first paramedic asked.

"Over here," Yates replied as he motioned with his hand.

"My shoulder, I've been shot," Scott said.

The two paramedics tended to Scott's wound as they helped him into the back of the ambulance.

"I'll follow along behind and go with him to the hospital," Dylan said. He got into his car and followed the ambulance out of the parking lot and onto the main road, heading to the hospital.

"Shit, we really shot my place up!" Jack said.

"You're lucky there was only one injury," Yates replied. "Bonnie, are you done?"

"Yup, I got everything I need," Bonnie replied. "And I got photos, too."

"Jack, call me if you remember anything else and thanks for replacing my tire," Yates said. "And if I can make one suggestion to you, remember to lock your doors."

Jack's jaw dropped as he now remembered leaving the reception area entrance door unlocked after Dylan and Scott arrived.

The two officers left the scene.

# 16

Cornelius arrived at his girlfriend's property outside of Lancaster Falls and parked his truck out of sight, under a tree in back. He entered the house and found Shawna glued to the TV watching a late-night talk show. She was wearing a pair of hot pants and a tank top with no bra underneath leaving nothing to the imagination. She did not notice Cornelius enter the home until he walked over to her and sat down beside her on the couch. Cornelius leaned over, took a pack of cigarettes off the coffee table and struck a match.

"Did y'all get another job done, suga'?" Shawna asked.

Cornelius took a long drag from the cigarette and placed his arm around her. "Sort of. The law showed up, so I had to get out of there," he replied.

"Did you find the money yet?" Shawna asked as she took a drag from her cigarette.

"I'm getting closer," Cornelius replied.

"You sure are smart keepin' things from John and Charlie. I bet you're hungry. Why don't you relax, while I whip somethin' up for y'all to eat."

Cornelius took a drag from his cigarette, nodded his head,

and stared at the TV. Shawna rose from the couch and headed towards the kitchen. Cornelius leaned over, grabbed the phone off the table and dialed John's number. The phone rang and rang while Cornelius looked at his watch. "Come on man. Answer the damn phone you fucker," he muttered to himself.

John was also in front of the TV watching the same late-night talk show and barely heard the phone ringing. He rose from the couch and ran down the long hallway to his office.

Upon hearing his father, Peter placed the magazine he was reading down on his bed, walked over to his bedroom door and opened it a crack, but did not see anyone. He started down the hallway quietly in his socked feet and heard his father talking on the phone. Peter stood motionless carefully listening.

"Yeah, I'll send a guy over tomorrow morning to fix your truck. Stop worrying," John said. "Fuck the cops. Shoot 'em if they get in the way."

Peter's jaw dropped to the floor. He had heard enough. He quietly retreated to his bedroom and left his father talking on the phone.

Shawna came out of the kitchen with a platter of sandwiches and a couple of beers just as Cornelius hung up the phone receiver. She happily placed everything on the coffee table in front of Cornelius and sat down beside him. She took a sandwich for herself and began to eat. Cornelius did the same and opened a beer bottle. Shawna leaned back on the couch and a glob of ketchup and mustard fell out of the sandwich onto her tank top. She looked down at her ample chest, took her finger, dabbed it on the ketchup stain and licked her finger with a smile. "Silly me. Whatever should I do?" she asked innocently.

Cornelius looked at her while taking a swig of beer and let out a loud belch. "I don't know. Use a tissue," he replied sarcastically.

Shawna looked at him disappointedly. She leaned over to kiss Cornelius and smelt a faint odor of perfume on his clothes and saw a faded smear of lipstick on his neck, above the collar, under his ear. She blinked twice and moved her head back. "What's a girl gotta do to get some lovin' 'round here?" she said as she got up and walked back into the kitchen.

"Bring me some more beer while you're in there!" Cornelius hollered.

Shawna took a towel and wet it under the faucet. She took her top off, wiped her chest with the wet towel and washed her tank top in the sink. She slipped her wet top back on and thought to herself: *Who the hell has he been seein' behind my back? As if I even have to ask. If I could just kill him in his sleep, then I wouldn't have to deal with his bullshit anymore.*

"Hey, where's the beer, man!" Cornelius yelled out.

Shawna opened the fridge, took four beers, walked back into the living room and placed the beers on the coffee table in front of Cornelius. She then stood in front of the TV blocking it. All you could see was Shawna's long bare legs and hot pants. Cornelius took a cold beer from the table, opened it and took a swig while smoking his cigarette. "Get out of the way, woman. This guy's funny tonight," he said rudely.

Shawna was about to burst with anger and frustration. She stormed out of the living room. "You're impossible!" she screamed as she ran upstairs and locked herself in her bedroom for the night. She stood in front of the mirrored closet and stared at herself. She began to dance to the music in her head. "You're such a dish. Why do you waste your time with a two-bit, cheatin' hood like him?" She began to strip in front of the mirror. She took her top off and grabbed her ample chest with her hands. "You're not gettin' any of these tonight, Cornelius." She bit her finger seductively and shook her head as if to say *no* to herself in the mirror. She bent down, sat on the floor and slid out of her hot pants. With her legs high in the air, she spun around on her backside and kicked her shorts onto the bed. She rose to her feet, looked at herself in the mirror, turned around, ran and jumped naked onto her bed and curled up under the sheets. "Maybe, I'll find a new man. One that won't cheat on me! Then I'll take that heist money all for myself," she said as she closed her eyes and went to sleep with a smile on her face.

Meanwhile, Cornelius polished off the food and beer that Shawna had prepared for him and fell asleep on the couch, snoring in front of the TV.

# 17

THE NEXT MORNING, Cornelius was sitting on the porch steps waiting on the repairman that John had promised. Cornelius was smoking a cigarette and drinking his morning coffee when Shawna came out of the house in her high heels and took a seat beside him. She was wearing almost nothing and was never shy about flaunting her assets. She took a pack of cigarettes out of her rear pocket and nudged Cornelius with her elbow for a light.

"Put some clothes on woman. The guy's comin' to fix the truck," Cornelius ordered.

Shawna gave him her saddest look. "Please, suga' bear, a light?"

Cornelius turned to her and flicked his lighter.

Shawna inhaled the smoke and felt the effect of nicotine. "Now if you'd only flick your other lighter."

At that moment, the repairman John had promised rolled up the driveway.

"Get in the house. Maybe later. I've got jobs to do," Cornelius barked.

Shawna rose from the steps and waved to the repairman,

then turned around and walked back inside the house. She was still mad at Cornelius and still wanted a new man, a man who would pay more attention to her needs and wants. Shawna did not need Cornelius for much of anything anymore. She had her own money now. Shawna did not care for the secrecy of the jobs he did either and despised his drug addiction. Cornelius had not been addicted to drugs when they first met a decade ago. The Romano family did not deal drugs back then, but over time things changed. What made matters worse was now Shawna suspected Cornelius of seeing someone else behind her back and she had a pretty good idea of who it was.

The repairman parked near the carport. Cornelius rose from the porch steps and walked over to him.

"David Wilks, here. John says y'all got a truck needs fixin'." David's right cheek was swollen with tobacco. He turned his head and spat a wad of brown spittle into a puddle of water. He reached into the bed of his truck and grabbed the toolbox.

"Over this way," Cornelius said.

"Nice place y'all got here," David said. He looked around at the trees, green grass, flowerbeds, gazebo, and then eyed Shawna in the second floor window doing her bra and putting on a T-shirt. His eyes almost popped out of their sockets. "Real nice place."

The two men walked over to Cornelius' truck. David looked at the damage on it. "Think you can fix it?" Cornelius asked.

"Y'all gonna need a new rear window and a new taillight." He tapped the broken light with his knuckles and stuck his finger into the bullet holes on the tailgate, "…

and a bullet hole here and here. I can fix that too with some filler and paint. I reckon that should about do it. I'll leave my toolbox here by yer truck, and I'll git the parts I need and come back in about an hour," David said.

The two men walked back to David's truck. Cornelius took a drag from his cigarette. "I may not be here when you get back, so just do the job and leave."

David opened the door to his truck, jumped inside, started the engine and stuck his head out the window. "Will do," he said. David backed out of the driveway onto the main road and headed in the direction of the car parts store with a wad of John's cash in his pocket to buy the necessary parts.

Around an hour had passed when David returned to Shawna's house to fix Cornelius' truck. David pulled into the driveway, honked his horn and waved at Shawna who was watering her flowerbeds. He stopped his truck shy of the carport, took a wad of fresh tobacco and jammed it into the right side of his mouth. He walked over to the rear of his truck, opened the tailgate and began unfastening the new glass window panel. Shawna saw David struggling. She dropped the water hose and walked over to him. "Would you like a hand with that?" she asked.

David managed to unfasten the first strap. "Yes, ma'am," he replied.

Shawna nodded, climbed onto the truck and the two unfastened and unloaded the glass panel. They walked over to Cornelius' truck and carefully sat the glass panel down on the ground. "By the way, where is Cornelius?" David asked.

Shawna leaned against the truck and let out a sigh. "Oh, he left after you did with someone to do some job or some-thin'. I don't even bother anymore," she replied.

David hopped onto the bed of the truck with his toolbox and began removing what was left of the old glass panel. Shawna went over to him, sat down on the open tailgate and began swinging her legs back and forth as he worked.

"I'm done here. Can y'all give me a hand with the new glass panel?" David asked.

"Sure can!"

The two walked over to the glass panel, lifted it, carried it onto the bed of the truck and very gently positioned the panel into place. "Hold it with those thingamaboobs… I mean bobs while I go inside the truck," David reddened.

Shawna smiled mischievously and pressed her body up against the glass panel. David stepped into the cabin of the truck and was greeted with Shawna's chest pressed up against the glass. He almost choked on his tobacco. David coughed, spat a large wad of saliva on the ground, and then coughed again. "Okay, you can let go now," he said.

Shawna let go of the glass leaving an imprint of her body behind. She jumped off the bed of the truck, threw her arms around David and walked her fingernails up his chest. "What now, suga' plum?" she asked with a smile.

David coughed and spat on the ground again. "Please, Miss Shawna, you're gonna give this ol' man a heart attack."

Shawna giggled and released David. David walked over to his truck, grabbed the new taillight and came back to install it.

Shawna watched David. She gave him the tools he needed from his toolbox. It was a quick job for him to do.

"Now to fill these bullet holes and paint over the filler," David said.

"Great! Where's the filler? I used to do this stuff with my pa," Shawna exclaimed.

"In the toolbox. Lift up the first drawer. It's under that," David replied.

Shawna took the filler from the toolbox and handed it to David. "Tell me somethin'. Have you heard anythin' 'bout the lost heist money?" she asked.

David began to work on the first bullet hole. "I shouldn't be talkin' about it," he replied.

"Come on, now. You can tell me. We both work for the same man," Shawna said as she leaned over and whispered in his ear. "Maybe we can do somethin' together, suga'."

David's eyes popped out and he dropped the filler on the ground. "I'm a married man and I don't particularly want Cornelius to kill me!" he said.

Shawna began to walk her long fingernails up David's shoulder and started to scratch the back of his neck in an attempt to further persuade him. "Please," she panted in his ear. "I'll make it worth your while."

The hair on the back of David's neck stood erect. He thought for a brief moment and cleared his throat. "If I tell you what I know and you find it, y'all have to promise to cut me in."

"It's a deal," Shawna replied.

"Alright, but you didn't hear anythin' from me. Remember that," David said with a smile. "John has narrowed it down to the last two mines where Joshua and Doug work. But I've been doin' my homework and my money is on Miller Hill Mine where Doug works. It's the oldest and biggest mine in the area and dates back to the time of the heists. It has a lot of closed up tunnels inside. The loot has to be down one of those tunnels no longer in use and before you go askin', I'll tell y'all straight away, that I'm too damn old to go on any damn treasure hunt and I ain't fixin' to get my ass shot off anytime soon either."

"Was that so hard," Shawna whispered as she leaned over and kissed him on the cheek leaving a pair of red lips behind on his skin.

"No, I suppose that wasn't," David replied.

The two continued to fix the bullet holes, sanding them down and painting them over until the job was done.

"What are y'all gonna do with the broken glass and junk?" Shawna asked.

"I'm just gonna bring it to the dump," David replied. He walked over to the cab of his truck and hopped inside. "It was my pleasure meetin' y'all. And thanks for the help!"

"Anytime suga' and I'll see y'all real soon," Shawna said and blew David a kiss.

"I'll hold you to that," David smiled.

David backed out of the driveway and honked his horn a few times at Shawna as she waved goodbye to him and blew him another kiss.

# 18

PETER WAS EATING a club sandwich in the kitchen when he heard his father walk down the hallway heading for the front door. Peter placed his sandwich down on the plate and rose from his stool to see if his father had left. He walked down the hall, into the living room and pulled the window curtain open a crack. He watched his father drive down the long laneway of the property and disappear out of sight. Peter decided that now was the perfect time to do some investigating.

Peter hurried to his father's office, opened the door and entered. Peter was not sure what he would find, but was looking for anything that would confirm his suspicions about his father. Peter tried to open the desk drawers, but they were all locked. He quickly scanned the office and walked over to the filing cabinets near the wall. He began opening the drawers, looking at the names on the files. He recognized all of the names. Nothing stood out. They were all names of mine workers, foremen and managers, files for accounts payables and receivables. He walked around the office to the bar at the far end of the room. He began opening cabinets and drawers, moving bottles of alcohol and rifling through papers until he came upon an unknown ledger. He placed the ledger on the counter top and opened it. He rifled through the pages, but it was all numbers front to back. He looked at the last entries and noticed the dates and dollar amounts. Peter turned white as a sheet. The last date matched the disappearance of Foreman Nathaniel Thompson. Peter remembered Jeb, the strange bald-headed man who came to Peter's house looking for his father. Peter speculated that Jeb had been looking for his payment for murdering Thompson and Thompson was dead just as the sheriff had concluded. There were two more dates and dollar amounts listed, and Peter guessed that these were payments for the murders of Foreman Raymond Moore and Manager Ben Stevens.

Peter placed the ledger back where he had found it. He left his father's office and walked down the hallway to the front entrance. He exited the house and walked to the garage, got into his '65 Ford Thunderbird and drove down the laneway and onto the main road.

Peter drove for a good five minutes when he suddenly spotted the orange Honda dirt bike with the broken fender that the sheriff had said to look for. The dirt bike turned onto the road three car lengths ahead of him. Peter began to follow at a distance. They drove by the filling station and along the river. The dirt bike turned into town and Peter continued to follow. The dirt bike did not have any rearview mirrors and the driver who was wearing a helmet never turned around to look behind. Eventually, the driver led Peter straight to the Rusty Mule. Peter pulled off to the shoulder of the road and watched the dirt bike disappear behind the building. He parked by the roadside in front of the bar and waited.

# 19

Shawna Ray strolled into the police station and approached Beth who was sitting at the desk near the front door. Shawna was wearing high heels, bell-bottom blue jeans and a white men's dress shirt tied at the waist. She carried a small red leather clutch in one hand. She wore makeup, perfume and her long yellow feathered hair flowed down her back. She pursed her red lips together and sucked down the last fumes from her cigarette before mashing it into the crystal ashtray on Beth's desk.

"Can I help you, Miss?" Beth asked.

Shawna tossed a loose strand of hair over her shoulder. "I'm here to see the sheriff."

"Do you have an appointment? What's this about?" Beth asked suspiciously.

Shawna smiled as innocently as she could manage. "I think I have a lead for him on a case. I need to see him."

Beth rose from her chair. "Wait here a minute, and I'll go see if he's busy." She walked to the sheriff's office and knocked on the door.

"Come in!" Yates said.

Beth opened the door and stuck her head inside. "There's a young lady here to see you. Says she has some information on a case that you're working on. Not sure if I believe her. She looks like a hooker!" Beth whispered.

Yates smiled. "Thank you, Beth. You can send her in. We'll see what she has to say."

Beth shut the office door, returned to her desk and sat down. "You can see him now. It's the last door. His name is on the door," she said.

"Why bless your heart," Shawna said sarcastically.

Shawna sauntered over to the sheriff's office, shaking her hips and making a loud noise with her high heels on the hardwood floor. She passed Bonnie's office and knocked on the sheriff's door. Bonnie rose from her chair, stuck her head out of her office and saw a woman opening the sheriff's door and entering. Bonnie wondered who this mysterious woman was and what she was doing. Shawna closed the sheriff's office door.

Yates looked up from behind his file and rose from his chair. "Please, come in. Have a seat."

Shawna walked over to Yates and took a seat on the empty chair in front of his desk. She put her red clutch down on the empty seat next to her, reached out with her hand and introduced herself: "My name is Shawna Ray."

Yates took her hand. "Pleased to meet you. What do I owe this pleasure?""

"Well, I'm here about my boyfriend. I think he's involved with somethin', but I'm not sure what it is." Shawna suddenly burst into tears. "He's always off doing jobs late at night, or strange hours of the day. He comes home and hardly pays any attention to me. I think he's doin' somethin' illegal." She reached into her clutch and pulled out a tissue to dry her crocodile tears.

Yates took a pull from his cigar, walked around to her and sat down on the corner of the desk in front of her. "Please, go on. What's his name?"

Outside Yates' office, Bonnie had her ear pressed to the door listening and motioning to Beth that Shawna was off her rocker. Beth smiled and began to laugh.

Shawna wiped more crocodile tears from her cheeks. "His name is Cornelius, Cornelius Bennett. He's my boyfriend. A good-for-nothin' two-bit cheatin' hood," she said.

"Cornelius? Does he live with you?" Yates asked.

Shawna rose from her chair, put her head on Yates' shoulder, and started to cry even more. "He sure does. I just don't know what to do anymore. The other night, I thought he was fixin' to beat me, so I locked myself in my bedroom, and he fell asleep in front of the TV, drunk and stoned," she said.

Yates stood up from the corner of his desk, put his cigar in the crystal ashtray and placed his hand on her shoulder to console her. "Does he smoke?" Yates asked curiously.

"Who doesn't? Of course, he does."

"What kind of cigarettes does he smoke?"

"I don't know. Why does it matter?" Shawna replied defensively as she took a pack of cigarettes from her clutch and stuck a match.

Yates recognized that the brand she was smoking matched the cigarettes he found at Jack's garage and changed the question. "And what does he look like? So, I can tell my deputies to watch out for him."

"Bald, tall like you, muscular with tattoos," Shawna replied as she touched Yates' bicep.

"Does he wear anything that would stand out, that is noticeable? Let's say a piece of jewelry?" Yates asked.

Shawna began to sniffle as she caressed his arm. "All these questions are gonna tire a girl out."

"It would help a great deal."

"Alright suga', he wears crystal rings on his fingers in the shape of skulls."

"Okay, I want you to leave your telephone number and address with me. If he tries anything, you contact the station straight away."

"Oh, thank you, suga'!" Shawna said in an innocent voice. She stopped crying immediately and did not say anything further. She stood there for a moment and suddenly reached out, grabbed Yates and pulled him to her chest, squeezing him tight. "I could eat you up," she whispered breathlessly.

At that point, Bonnie had heard enough and burst into Yates' office. "I need that file you were working on," she said calmly.

Yates scanned Bonnie with relief and began to break Shawna's lock on him. "Please, Miss. Shawna!" He removed her arms from around his back.

Shawna looked at Bonnie and gave her a wicked look which Bonnie returned. "I think the gentleman was asking you to leave," Bonnie said.

"Oh, I see how it is. You can't compete with me, suga'," Shawna exclaimed.

Shawna grabbed her clutch and passed Bonnie on the way out. The two ladies glared at each other and gave each other the *malocchio*. Shawna walked through the station and out the entrance door, heading to her convertible, '72

Corvette that she had parked in front of the police station. Shawna smiled to herself and was content with what she had done. Her plan was coming together perfectly. She popped her car in gear and sped off across the town square, heading back to her home.

Shortly, Peter pulled his Thunderbird into the police station parking lot. He got out of his car, headed inside and greeted Beth who smiled at him from her typewriter. "Peter! How are you feeling today?" she asked.

"I'm feeling better. Is the sheriff in and Bonnie too?"

"They sure are. Go say hi!"

Peter walked through the station to Bonnie's office and knocked on her door. She was doing some paperwork when he entered. "I have to talk to Robert. Let's go," Peter exclaimed as he grabbed Bonnie by the hand and yanked her from her chair. The two deputies entered the sheriff's office.

"Look who I found, Robert!" Bonnie said as she stood at the door.

"Peter! Come in. Please, both of you, take a seat."

Peter sat down and began to tell his story. "I decided to do some snooping at home after I saw my pa leave."

"Oh! Please, do tell," Yates said.

"I snuck into his office and started looking around. I didn't find much at first, but I did find a ledger with dates and dollar amounts. One of the dates matched the day that Foreman Nathaniel Thompson disappeared. It was around the same time a bald-headed man with tattoos came looking for my pa. There were also two more dates with dollar amounts next to them. I'm thinking the dates coincide with Ben Stevens and Raymond Moore's deaths."

"Did you say a bald-headed man with tattoos?" Yates asked.

"Yeah, why? Did I miss something today?" Peter asked curiously.

"The girlfriend showed up while you were out. The man's name is Cornelius Bennett," Bonnie replied.

"He told me his name was Jeb when he showed up at my place and he spoke with a Florida accent," Peter said.

"He lives with his girlfriend and she has a Florida accent as well. I have her address and phone number. Peter, see if you can find any information on this man," Yates said.

"There's one more thing," Peter said. "When I left my place, I spotted that orange Honda dirt bike with the broken fender you told us to watch out for. I followed the driver along the river and into town until the bike finally turned into the Rusty Mule and drove around to the back of the building and disappeared."

Yates and Bonnie both looked at each other. "Disappeared?"

"Yeah. I waited for over an hour in front and never saw the bike leave. So, I finally drove around back and no bike."

"Did the driver see you?" Yates asked.

"No, sir. I kept my distance. The driver had on a helmet and never turned around to look."

"That's curious," Yates said. "Now, I'm definitely there's convinced something's going on. Good work!"

Peter left the office. Yates took a pull from his cigar and walked towards the window. Bonnie followed. "This case keeps getting more and more intriguing," he said.

# 20

JOHN ARRIVED AT the Rusty Mule just in time for his weekly meeting with Charlie. John stepped out of his truck and lit a cigarette. He walked into the bar and waved at Charlie who was exiting the kitchen. John sat on a bar stool, tapped the cigarette ash into the ashtray and whistled for Samantha. Sam finished mixing drinks and drifted over to him at the far end of the bar counter. "What's your fancy?" she asked.

"Just a beer," John replied.

Sam nodded her head, poured a cold beer from the keg and slid it over to him. John grabbed his beer, took a drag from his cigarette and disappeared in back.

No sooner had John stepped into Charlie's office when Cornelius arrived. He too waved to Charlie, took a seat on a bar stool and motioned for a drink. "Cold beer," he said.

Charlie provided the beer. Cornelius took a swallow and followed Charlie to the back office where John was already waiting for them, sitting at the desk with his feet up, drinking his beer and taking a drag from another freshly lit cigarette. Cornelius took a seat on the leather couch, while Charlie sat down in front of his desk.

"Comfortable?" Charlie asked sarcastically.

"Yes, I do think I am rightly so," John said with a sneer. He placed his beer down and leaned up against the desk. "Alright, I called you both here to tell you that the Earl Hopper Mine is a no go. The foreman got back to me and said there was nothing."

"Isn't that the mine that Ben Stevens managed?" Cornelius asked.

"Yeah, lucky for us the foreman is on our side," John said.

"Well, that narrows it down," Charlie added.

John got up from the chair with his beer and took a gulp. "Yeah, just the River View Mine and Miller Hill Mine are left."

Cornelius took a drink from his beer and put the mug down on the coffee table in front of him. "Now we're getting somewhere," he said with a smug grin.

"You still need to knock off that drunk," Charlie said angrily.

"Yeah, I'll get the sorry son of a bitch," Cornelius replied.

"Now that that is out of the way," John said, "when are you expecting the next shipment from Florida?"

"The boys are bringing it in a food delivery truck by the end of the week. Enough smack to sell on the streets of this shithole for a month," Cornelius replied.

"Good, good," John said.

"Speaking of which, where's mine?" Cornelius demanded.

"Not again. Follow me," Charlie said.

The three men left Charlie's office together and headed to the stockroom. Charlie unlocked the door, flipped the lights on and the three entered the room. They walked to the very back where Charlie and Cornelius moved a cabinet out of the way to reveal a secret door. Charlie took his key chain from his pocket, unlocked the door and the three entered another room. This room was much smaller than the actual stockroom itself and had shelves of drugs, with a lab in back. Charlie grabbed one tiny bag of white powder and handed it to Cornelius. "You need to get off this shit," Charlie said.

"Shut your damn mouth and do your fuckin' job. Without me, you'd both be dead," Cornelius barked.

Charlie stood right up to Cornelius' face. "You think we can't handle things without you?"

"No, I don't think you can," Cornelius yelled as he pushed Charlie back.

John immediately stepped between the two. "Let's all be friends here," he said calmly.

Cornelius turned around, emptied the contents of the bag onto a shelf and began to snort the powder. John and Charlie left the room and started bickering in the stockroom.

"That guy's a liability. He'll fuck up everything!" Charlie said.

"Keep your voice down," John said as he put his arm on Charlie's shoulder and turned Charlie away from the secret room. The two men began to walk to the front of the stockroom, away from Cornelius.

"Just let him do the dirty work. If we're lucky, the sheriff will take care of him for us," John whispered.

"You'd better be right about that," Charlie said angrily. "Cornelius, you finished in there?" he barked out.

Cornelius walked out of the secret room rubbing his nose. "Throw me the keys. I'll lock up.'

"You got to be kidding me," Charlie said to John.

"Just throw him the damn keys," John said.

Charlie shook his head and threw Cornelius the keys. Cornelius closed and locked the secret door. He muscled the cabinet back into place by himself and tossed the keys back to Charlie. The three men walked out of the stockroom, down the hall and into the bar. Charlie settled behind the bar counter while John and Cornelius took a seat at one of the booths near the window and ordered something to eat.

## 21

Sue-Ellen and Sara were saying their goodbyes to Dylan and Scott. The two girls had spent a good part of the day with the boys at the hospital and now it was time for them to go to work, waitressing at a local restaurant. Dylan put his magazine down on the counter, approached the window and looked outside.

"What're y'all thinkin' about?" Scott asked.

Dylan turned around and took a seat on the chair next to the bed. "I was thinkin' about what occurred the other night."

"I've been thinkin' about it too."

"Considerin' what happened to Ben, I think someone might want Jack dead because of what he knows about the money."

"But they don't know that we know what Jack knows."

"Keep your voice down," Dylan whispered.

Outside in the hallway, Lisa LeBlanc, an intern doctor, heard the two friends talking and stopped next to the door to listen. She bit her lower ruby red lip as she strained her ears to hear what the two friends were saying.

"No one knows that we know, except Jack. We have to keep it that way, or we might be next," Dylan said.

"Do you think that Jack knows that someone is out to do him in?" Scott asked.

"If he's smart, he does and he'll be more careful from now on, which is exactly what we need to be," Dylan said.

"Man, I'll be glad when I'm outta here."

"Me too."

Lisa quietly darted down the hallway to the pay phones near the nurses' station. She stuck her bubblegum under the phone, took a dime from her pocket and began to dial the private office number of the Rusty Mule.

"Rusty Mule, speakin'?" Cornelius said.

"Oh, Cornelius, baby! We've got a problem," Lisa said in a sultry voice over the phone receiver.

"What?"

"You know that guy you shot at Jack's place, he and his friend are here."

"Who?"

"They know what Jack knows."

"What're you talkin' about?"

"What are we gonna do?"

"You're the doctor, you figure it out."

"Well, I could… Oh, Cornelius baby, did you find the money yet?"

Cornelius belches.

"When do I get to see you again? Oh, I know what to do. Plenty of pillows 'round here."

"Meet me at the hideout."

"Fuck that. I'm not going to no abandoned mine again."

"I have to meet John later tonight. I don't have time for this!"

"What about the waterfront after I get off work?"

"Ah, no. Shawna might find out. Call me here first, after you've taken care of the boy."

"Done and done," Lisa replied as she hung up the phone with a grin from ear to ear.

## 22

A WOMAN WEARING a sundress, high heels, and a fashionable hat stepped out of the rear seat of a taxicab. Her long strawberry blonde hair curled down her back, and shone in the sun. She leaned into the open passenger car window and handed the driver a hefty tip. "Wait here a lil' while for me, please. I'll be back soon," she said. The cab driver nodded, grabbed the newspaper from the passenger seat and began flipping through the sports pages while watching the meter.

The lady walked into the police station and stood looking around wide-eyed and nervous, not knowing what to expect or say, even though she had gone through everything in her mind hundreds of times before arriving. Beth saw the lady standing at the entrance and wondered who she was. "Can I help you, Miss?"

The lady approached Beth at her desk. "I'm looking for Sheriff Robert Yates. Is he here today?" she asked.

Beth looked at the lady suspiciously and thought, not another Shawna. "Who may I ask is enquiring?" she said.

"My name is Melanie Yates. I'm Robert's wife."

Beth was surprised. "Just a minute, please. Let me see if

he's in." Beth rose from her chair and left Melanie standing nervously. Beth approached the sheriff's office and rapped the back of her knuckles on the door, opened it a crack and poked her head inside. "There's a lady here to see you. Says her name is Melanie Yates, your wife?"

Sitting at his desk reading a file, Yates' heart skipped a beat. He picked up his cigar and laid the file down. "I should've seen this coming," he muttered to himself.

"Pardon?"

"Never mind. Send her in."

Beth nodded and closed the door. She returned to her desk and looked at Melanie still standing in the same place, fidgeting with her purse strap. "He's in his office. Last door," Beth pointed.

Melanie thanked Beth and walked through the station. First, she passed Peter's office and then Bonnie's office before arriving at the sheriff's door. Melanie took a nervous gulp, turned the doorknob and entered. Bonnie who was working at her desk caught a glimpse of a strange, attractive, middle-aged, tall woman walking by and wondered who she was. Melanie closed the office door behind her and removed her hat and sunglasses. "Hello, Robert," she said.

Yates put his cigar down and rose from his chair. "What in the hell are you doing here?" he demanded.

Melanie sat in the chair in front of his desk and put her purse down on the opposite seat. "You're not making this easy for me. I'm nervous enough as it is, Robert," she said.

"You got some nerve coming here after what you did. What the hell do you want?" Yates shouted.

Melanie burst into tears. "I know I made a mistake. I didn't want that, Robert. I was lonely. You were gone all the time at work, being a cop, putting in long hours. I didn't know what to do. It just happened."

"Just happened? Let me get this straight. You cheating is somehow my fault? Why did you come here?"

Melanie got up from her chair, took the divorce papers out of her purse and waved them in the air. "I came here to ask for forgiveness and reconciliation. I thought maybe we could act like two grown adults and try again," Melanie yelled out. She threw the papers down on Yates' desk in front of him.

Bonnie was standing outside of her office and heard the estranged couple arguing and yelling at each other. She shook her head, walked back into her office, grabbed her coat and hat and approached Beth at her desk. "I'm not gonna stick 'round here to hear those two fightin' all afternoon. I'm goin' out for a bit," she said.

"What do you want me to tell Robert?" Beth asked.

"Tell him whatever you want."

Beth looked curiously at Bonnie as she exited the station. Beth turned her head towards the sheriff's office and heard the couple still bickering.

"Robert, I still love you. Can't you see that? What am I supposed to do? I know I made a mistake. We all make mistakes," Melanie yelled out.

"You slept with another man! That's more than a mistake. I've moved on with my life. Why do you think I travelled halfway across the damned country!?" Yates shouted.

"Is this really about my affair or is it just an excuse to end things because I can't have children."

"We've been through this story countless times, so don't try to change the subject, Melanie." Yates said. "I accepted your condition a long time ago and I still married you because I loved you."

Melanie calmed down a little. "I didn't realize Robert," she said.

"You didn't realize a lot of things, Melanie. If you were lonely, you should've talked to me about it, instead of having a damned affair," Yates shouted as he walked over to the window and stood there with his back to Melanie, not saying anything.

Melanie saw how Yates was standing and walked over to him. It had been a long time since she'd seen him that mad. She put her arm around his shoulder and grabbed his other arm, holding him tightly to her body. "Robert, I'm sorry. Please forgive a foolish woman. I guess you don't know what you've got 'til it's gone," she said sadly.

Yates turned around and held her in his arms: "Melanie, look at me."

Melanie looked at Yates with sorrow in her eyes.

"I can't reconcile with you. But for what it's worth, I do forgive you. We were married for fifteen years, and that has to count for something. We had a lot of good times together in Montana, but I've moved on with things. I'm sorry it has to be this way. I just want the divorce to be final and over with," Yates said.

Melanie put her hand on his chest and looked him in the eyes. "Okay Robert, I owe you that much at least," she said.

"Thank you, Melanie," Yates said and kissed her on the forehead.

They walked back to the desk and sat down. Melanie grabbed the divorce papers and signed them. Yates picked up his cigar and took a deep pull.

"I never could get you off of those nasty cigars," Melanie said jokingly. "You aren't still eating beef jerky… are you?"

Yates sniffed the tobacco aroma from the cigar. He took another pull from his cigar and placed it down in the crystal ashtray. "No, I don't think anyone can get me off cigars," he said. "And beef jerky is good for me. If it's good for BJ, it's good for me."

"And how is that mangy BJ doing?"

"Just because you never liked BJ doesn't make him mangy."

Melanie rolled her eyes. "I'd better go. The cab driver is waiting for me."

"Let me at least see you to the door."

Melanie smiled at Yates as they both rose from their chairs. "How long will you be in town?" Yates asked.

Melanie grabbed her purse, hat, and sunglasses. "Just a few days. Then I'm flying back to Montana," she said.

"You should go on the riverboat tour. But be careful while you're here. There's something strange going on. Big case, can't discuss it," Yates said.

"Okay, I'll be careful," Melanie said with a chuckle. "But just one last thing before I go."

"What's that?" Yates asked.

Melanie threw her arms around Yates, held him tightly against her and gave him a long kiss that seemed to go on forever. "I'm gonna miss that," she said as she looked into his eyes.

Yates smiled and smacked her bottom. "Oh, I'm sure you won't have any problems nabbing a new hubby," he said. The two walked out of the office. Yates closed his office door behind him. "Call me before you leave and we'll have a drink. You can tell me how Sean is doing," Yates said.

Melanie turned to Yates and kissed him again. "I'd like that," she said. They walked through the station to the front entrance door. "I'm glad we managed to part on good terms."

Yates stuck his hand out to shake hers. "No hard feelings," he said.

The two shook hands. Melanie exited the police station. She climbed into the rear seat of the cab, and the driver took her to the nearest motel where she would spend a few days playing tourist in and around the county.

Back inside the station, Yates was standing near Beth's desk. "That's now my ex-wife," he said.

"Oh, no. Is that good?" Beth asked.

"Yeah, I think it is," Yates said. "Where's Bonnie?"

"She heard you two arguing and left."

"Do you know where she went?"

"No, she didn't say, but she tore outta here pretty quick."

"Did Peter go home?"

"No, he's downstairs in the basement."

"You can head home if you want."

"I think I'd rather stay here with you and Peter and see if Bonnie comes back."

"Sounds good to me. I could use the company."

# 23

Jacoby Nicholas arrived at the Rusty Mule in the pouring rain. Everyone who knew him called him Nickels, and it became his nickname over the years. Nickels pulled into the parking lot and drove around back to the rear of the building. He parked his Dodge Charger near the garbage container and headed for the rear door. He threw his cigarette in a puddle, rang the bell and waited for someone to let him in.

Freddie put his cooking tongs down and walked over to answer the door. He had no idea what Nickels really did. All Freddie knew was what everyone else knew, that Nickels came around once a week to make pick-ups and drop-offs. No one knew what his pick-ups and drop-offs entailed, and no one ever asked because they all trusted and respected Charlie, and at the end of the day, no one wanted to lose a good paying job for being nosey.

Nickels entered the kitchen. "Where's ol' Charlie at?" he asked.

"He's tending bar. I'll go fetch him. There's some food on the counter if you're hungry," Freddie said.

Nickels nodded. Freddie turned around and headed towards the bar. He opened the kitchen doors, looked into the crowd and waved at Charlie. Charlie noticed Freddie waving and knew right away that Nickels had arrived. Charlie undid his bar apron and tossed it over one shoulder. He entered the kitchen and found Nickels standing beside the oven eating a burger with fries on a plate. Charlie motioned to Nickels. Nickels wolfed down the last piece of burger and followed Charlie out of the kitchen and into the stockroom.

"Give me a hand with moving this cabinet out of the way," Charlie said.

The two men moved the cabinet, pushing it to one side. Charlie unlocked the secret door behind the cabinet, and they entered the next room. Charlie pulled the string and the light flickered on. The two men walked further into the room before stopping near a shelf of boxes. Charlie pulled down four boxes containing various drugs and gave two boxes to Nickels.

"Looks like we're running low. When's the next shipment?" Nickels asked.

"Should be here by the end of the week. Cornelius didn't send for a restock shipment last month. I swear he does as much drugs as the rednecks around here. You got my cash?" Charlie said.

Nickels took a bulky manila envelope from the inside pocket of his duster and handed it to Charlie. "About five-grand in there," Nickels said.

"I love the smell of money!" Charlie commented. He opened the envelope and looked inside.

Nickels laughed. The two exited the secret room. Charlie and Nickels put their boxes down. Charlie turned off the light and locked the door. The two men moved the cabinet back into place, grabbed their boxes off the floor and exited the stockroom, locking the door behind them. Charlie went to his office and dumped the money in his wall safe while Nickels went to the kitchen. Charlie returned moments later and found Nickels opening the rear exit door. It was still raining heavily outside. "See y'all next time and thanks for the grub!" he said. Nickels ran to his car, backed it up to the rear door and opened the trunk. Charlie placed the boxes inside and slammed the trunk shut. Nickels drove out of the parking lot onto the main road with a thunderous rumble from the exhaust.

It was an operation that had started after Charlie had moved into town and bought the Rusty Mule. He had managed to keep it secret from the previous, now retired, Sheriff Lloyd Callaghan, but now there was a new lawman in town who was asking the right questions and snooping in the right places.

# 24

A PICKUP TRUCK rolled onto Shawna's driveway late at night. The vehicle stopped near the carport and Cornelius climbed out of the passenger side. John took a drag from his cigarette. "Did you hear anything from that intern doctor?"

"No, and I don't like it," Cornelius snapped back.

"Well, you'd better find out what happened."

Cornelius slammed the passenger door. "I will."

"And don't forget about Jack."

John backed onto the road and tore off. Bonnie was approaching from the opposite direction and passed John. She turned her head around and took a second look. "That pickup truck looks familiar," she said to herself. She drove by Shawna's house and saw Cornelius and Shawna standing in the driveway under the porch light, near the carport. Bonnie drove until she was out of sight of the house and pulled onto the shoulder of the road. She spun the police car around and headed back.

Cornelius and Shawna entered the house. Cornelius headed straight for the living room and Shawna stepped into the kitchen. Cornelius flopped down on the couch like a sack of potatoes and switched the TV on. Shawna brought out a few bottles of cold beer and placed them on the coffee table in front of him. Cornelius tried to grab Shawna, but Shawna dodged his advance and moved out of the way. She walked back into the kitchen and started making sandwiches on the countertop. "Now, he wants some of me. That's not happin' anymore. I'll get him so full of beer and food that he'll just fall asleep like last time," Shawna said to herself.

Outside, Bonnie stepped out of her car. Under the cover of the night, she walked across the road, jumped over the small picket fence that surrounded Shawna's property and crouched down. Bonnie could see into the windows of Shawna's home. The lights were on inside, and Bonnie noticed Shawna and Cornelius sitting on the couch. Bonnie slowly made her way closer, passing a flower bed and stopping at the gazebo. She crouched down behind the gazebo in the front yard and continued watching.

Back on the roadside, at the end of Shawna's property, another car pulled onto the shoulder of the road. Joshua Doyle stepped out of his '69 Oldsmobile 442. He was on his way home from his girlfriend's house and noticed a police car parked in front of Shawna's property. Joshua strained his eyes and saw someone crouched down behind the gazebo. He silently closed the car door and carefully made his way through the tall grass in the ditch. Over the picket fence Joshua climbed and stealthy approached Bonnie. As he came closer, Joshua recognized who it was. He took a blunt weapon from his backside, quickly approached and smacked Bonnie in the back of the head. Bonnie fell to the ground behind the gazebo. Joshua darted back to the roadside and slashed the tires on the police car before jumping into his

Oldsmobile. He sped off into the night, leaving Bonnie lying unconscious on the grass.

"Did you hear somethin'? I thought I heard somethin' outside?" Shawna asked curiously. She shoved Cornelius but he was fast asleep, full of food and beer. "Great!" Shawna rose from the couch, turned off the TV and lights and peered out the living room window, but saw nothing. She went around the house, locking doors, closing windows, and even got her shotgun out of the closet. She wasn't taking any chances and hurried upstairs, locked herself in her bedroom and left Cornelius snoring on the couch.

Back at the police station, Sheriff Yates was pacing in his office, smoking his cigar. It was nearly midnight, and he was concerned about Bonnie and where she had gone off to. He thought for sure she would have shown up by now, but she hadn't and no one knew where she was.

Yates started thinking about Bonnie and the time they had spent together since his arrival in Lancaster Falls. He thought about how good of an officer she was and how her intuition was always right. He thought about how strong and smart she was and how thickheaded she could also be and then it dawned on him where Bonnie might be, and a smile came over his face. He grabbed his coat and hat, and left the police station. A cloud of cigar smoke followed Yates as he walked to his police cruiser, got inside and left for Shawna's house hoping that his hunch was right.

The road was deserted except the occasional stray animal. Yates tore onto the back roads to make better time. Up and down, the car bounced on the dirt until he finally arrived at Shawna's property. He slowed and passed by Bonnie's car parked on the shoulder of the road. A grin came over his face as he pulled his cruiser in front of hers and exited the car. He drew his revolver and took one final pull from his cigar before tossing it to the ground and walking across the road. He crouched down behind the picket fence and wondered where Bonnie might be. He poked his head over the fence and scanned the area. All of the house lights were off except the porch light. Yates jumped over the picket fence and swiftly walked towards the house. He looked around and saw a gazebo. He headed towards it for cover and saw a figure lying on the ground. He looked more closely as he advanced and saw that it was Bonnie lying in the grass, not moving. He fell to one knee in front of Bonnie, put his gun in its holster and bent over to see if there was a pulse on her neck. He felt a faint pulsation and a sigh of relief came over him. She was alive but unconscious.

A light popped on, on the second floor of Shawna's house and the hourglass silhouette of a naked woman appeared behind the window curtain. It was Shawna, peeking out from her bedroom window. She saw a figure of a man wearing a hat holding another person in his arms and wondered what was going on in her front yard and if it was related to the noises she had heard earlier. Shawna threw on her pink robe and pink slippers, grabbed the shotgun by her bedside and walked out of her bedroom and down the stairs. She entered the living room, saw Cornelius asleep on the couch and walked by him. She unlocked the front door and stepped out onto the front porch. She looked at her gazebo and saw the two figures in the dark. She hastily pointed her shotgun at the two shadowy figures and quickly started walking towards them. Yates was so fixated on Bonnie that he did not hear Shawna who was rapidly approaching. He had almost reached the road when Shawna came right behind him and pointed her shotgun at his back. "Hold it right there!" she exclaimed.

Yates turned around with Bonnie in his arms. "It's me, Miss. Shawna. Please, we have to get Bonnie to the hospital. I found her unconscious in your front yard!"

"Oh, my. I'm sorry, Sheriff. Let me come with you."

"Not dressed like that you're not."

Shawna looked at him, then at herself and saw that her robe had come completely undone. She quickly covered her naked body and smiled at Yates. "Usually, men have to pay to see the girls. I'll get dressed and meet you at the hospital!" she said coyly. Shawna turned around and ran towards the house while Yates went in the opposite direction to the police cars.

Yates placed Bonnie down gently on her back on the rear seat of the sheriff's cruiser. He got in the front seat and radioed the hospital to expect two officers with one injured.

Yates pulled up to the emergency entrance of the hospital and parked near the front doors. He exited the car, opened the back door, and ever so gently took Bonnie in his arms. He closed the door, ran inside the hospital and approached the nurses' station. "Officer down!"

"Follow me," said an attending physician.

Yates followed the doctor down the hallway to the emergency room. Bonnie began to stir in his arms. He placed Bonnie down on the bed. The doctor tended to her. She awoke and sat up. Everyone breathed a sigh of relief. "Where am I? What happened to me?" Bonnie asked. "My head."

By now, Shawna had arrived at the hospital, fully

dressed. She parked her Corvette next to the police car, ran inside the hospital in her high heels as only Shawna could and approached the nurses' station. "Where did the handsome sheriff go with the officer in his arms?" she asked. The nurse pointed down the hallway to the emergency room. Shawna ran down the hall, burst into the emergency room and saw Bonnie sitting up on the bed. "Well, shoot! Thank heavens you're alright, suga'," Shawna exclaimed.

"Thank you for coming," Bonnie said. "I remember what happened now. I was in Shawna's front yard, behind the gazebo when someone hit me on the back of the head."

"Yes, they hit you with a blunt weapon," the doctor said.

Bonnie touched the back of her head. "Just like Peter."

"Well, it wasn't me, suga'. My boyfriend and I were, well, you know…"

Bonnie and Yates both looked at each other.

"You're free to go home tonight, Officer. But please, try to stay light on work. You suffered a mild concussion," the physician said.

"Thank you," Bonnie said.

"Since we're here, I'm going to check on Scott before we leave. Shawna, stay here with Bonnie 'til I get back, please. I won't be long," Yates said.

Shawna nodded.

Yates left the room.

On the other side of the hospital, Lisa Leblanc approached Scott's room and slowly opened the door. Scott was asleep from the medication that he had been given hours earlier. Lisa quietly walked over to an empty bed and grabbed a pillow. "Gonna be a shame to do you in, sleepy head," she said as she chewed her bubblegum. Lisa held the pillow down over Scott's face and pressed as hard as she could.

Outside of Scott's room, Yates turned the doorknob. "I hope I'm wrong," he said to himself. Yates entered Scott's room, reached for the lights and found Lisa with a pillow pressed down on Scott's face. "Hold it right there, lady!" Yates yelled out. He grabbed Lisa by the arm, threw her against the wall and handcuffed her on the spot.

Lisa stood with her face against the wall. "Let me go!" she screamed.

"You're under arrest for the attempted murder of Scott Rogers," Yates said.

Scott sat up in bed, looked at the sheriff and said, "What in the hell just happened?"

"Are you alright?" Yates asked.

"More or less," Scott replied.

"Can you hold her while I call hospital security," Yates asked.

"Sure can!" Scott hopped off the bed, grabbed Lisa by the arm, turned her around and held her. "Stop squirmin' around," he said.

"Honey, I'm kinda glad I fucked that up. You're too hot to kill."

"You're crazy, girl. Stop squirmin'!"

Lisa began to laugh, reached out and dared Scott to kiss her. "Stop that. You're nuts!" he said.

Yates returned and read Lisa her rights. Lisa did not pay attention. "Thanks Scott. I'll take it from here. A hospital security guard will be by shortly to guard you. In the meantime, there's a physician down the hall if you need anything." Yates grabbed Lisa and the two walked out of the room and down the hallway. "What's your name, Miss?" Yates asked.

"Lisa Leblanc."

"Come with me. We have to meet up with my deputy before bringing you to the police station."

The two approached the emergency ward and entered the room where the ladies were waiting. Bonnie and Shawna turned their heads and looked at Yates and Lisa as they entered the room. Lisa's eyes suddenly grew as large as saucers. "Shawna, you tramp! What're you doin' here?!" Lisa shouted.

"Lisa, you whore!" Shawna barked out.

Lisa wrestled away from Yates unexpectedly and lunged at Shawna. Bonnie got in between the two ladies and stopped them before a fight could break loose. Yates grabbed Lisa and dragged her away from Shawna as Bonnie held Shawna back.

Yates clutched Lisa's arms. "It's quite apparent that you two ladies know each other."

"Stay away from Cornelius! That money's mine!" Lisa shouted.

"You can have the two-timin' louse!" Shawna yelled back.

"Let me go! You're hurtin' my arms!" Lisa said through clenched teeth as she frantically tried to wrestle away from Yates again.

"Shawna, I think you'd better go," Yates exclaimed.

"I hope you rot in jail!" Shawna yelled as she exited the room.

"Where did you find her?" Bonnie asked.

"In Scott's room. I caught her attempting to suffocate him with a pillow," Yates replied.

"Oh, my! Is he alright?" Bonnie asked.

"Yeah, the hospital security will guard Scott overnight," Yates said.

The three left the room and walked down the hallway leading outside. They reached the police cruiser. Yates shoved Lisa inside and secured her in the rear seat. The two officers climbed into the front seats and headed back to the station.

# 25

Yates parked the sheriff's cruiser in front of the police station. He opened the back door and grabbed Lisa's arm, pulling her out. Bonnie opened the entrance door and the three walked into the station. Yates turned the lights in the back of the station on and dragged Lisa to the jail cells. Bonnie unlocked the cell door. Yates undid Lisa's handcuffs and shoved her into the jail cell, slamming the door shut. "What did you mean before when you told Shawna that the money was yours?" Yates asked.

"Why should I tell you anything," Lisa said.

"It would be in your best interest to cooperate with us," Yates said.

Lisa sat down on the bench, looked at her captors and thought for a moment before she rose from her seat and approached Yates. "Gimme a cigarette first," she demanded.

"Sorry, I only smoke cigars," Yates said.

"Don't look at me," Bonnie said.

Lisa rolled her eyes. "I take it you don't know about the heist money that everyone is looking for?"

Yates shrugged his shoulders pretending not to know. "What heist money?"

"The money that the Rhodes and Thomas families stole all those years ago," Lisa said.

"You and Cornelius are looking for it?" Bonnie asked.

"It's our money! We have just as much right to it as anyone else. The statute of limitations ran out a long time ago," Lisa said.

"Wait a minute. I thought Shawna was Cornelius' girl-friend!" Bonnie exclaimed.

"Why do you think we hate each other," Lisa said.

"Aren't you afraid that Cornelius will screw you over and keep the money for himself?" Yates pointed out.

Lisa paused for a minute, sat down on the bench and looked at the ceiling. "I never thought of that," she said dejectedly.

"You're a bright girl, Lisa. Think about it. We'll talk again soon," Yates said.

The two officers walked away from the jail cells and entered the sheriff's office. Yates closed the door behind him and sat down at his desk while Bonnie took a seat on the couch near the window.

"I think I owe you an explanation for what happened today with Melanie. I had no idea that she was coming here with divorce papers in hand, looking for reconciliation," Yates said.

"I know. I heard you two yelling through the door," Bonnie said. "But you don't owe me any explanation."

"Well, I feel like I do," Yates said. "I told her that I had moved on with my life and that it was over between us. In the end, she signed the divorce papers."

Bonnie lay down on the couch and stared at the celling. "You got what you wanted."

Yates struck a match and lit a cigar. "Yeah… We were all worried about you when you took off like that, you know."

"I couldn't stand listening to you two fighting. It reminded me too much of my own past relationship."

"Divorced?"

"No, thankfully, I never made it down the aisle."

"Want to tell me about it?"

"Another time. My head hurts too much from the blow I took."

"How did you wind up at Shawna's house tonight?"

"I was passing by and saw John dropping Cornelius off and leaving, so I parked my car on the roadside and went to see what Cornelius was up to. That's all I remember."

"You should be more careful next time."

"I know… Shit, my squad car is still there."

"We'll get it in the morning."

"How did you know where to find me?"

"Just a hunch."

"Like with Scott before?"

"Something like that."

"What do you mean?"

"With Scott, I knew he may have been in trouble after the shoot-out at Jack's place. But with you, it was different. I knew because I've gotten to know you since I've been here."

"I'm not that predictable, am I?" Bonnie asked.

"Chalk it up to human nature," Yates said with a smile.

# 26

YATES AND BONNIE drove to Shawna's house early the next morning. The officers approached the police car that Bonnie had left by the side of the road and began to inspect it. "Robert, I got two flat tires on this side," Bonnie said. "They've been slashed. You don't suppose it was my assailant, do you?"

"I'm thinking so. The question is how did the assailant know to find you here. We know it wasn't Shawna or Cornelius. We should look over the car, both inside and out," Yates said as he opened the car doors. Bonnie agreed and looked around the wheel wells and underneath the car. Yates popped the hood and looked at the engine, but there was nothing unusual. Then he went into the car and turned the engine over. The car ran fine. Bonnie opened the trunk while Yates took pictures. "Everything looks okay. We'll wait on the tow truck while you finish looking," Yates said as he leaned up against the door and took a bite of beef jerky.

"Good thing you put in the call before we left the station," Bonnie said.

Across the road, inside Shawna's house, Cornelius was

peeking out the window through the curtains watching the two officers.

Shawna came down the stairs from her bedroom and walked by Cornelius on her way to the kitchen. "What are y'all doin' starin' out the window like a badger starrin' at a mirror?" she asked.

"Fuckin' cops are sittin' on the side of the road!" Cornelius exclaimed.

Shawna shoved Cornelius out of the way and stuck her head through the curtains. "Looks like there lookin' for somethin' or maybe someone," she said sarcastically.

Cornelius did not like that answer at all. He grabbed Shawna by the arm and pulled her away from the window. "I've got a good mind to get my gun out!" he shouted.

"Oh, calm the hell down. They haven't done anythin' yet. Play it cool and wait. Let them make the first move. Now come with me to the kitchen for some food. I have somethin' important to tell you."

Cornelius looked at Shawna curiously and calmed down somewhat. The two walked into the kitchen to eat.

Maverick's tow truck pulled in behind the squad car, and Marty Maverick hopped out of the truck. He shut his rusty door and walked over to Bonnie and the sheriff. As he approached, Bonnie caught a whiff of the marijuana that he had recently smoked inside the cab. "What do y'all call that smell? Eau de grass?" she asked jokingly.

Marty looked at the two officers, became very agitated and waved his hands in the air: "Whoa now! I didn't do anythin' wrong! I'm just here to pick up a car!"

"Just make sure you bring it to Jack's garage. Tell him

we'll drop by to pick it up. And don't make me look in your truck either," Yates said.

"Yes sir, Sheriff, sir. I'll be doing that right away," Marty replied as he walked back to his truck.

"Hey, my car's over here," Bonnie said.

"Yes, ma'am. I'll hook it up right away," Marty said anxiously.

"Keep your eye on this clown. I'm going to look around, see if I can find any clues left behind by your assailant," Yates whispered. He walked up and down the shoulder of the road and in the ditch. He saw tire tracks in the dirt and photographed them. He noticed the tall grass in the ditch was parted, so he knew the assailant had parked his car and crossed by foot onto the property. But the question remained as to who the assailant was, how he even knew to find Bonnie there and whether it was just dumb luck that he did. Yates walked back across the road, over to Bonnie and saw Marty pulling away with the car in tow. "I found evidence of another car," Yates said as he turned around and pointed across the road. "I'm concerned as to how the assailant knew to find you here."

"Do you think I was followed?" Bonnie asked.

"We can't rule it out. John may have noticed you in the squad car as you passed by him. Maybe he sent someone."

"But there wasn't enough time for him to get back home and call someone unless he stopped at a pay phone. Even if he did, why didn't he just call Cornelius and tell him instead?"

"Shawna said he was sleeping on the couch. Maybe he didn't hear the phone ring, but then again why didn't Shawna answer it?"

"Too many holes."

"Well, either that or it was just dumb luck that the assailant found you here last night. He may have been dropping by to see Cornelius or he was just driving through and found you lurking on the front lawn. Whoever it was, he knows Cornelius and is mixed up in this," Yates replied as he opened the car door.

"Maybe Lisa knows somethin'," Bonnie said.

"If she's willing to talk," Yates replied.

"It's worth a shot. Do you think we gave ol' peep through the curtains a good scare?" Bonnie asked jokingly.

"I hope so," Yates replied.

Back inside Shawna's house, the two had finished breakfast. "Now, remember where I told y'all to look, and don't fuck it up," she said as the two exited the kitchen. Cornelius went back into the living room and stuck his head through the curtains once more. He looked in every direction, but the officers had gone. He closed the curtains and began grumbling under his breath to himself. "Damn cops, who the fuck do they think they are? I'll show them. They ain't got shit on me." He stomped through the living room passed Shawna and exited the house.

"Good riddance!" Shawna muttered to herself as she eyed the handgun that Cornelius had forgotten on top of the counter next to the phone. She stepped out onto the porch and saw Cornelius tearing out of her driveway. "Cornelius, you forgot your..." she started to yell but stopped in midsentence. Her ruby red lips suddenly turned up and a partial smile crept onto the corner of her face. She stomped her foot on the porch step, turned around and walked back inside her house. "I hope you rot in hell!" she said as she slammed the screen door shut.

YATES AND BONNIE arrived at the police station. The sky above them had grown dark. Large rain drops began to fall. Buckets of water came down from the sky and a loud clap of thunder resounded in the distance. The two officers scrubbed their boots on the front entrance floor mat. Beth greeted them. "Rain again," she said.

"Got that newfangled whatchamacallit working?" Yates asked.

"You mean that thingamabob," Bonnie giggled.

"No, not yet, but I'll figure it out or die tryin'," Beth replied as she shook the answering machine.

"Just hit it a few times. I find that always works!" Yates laughed.

"Or just shoot it. That's what I do!" Bonnie also laughed.

"Don't tempt me," Beth retorted. "Don't tempt me!"

"So, how's our prisoner doing?" Yates asked.

"Peter's been watching her, but she's a little restless. You'd better go check in with him," Beth replied.

The two officers walked through the station to the jail cells in back, only to hear Peter and Lisa arguing. "Well, maybe if y'all ate the food, and not tossed it about, I wouldn't be shouting!" Peter yelled.

"Well, maybe if you brought me something besides donuts, bagels, and coffee, I'd eat it!" Lisa yelled back.

Yates tapped Peter on the shoulder. Peter stepped aside and Yates approached the jail bars. "Lisa, you should be a little kinder to my deputy. He did bring you food."

Lisa grabbed the jail bars in front of Yates. "When do I get out of here?"

"You know I can't do that, Lisa," Yates said.

Lisa let out a sigh: "I thought about what you said to me, about Cornelius cutting me out. I think you're right. That sounds like something he'd do."

"What can you tell me about him?"

Lisa paused for a moment. She crossed her arms and walked back to the brick wall behind her. "He's from Florida and works for the Romano crime family. I thought I was smarter than him, than both of them. I hate Shawna. She's nothin' but trouble."

"What do you know about her?" Yates asked intriguingly.

"I wouldn't trust her, Sheriff. She's a grifter. She'll try to swindle you out of anything given the opportunity. She only cares about money and I wouldn't put murder past her either. She hustled my brother out of his life savings. Said everything he wanted to hear. She plays the innocent role, but she's hardly that," Lisa said.

"Do you know anything about who hit me on the head?" Bonnie asked.

"Someone hit you?"

"In front of Shawna's place. Peter was also wacked by the roadside a few days ago."

"I don't know anything about that, honest."

"Thank you, for now Lisa," Yates said.

The three officers left the jail cells, entered Yates' office and sat around his desk. "Do you think she's telling us the truth?" Bonnie asked.

"I think so. But we'll talk to her again," Yates replied. "Peter, I'm gonna head over to your place and have a word with your father."

"I understand. You do what you have to," Peter said.

Yates got up from his chair and headed for the office door. "You two stay here and look into the Romano crime family. I won't be long."

## 28

SHERIFF YATES PARKED his car beside the large fountain in the middle of the driveway. He almost wished it was a better day so that he could enjoy the scenery, but he had work to do. He ran through the rain and approached the large white columns. He rang the front doorbell and wondered about Peter, and if John would do anything to harm his own son because of this visit. Yates was more concerned about his deputy's well-being than questioning John. Yates always expected the worst in any situation. It's what kept him alive to this day. A maid opened the front door and greeted Yates. The maid was a short slender woman, dressed in a maid's outfit. "Come in please. Come in from the rain," she said.

Yates stepped into the home and removed his hat. "I'm here to see John, Peter's father. I didn't catch your name, Miss?"

"My name is Nina. I'll call Mr. Thomas. It'll just be but a minute. Wait here, please," the maid replied.

The maid vanished down a hallway, leaving Yates dripping rainwater onto the rug. Yates turned his head to the window and looked outside. Watching the rain fall to the ground, he saw a frog hopping along the gravel and disappear into the grass. His mind began to drift as he recalled a past event in Montana that happened over twenty years ago, after the war, when he was a young deputy. Yates remembered it was a deadly case that he and his partner were on. They had been trapped in an alley by two perpetrators. A gunfight broke out. His partner shot one fugitive dead and then was shot in the chest by the other assailant. Yates returned fire on the remaining fugitive, but it was too late. Yates' partner started coughing blood and died. Even though Yates had seen far worse in war, and shot down many enemy pilots in the skies over Korea, that moment in his life changed him because his partner was someone Yates had looked up to, someone who had helped Yates get a job when he was down on his luck. For better or for worse, that moment in his life made him into a damn good sheriff years later. Yates had demons that haunted him. *Everyone has at least one*, he thought to himself. He then heard a voice calling him back to reality.

"Robert Yates? Is that you?" John asked.

Yates turned his head away from the window and the two men shook hands. "You got some spare time for me?"

John let out a chuckle and slapped Yates on the back. "That's what I like about you, Sheriff. You don't mess around. Always to the point. Come, follow me to my office."

Yates followed John through the hallway to his office. John opened the door, and the two men walked into the room. John approached his desk, while Yates looked at an oil painting of a wild stallion galloping in a meadow with a large orange sunset in the background.

"Would you like a drink, Sheriff or a cigar maybe? Peter tells me you're very fond of them," John asked.

"No, thank you," Yates replied as he turned away from the painting.

"Suit yourself. I see you like my paintings. You have a good eye, Sheriff. That particular painting dates back to the Civil War. By an unknown artist," John said as he poured himself a glass of cognac from the bar and sat down at his desk. "Please, have a seat, Robert."

Yates sat on the leather chair in front of John's desk. "I hope I'm not interrupting your day," Yates said.

"Nonsense."

"We're working on a case back at the office, and I believe you may be of some help."

"There you go again. Always to the point," John commented as he sipped his cognac and countered. "How can I help you? Is my son not doing a good job?"

"This isn't about Peter, John. It's about you."

*I'd better choose my words wisely,* John thought to himself and said "Me? How could I possibly help a man like you?"

"Well, it's like this. We've been doing some investigating into the recent murders, and they all seem to point back to your mines."

John's eyes narrowed as he leaned forward in his chair and clutched his glass of cognac. "I'm not sure I like what you're implying, Sheriff. Are you accusing me of something?"

Yates rose from his chair. "No, I'm just here paying a friendly visit and letting you know that I've got my eye on your mines from now on," he said trying to intimidate John.

John rose from his chair. "Sheriff, you have nothing to worry about with me. I run a legitimate business here."

"I'm sure you do, but do you know anything about a man by the name of Cornelius Bennett?"

John became agitated. "Who?"

"You know, Cornelius. He works for you, doesn't he?"

"There are so many people working for me, Sheriff."

"You can't miss the guy. Tall, bald and bulky with tattoos. Likes to go by the name of Jeb sometimes and wears crystal skull rings on his fingers."

"Skulls and tattoos," John paused for a moment: "Sheriff, if there is such a man in these parts, I'm sure you'll find him sooner or later."

Yates started for the office door. "You can count on it," he replied.

"Let me walk you out, Sheriff. We must do this again," John said as they walked into the hallway.

"I'm sure we will, John. Let me leave you with this before I go. How well do you know Charlie Rhodes?"

John became annoyed with Yates. "Everyone knows Charlie. He owns the bar."

"I was just curious if the two of you ever worked together in the past?"

A drop of sweat formed on John's brow. "I reckon not."

"Are you sure? I've heard all sorts of rumors saying that your families go way back," Yates said.

John remained silent for a brief moment, thinking of what to say: "You shouldn't listen to these yokels, Sheriff."

"Well, thanks for your time, John. Let's keep in touch," Yates said with a smirk. He exited the home and walked out into the rain, thoroughly satisfied that he had stirred up enough shit.

John stared out the window and watched Yates drive off into the distance. "Damn that sheriff. Who the hell does he think he is?"

Yates started down the road that runs parallel to the river and saw in the distance Peter's Thunderbird parked on the shoulder of the road, near the bridge. Bonnie and Peter were at the riverbank near the base of the bridge with Brian Long and Ted Tillman. Yates pulled onto the shoulder of the road, and began to walk over to where the others were standing. Bonnie saw Yates approaching and met him halfway. "Robert, we found Nathaniel Thompson's body," she said.

"Where?"

"Brian and Ted were walking across the bridge when they spotted something bobbing in the water near one of the bridge pillars. A rope tied around the body had snagged a rock under the water near the base of the pillar and kept the body in that one place bobbing in the current. I assume the body had been tied to something heavy at some point and the rope snapped and the body drifted until it reached the bridge pillar here and became snagged. Part of the rope was still tied around both ankles."

"Did you take their statements?"

"Yes and we tried getting a hold of you on the radio, but we couldn't reach you. We assumed you were still at the Thomas estate."

"Yes, I was. Where's the body now?"

"It's over this way."

The two approached the riverbank. Yates bent down in the mud and looked closely at the body of Thompson. "There's a lot of bruising here and it appears that he was shot. Tell Peter to have them come and pick the body up for autopsy. How are Brian and Ted holding up?" Yates asked.

"Peter calmed them down. They were upset at seeing the body," Bonnie said.

Yates looked at the body again. "I'm betting the slug in Thompson will match the one they pulled out of Scott's shoulder," Yates said. He waved at Peter: "Pete, come here a minute."

Peter thanked Brian and Ted and told them they were free to leave. Peter walked over to where Yates and Bonnie were standing, near the body. "Yes, Sheriff, sir?"

"My visit with your father went well. But watch what you say around him from now on."

"Do you think he'll give me any trouble?"

"No, after talking to him, I don't think he will. But I also don't want you to accidently tip him off on any activity we may be doing. If he asks you any questions, keep your replies short and to the point and don't let on that you know anything."

"I'll make sure, sir."

The three officers began to walk back up the inclination of the riverbank when suddenly they heard in the distance the faint sound of a dirt bike coming in their direction. Yates stopped in his tracks as they came to the roadside and put a finger to his lips. "Quiet," he said. The sound got louder as the officers saw that same orange Honda dirt bike with the broken fender approaching rapidly. The dirt bike came to a stop on the opposite side of the road. The exhaust of the bike belched balls of smoke as the driver revved the engine. The driver was wearing a full leather bodysuit and helmet. No one knew who it was. The driver unzipped the leather bodysuit and pulled out a handgun. Bonnie and Peter immediately pulled their revolvers out, but Yates held them back. "Wait a minute," he said. The driver leaned over, placed the handgun on the ground and kicked it over to the officers. Yates took a rag out from his pocket and bent down to retrieve the weapon just as the driver revved the engine and tore off down the road.

The three officers looked at the weapon sitting on the rag in Yates' hand.

"What do you suppose that was all about?" Bonnie asked.

"I don't know just yet, but I have a notion that someone is up to something and that gun might be the one piece of evidence we need," Yates replied.

"Wow! She's smokin' hot!" Peter drooled.

"Whoa, Nellie! Down boy!" Bonnie said.

"Who do you suppose that was?" Peter asked.

"Are you kiddin'! Her boobs were burstin' out of her leather suit! I'd bet it's Shawna," Bonnie said.

"Hey! Was she the one who conked me on the head?" Peter asked.

"Probably," Yates said.

"If she conked Peter, then who conked me?" Bonnie asked.

"I'm sure we'll find out soon enough, but for now, we'll play along," Yates said.

# 29

Dylan Sanders went to pick up his good friend Scott Rogers at the hospital. Dylan knocked on Scott's open door, entered and found Scott sitting on the bed. "How's the shoulder today," Dylan asked.

Scott grabbed his belongings. "Hurts, but good. They took out the one bullet and the doc gave me some medication. Told me not to work for a while. Nothing I haven't been through before."

The two friends walked out of the room and over to the nurses' station to checkout. The nurse handed Scott some paperwork to sign. Scott signed the papers and handed them back. The two friends began walking down the hallway. "Don't suppose you know who my new mine foreman is?" Scott asked.

"Nah. They should be back to work today, though," Dylan replied.

Scott stopped in his tracks and grabbed Dylan by the arm. "Wait, stop!"

Dylan stopped and turned around. "What?"

"Last night a doctor tried to suffocate me in my room with a pillow," Scott whispered.

Dylan's mouth dropped open.

Scott started to walk again. "The sheriff got her just in time. He came to check on me and found her with a pillow pressed against my face. He arrested her and called hospital security to guard my room."

"Man, we're neck deep into this one."

"Yeah, I'm thinkin' maybe you should snoop around work, see if you can find out anything more."

"I might just do that. Bug ol' Doug!"

The two friends reached the hospital exit and walked across the parking lot to Dylan's Camaro. They both got inside and drove off in the direction of Scott's home.

After dropping Scott off at home, Dylan arrived at work. He grabbed his gear from the trunk of his car, punched his time card and strolled past Doug's shack. Doug was standing outside, leaning against the front door when he saw Dylan pass by. "Dylan, where the hell have you been? You're late!"

Dylan cringed and stopped in his tracks when he heard Doug's voice. "Nah, I'm sure I'm on time somewhere in this world!"

"You don't get paid for tellin' jokes. Now get to work!" Doug barked out.

Dylan muttered to himself under his breath as he walked past a few workers and stopped at the entry of the mine. He put his work tools down and began looking at the map of tunnels posted on a wooden board. He looked over each area of the mine, trying to figure out where the buried heist money might be. He knew that Miller Hill Mine dated back to the time of the bank robberies and thought that he may have a good chance at finding something. He grabbed his tools and began to walk down the first tunnel, nodding as he passed by his fellow miners. He went down one tunnel after another until he was far enough away from everyone in a different part of the mine. Dylan plunked his tools on the ground, except for his pickax and started walking around the tunnel. He poked at the rock wall on the right side with his pickax, seeing if a stone would break lose revealing a clue of some sort. Then he went to the left side, doing the same. From left to right and side to side he went, but he did not find anything. He walked back to the beginning of the tunnel, gathered his tools and started walking to the next tunnel. Dylan plunked his tools down again and began doing the same thing as before, but found nothing once more. Quite a bit of time had passed by now, or so it seemed to Dylan. He became frustrated with not finding anything and took a different route back to the workers when he came upon an old unmarked tunnel that wasn't on the map. He saw that the entrance of the tunnel was boarded with old rotted pieces of wood. He began to pry the middle board loose with his pickax. Several boards fell to the dirt with a thud. He put one leg through the opening, bent down and managed to squeeze the rest of his body through the slot. There were no lights dangling from this tunnel ceiling which made it hard for Dylan to see with just his hard hat light, but he ventured on. Some soot fell from the ceiling onto his face, then some rock pebbles bounced off his hard hat, but he continued. The tunnel was very narrow and descended in height the further he walked. Then suddenly, he tripped on what he thought was a rock on the ground. "Shit!" Dylan said to himself. He looked down to see what he had tripped on, but could not tell. He got down on his knees and began to dig with his hands. The more dirt he brushed away, the more he realized that he had unearthed human remains.

Dylan was startled for a moment, but only a moment. Any misgivings he may have had quickly gave way as he continued digging. First, he revealed the entire skull, then the neck but stopped at the collar bone. He stared at the skeleton and wondered who it might be when something caught his eye. Dylan leaned forward and saw a rusty chain around the neck of the skeleton. He unearthed more of the skeleton until he felt an old brass key. Dylan tugged the chain and snapped the key free. The key was covered in soot and dirt. He spat on the key and cleaned it off on his coveralls. Dylan looked at the key under the light of his hard hat and wondered if it would open a strong box or trunk containing the missing stolen money. "Wait 'til I tell Scotty what I found," Dylan said out loud as he stuffed the key in his pocket and gently covered the skeleton with dirt. He did not want anyone else to know what he had found.

Dylan returned to the entrance of the abandoned tunnel and exited through the opening he had made. He picked up the boards that he had pried loose and nailed them back into place so no one would be the wiser. He grabbed his work tools, walked through the tunnels back to a small group of workers and went to work. No one had even noticed that he had been gone for over two hours.

# 30

Yates, Bonnie and Peter were sitting in the sheriff's office early that evening, diligently going through paperwork from the case. Yates took a pull from his cigar and turned the page. "The lab found the .32 caliber bullet from Thompson's body, from Scott's shoulder and the shoot-out at Jack's place all match the gun the dirt bike driver gave us. Gun used was a Beretta .32 caliber semi-automatic handgun. Cornelius' prints were all over it," Yates said.

"Anyone else's prints?" Bonnie asked.

Yates handed the file to Peter. "No, they only pulled Cornelius' prints."

Peter opened the file and continued. "That gun was also used in shootings in south Florida along with a .40 caliber Smith & Wesson revolver that was additionally pegged to Cornelius. He has a long list of offences," Peter said. "I had to go to the federal level to get information on him. He's a hitman for the mob. He's part of the Romano crime family and get this, he also has an older brother who goes by the name of Bulldog Bennett. Jebediah or Jeb Bennett is his real name. Jeb is also the fake name Cornelius used when he came to my house to see my pa."

"A brother?" Yates commented.

"Yes," Peter said and continued. "I pulled information about the Romanos. Fernando Romano runs the Romano crime family. His cousin Marcus Romano plays a role and so do a few other family members. Charlie works for them. They're based in south Florida. Mostly deal in counterfeiting, prostitution, illegal gambling and money laundering, but have branched out into drugs as of late."

"So, it's true what Lloyd told us," Bonnie said.

"Callaghan? What did he tell y'all?" Peter asked.

"He said your father ran into Charlie Rhodes on vacation in Florida a few years ago," Yates replied.

"I wonder how they met?" Peter queried.

"That's the million-dollar question," Yates said. "What about the beer bottle we found at the cabin?"

"Almost forgot. Cornelius' prints were on that as well," Peter said.

"And the barbed wire?" Yates asked.

"The barbed wire matched the barbed wire taken from Ben Stevens wrists," Peter said.

"What about the wire cutters?" Yates asked.

"Cornelius' prints again. No one else," Peter said.

Yates took a pull from his cigar. "She's a sly one," he said.

"Hot too!" Peter said.

"You don't want to get mixed up with her. She's bad news," Bonnie warned.

Peter smiled. "I know, but a boy can dream."

Bonnie rolled her eyes. "What about the dried blood from the office shack where Thompson disappeared."

"It matches the blood type of Thompson and we already know he's dead," Peter said.

"And the old papers that I found at the cabin?" Yates asked.

"Cornelius' prints again. No one else," Bonnie said.

"There's one other part before we finish. Cornelius' older brother," Peter said.

"Does he also work for the Romano crime family?" Yates asked.

"No, he's strictly independent, but his rap sheet is much worse than Cornelius," Peter said.

Yates quickly looked through the Bulldog's record. "He's some piece of work, this one."

"Great! So, what's the plan now?" Bonnie asked.

"We have the evidence we need, but the second squad car is in the shop for repairs and I want it for backup. We'll visit Jack and see if the car is ready. I want to talk to Lisa first though. Then we can devise a plan to nab Cornelius. Come with me," Yates said.

Lisa was lying down on the jail cell bench. She sat up and looked at the officers as they approached. "What do you three want now?" she asked irritably.

"Are you willing to help out more and put an end to what's going on in this town?" Yates asked.

"Yes, but if I agree to help you further it's only because I want to see Shawna behind bars for what she did to my brother and the last thing I want is for her to get any of that lost heist money."

"That's good enough reason for me," Yates said. "And I'll look into a lighter sentence for you if your information pans out."

Lisa paused for a moment and rose from her seat. She approached the jail cell bars and looked at Yates. "When I started seeing Cornelius, I found out about the heist money and wanted a piece of it to spite Shawna. I got too involved with the whole thing," she said.

"Does Shawna work for the Romanos?" Bonnie asked.

"She's a feature stripper at a club in south Florida owned by the Romanos called The Lucky Dollar. She travels around the country when she's not on call there and runs con jobs on men just like she did on my brother. She came here the same time Cornelius and Charlie did. She's too smart to get caught, Sheriff," Lisa said.

"Is there anyone else locally involved?" Yates asked.

"There are a few people locally that John and Charlie bought off. Joshua Doyle, Doug Ramsey and someone named Nickels."

"Nickels? Where have I heard that name before?" Peter wondered aloud.

"Do you know him, Peter?" Yates asked.

"I don't know him, but I've heard that nickname before around town," Peter said. "I just can't place the nickname with the face."

"Do you know what he looks like, Lisa?" Yates asked.

"No, I've never met Nickels before. I only know the few things that Cornelius tells me," Lisa said. "There's one thing about John and Charlie that you should know though."

"And what's that?" Yates asked.

"From what I've heard, John was doing heavy betting on the horse races when he was vacationing in Florida. He was losing big and that's when he ran into Charlie Rhodes. They reunited their families past history, became friends and was introduced to Fernando Romano," Lisa said.

"Shit, I had a funny feelin' for a while that somethin'

was off at home, but I could never put my finger on it," Peter said. "I always assumed that pa was acting funny because ma had died."

"You're not the only one they've fooled. Callaghan was fooled by them too," Lisa said.

"How do you know?" Yates asked.

Lisa hesitated for a moment. She looked both ways as if checking to see if anyone else was listening and whispered. "They're running a drug ring out of the Rusty Mule and have been for years."

Yates' eyes widened as the three officers looked at each other.

Lisa continued. "John and Charlie's obsession with the lost heist money is driving them to become reckless and jeopardize the entire drug operation. They're relentless in their search for the treasure bothering anyone they think knows something and killing anyone who gets in the way or threatens to report them."

"You mean like Ben Stevens, Raymond Moore and Nathaniel Thompson," Yates said.

"Yes, Raymond Moore figured out what was going on and told Ben Stevens and Nathaniel Thompson. How Moore figured it all out I don't know," Lisa said as she turned around and walked back to the jail bench. "Could you bring me some cigarettes?" she asked.

"I'll tell Beth to bring you a pack," Yates said as he thanked Lisa for her information.

The three officers went back into the sheriff's office to review the files and formulate a plan to capture Cornelius.

**31**

It was eleven p.m. as Dylan and Sue-Ellen pulled into the parking lot of the Rusty Mule. Scott and Sara had arrived earlier in the evening. Jack was there too, and most of the locals from around town, as well as Cornelius who was sitting alone at a table in the corner.

Dylan and Sue-Ellen exited the Camaro and ran through the rain. They entered the bar, saw Scott and Sara sitting at a table and joined them. The friends sat together in the middle of the bar and ordered drinks. Jack turned his head and noticed the four friends from his bar stool. He downed the last of his whiskey and collected his half full mug of beer. He approached the friends dangling a cigarette from his lower lip and dragging a chair behind him. "Let me propose a toast to Scott. We're all glad he's still with us," Jack said as he sat down.

They all clinked their glasses together. "Here, here. Cheers!" everyone said.

"Scotty, how's the shoulder?" Jack asked.

"It could've been worse," Scott replied.

Jack took a swig from his beer mug and looked at Sue-

Ellen and Sara. "Ladies, your boys are heroes! You should've seen 'em in action." Jack rose from his chair and began mimicking a gunfight scene with his hands. "Pow! Pow! ol' Dylan here was shootin' the place up! Bullets were flyin' every which way!" Jack sat back down and took another gulp from his beer mug, drinking the last drop down. He let out a sharp, shrill whistle and waved his hands to get Samantha's attention.

Sam drifted over to the table. "Y'all want refills?" she asked cheerfully.

"Oh hell, yeah! We sure do," Jack replied.

Sam smiled, and turned to leave but was met with Jack's hand on her bottom. "Eek!" she squealed and shook her finger at Jack disapprovingly before heading to the bar.

"Sara, let's use the ladies' room and let the boys have some time with their new friend," Sue-Ellen said. The two girls rose from their chairs and walked by Cornelius on their way to the ladies' room. He was sitting at a table, smoking a cigarette and drinking beer, but they did not know him. No one knew Cornelius in the bar except Charlie.

Sam returned with five more beer mugs and placed them on the table. "Enjoy!" she said and left.

Jack started on what must have been his sixth beer of the night.

Dylan leaned up to the table and motioned with his hands for Scott and Jack to move in closer. "Psst," Dylan said, "I found somethin' today at work in the mine!"

"Shit, what?" Jack asked.

"I found a skeleton buried in an abandoned tunnel," Dylan replied.

"I guess you couldn't tell who it was, huh?" Jack joked.

"Uh, no Jack. That would be a little hard seein' how it was a skeleton!" Dylan replied sarcastically.

Scott almost choked on his beer as he laughed. "Did you find anything else?"

Dylan placed his beer down, reached into his jean pocket and pulled out an old brass key. "I also found this around the neck of the skeleton."

Jack placed his beer mug down. "Shit! That might be the key that makes us rich!"

Cornelius who had been keeping an eye on the three men rose to his feet to get a better look at what Dylan had in his hand. He saw something small and golden, glimmering in the dim light and knew right away that it was the key to the trunk full of money. Cornelius pushed his chair out of the way and headed over to the restrooms to use the pay phone. He glanced over his shoulder as he walked and saw Jack grab the key from Dylan's hand. Cornelius reached the pay phone and dialed John's number as the girls passed him heading back to the table. "John, sit down and listen," Cornelius said into the phone receiver. "I'm over at the Rusty Mule. Jack's here with the two guys from the other night at the auto body shop and one of 'em handed Jack an old brass key."

"Which guy was it? What does he look like?" John asked.

Cornelius looked across the bar at Dylan. "He's tall with a goatee and dirty blonde hair."

"That's Dylan Sanders. Get me that damned key!" John demanded.

"I'll take care of it," Cornelius said.

Back at the table, the three friends were still talking. Jack had given the key back to Dylan, unbeknownst to Cornelius who was still on the phone.

The girls returned and sat down. Jack put his empty beer mug on the table and rose from his chair. "I'd better head on back to the shop and call the sheriff, let him know his deputy's car is ready for pick up. I'll see y'all later!" Jack said and left the table.

Scott looked at Dylan, "At this hour?!"

Dylan laughed. "He's drunk!"

Cornelius glanced back into the crowd of people and saw Jack departing. "I gotta go," Cornelius said and hung up the phone.

Jack staggered across the bar in a drunken state and managed to reach the front door without annoying anyone. He did not notice that he was being followed as he stepped out into the pouring rain. The rain was oddly refreshing as it hit Jack's face. He staggered across the parking lot and reached his Chevy Impala, just as Cornelius exited the bar. Cornelius looked left then right, took a drag from his cigarette, and saw Jack driving off. Cornelius dropped his cigarette in a water puddle and walked through the rain to his truck. He tore out of the parking lot after Jack. Jack had a bit of a head start on Cornelius, but Cornelius saw Jack turn right, which meant he was heading towards his auto body shop. Cornelius turned on the radio in his truck and began to slow down on the wet asphalt. He wasn't in any hurry now that he had figured out where Jack was headed.

## 32

THE RAIN HAD gathered into a storm and the wind was blowing hard when Jack arrived at Hickory Creek Auto Body. He entered the building and fumbled around in the dark for the light switch, but the power was out again due to the storm. He stepped into the work bay and stumbled over to the cabinet against the wall. He took out a flashlight and approached the police car. He couldn't remember the work he had done to the car earlier and found it difficult to focus because of the alcohol in his system. He tripped over a wrench that was left on the floor and braced himself on a workbench to prevent from falling. "Easy does it, Jack," he said out loud to himself. He moved around the deputy's squad car and gave it a once-over. "Looks alright. I guess I fixed it," he said. He stumbled again and fell flat onto the floor dropping the flashlight. "Shit!" He bent down, collected the flashlight and slowly started to stand, but the flashlight wasn't working anymore. He wacked it against his hand a few times with no luck. "Dang it. What the hell else could go wrong tonight?" he complained. He stammered around in the dark and managed to find his way over to the phone.

Outside, thunder and lightning filled the sky as Cornelius slowly drove up to Hickory Creek Auto Body. He pulled over to the shoulder of the road and turned off the headlights and engine. He reached for his revolver in the glove compartment and put his ball cap and gloves on. He exited the truck and noticed immediately that the auto body shop sign was off, as were as all the lights inside and outside the shop. An evil smile came upon Cornelius' face. He ran through the rain, across the deserted road and approached Hickory Creek Auto Body.

Inside, Jack had picked up the phone receiver, but the line was dead. "Dang storm!" Jack said out loud.

Cornelius slowly entered the shop through the reception area door that Jack had forgotten to lock because he was inebriated. Cornelius carefully made his way to the work bay door, opened it and glanced inside. "Who's there?" Jack exclaimed as he placed the phone receiver down.

A flash of lightning lit the inside of the shop long enough for Cornelius to see a large torque wrench on a workbench and Jack on the opposite side of the deputy's squad car. "Who's there? I know someone's in here!" Jack barked out.

Cornelius began to walk towards Jack as Jack circled around the police car. A lightning flash struck again, but this time Jack saw a figure moving towards him with a gleaming torque wrench in one hand. Jack moved closer to the reception door as Cornelius reached Jack and stuck him on the head. Thunder shook the building. Jack collapsed onto the cold concrete floor. Cornelius stood over Jack, but Jack wasn't knocked out. Jack was a tough old sot. He reached over with his arms and grabbed Cornelius' legs in the dark. Cornelius fell to the floor and dropped the torque wrench making a loud clank on the concrete floor. "I got you now, you son of a bitch!" Jack yelled out.

The two men both tried to rise to their feet as they swung punches at each other. Back and forth they went, lefts and rights to the midsection and jaw until they were both on their feet. Jack swung a punch at Cornelius' stomach. Cornelius buckled over. Jack formed a fist with both hands and slammed it down on Cornelius' back. Cornelius fell to the floor, but picked himself up and tackled Jack down, knocking over a workbench with tools. The tools fell to the concrete making an awful noise as blood from both men was everywhere. They threw one punch after another until Cornelius had had enough and took his revolver out from his back belt and shot Jack once in the heart at point-blank range. Jack crumpled to the floor in a pool of his own blood. "Good riddance," Cornelius said.

Cornelius wiped the blood from his mouth, spat on Jack and searched through Jack's pockets for the brass key. He found nothing. Cornelius picked up Jack's flashlight lying on the floor and flicked it on, but no light emerged. He rattled the flashlight and flicked it on again. This time a beam of light shot across the bay. Cornelius began tearing the bay apart looking for the key. He opened cabinets, throwing the contents onto the floor and searched through toolboxes, but found nothing. He next went into the reception area and started riffling through the desk drawers and again found nothing. He then remembered the stockroom from last time. He entered the stockroom and began tearing the room apart, knocking down shelves and cabinets looking for the key and came up empty-handed one last time. He became enraged at not finding the key, but there was nothing more he could do.

Cornelius left Hickory Creek Auto Body and strolled across the parking lot as the rain washed the blood from his body. He crossed the deserted road, got inside his pickup truck, started the engine and sped off into the dark, wet, sinister night.

# 33

It was well past midnight and most of the patrons had left the Rusty Mule for home. Sheriff Yates and Bonnie entered the bar. They stood at the door dripping rain water onto the floor and looked around.

"Let's ask Dylan and Scott if they've seen Jack," Bonnie said.

Yates nodded. The two walked over to Dylan and Scott who were sitting with their girlfriends. "It's a good night to be indoors, huh," Scott said.

Yates looked at the four friends and smiled. "Have any of you by chance seen or heard from Jack? We've been looking for him for a while, but can't find him. I thought he might be here," Yates said.

"He was working on my car," Bonnie added.

"He was here earlier, but left to go back to the shop. I'm sure y'all find him there," Sue-Ellen said.

"That's the first place we looked. He wasn't there and he isn't answering his phone either," Bonnie said.

"Oh, he left here about an hour ago," Sue-Ellen replied.

"We'll go back. Much obliged," Yates said as he tipped his sheriff's hat to her.

The two officers exited the building. The rain was easing up, but it was still windy and thundering. They walked over to the sheriff's police cruiser, got inside and headed to Jack's shop.

When Yates and Bonnie arrived at Hickory Creek Auto Body, the rain had almost stopped. Yates parked the sheriff's cruiser behind Jack's Chevy Impala. "That's odd. His car wasn't here before when we drove by and all the lights are off. Think the power's out again?" Bonnie asked.

"Looks that way. Let's see where he is," Yates replied.

The two officers climbed out of the police cruiser and walked past Jack's car. Bonnie stopped at the first bay door, put her face against the glass window and peered inside, but she couldn't see anything. She cleaned the glass with her coat sleeve and looked again. "It's so dark. I can't see anyone. Let's check the door!"

They approached the reception area entrance door. Yates turned the knob and the door opened as the thunder above them resounded in the night sky. They entered the shop. It was eerily dark and silent inside. "I think I'm gonna go back and grab a flashlight," Bonnie said.

Yates nodded. "Okay, be quick about it."

Bonnie turned around and exited the building. Yates drew his revolver and began to look around the reception area. The place was a disaster. Papers littered the floor every-where. "Jack, you in here?! It's me, Robert Yates. Where are you, Jack?!"

Yates pushed the stockroom door open. Bonnie returned with a flashlight. "Now we can see what the hell is goin' on in here," she said.

Bonnie began shining the light around the stockroom. Files, boxes and papers littered the floor. Shelves had been tipped over, supplies and tools were in disarray and desk drawers were open. "Let's check the bay," Yates said.

They exited the stockroom and entered the bay. Bonnie flashed the light and the two officers saw the bay had been torn apart as well. It was the same scene as the other two rooms. Then they saw Jack's lifeless body lying on the floor. Yates bent down and placed his finger on Jack's neck and shook his head. "This didn't happen long ago," he said.

Bonnie flashed the light up and down Jack's body and saw he was shot. "What do you think the killer was lookin' for?" she asked.

"Considering Cornelius had been here a few nights ago and what we already know is going on, I'm betting he was looking for something related to the heist money," Yates replied. "I'll radio for help. Take a look around and be careful about it."

Bonnie began to search for evidence as Yates left the building and went back to the sheriff's car outside. The first object Bonnie found was a bloody torque wrench lying on the floor near the body. She bent down, took a rag from her coat pocket and grabbed the wrench. She placed it inside a plastic bag.

Yates finished his call and returned as the lights inside began to flicker on. Bonnie turned her flashlight off and waved to Yates from the bay. "Over here. Now that the power is back on, we can see what we're doin'. Place sure is a mess," she said.

"Storm seems to have stopped. Did you find anything?" Yates asked.

"Just a torque wrench with blood on it."

"You continue to search here, while I search the other rooms."

Bonnie nodded.

Yates walked back to the reception area and looked through the papers that littered the floor, but did not find anything useful as they were all client invoices and order forms for parts. He began to take pictures, documenting the crime scene. Next, he searched the stockroom, wondering to himself what Cornelius could have been looking for. Yates took pictures of the room and thought about what Callaghan and Lisa had said to him.

An hour had passed and Jack's body had been brought away. Yates and Bonnie had finished documenting the crime scene and searching for evidence, but the bloody torque wrench was all they found.

It was nearly two a.m. Yates struck a match and lit a cigar. He thought about the crime scene and how it was the same *modus operandi* as before with no prints left behind. No bullet casing was found either which suggested to Yates that Cornelius had switched to the .40 caliber revolver that was mentioned in the file. Yates speculated that the switch was made after the mystery dirt bike driver, which he deduced was Shawna, delivered to him Cornelius' semi-automatic handgun. The sheriff walked back outside to his police car and began to piece together the events of the past week in his head. The bay door suddenly opened and Yates watched Bonnie drive out the deputy's car that was parked inside. Bonnie exited the car. "Clean and not a scratch. Can you believe it! Wish we had gotten to him sooner though. If only he had called us earlier to pick-up the car."

## 34

Yates, Bonnie and Peter arrived at Shawna's home to arrest Cornelius early the next morning. With shotgun in hand, Yates exited his cruiser and crouched down near the trunk of his car. Bonnie and Peter joined him. "Stick to the plan and I'll tell you when to move towards the house," Yates said.

Inside the house, Shawna was scurrying around doing her morning chores, while Cornelius was coming out of the kitchen with his coffee mug in hand. He walked by the living room window and noticed two police cars that weren't there before, blocking the laneway. "Damn cops!" he exclaimed.

"What's wrong, suga?" Shawna asked as she rushed by him with her laundry basket.

Cornelius took a sip from his coffee mug and glanced back at Shawna. "Damn sheriff's outside with his two deputies!" Cornelius said. He shook his head, walked over to the counter, picked up the phone receiver and dialed John's number. "I got three cops sittin' outside the house!" Cornelius barked.

"What're they doing?" John asked calmly.

Cornelius dragged the phone cord over to the window.

"They're blocking the driveway using police cars. I see the sheriff with a shotgun."

John lit a cigarette. "You're gonna have to handle it. I'd say make a run for it," he said with a smirk.

"Can't you get a hold of Nickels and get me some damned backup?"

"Are you kidding? Do you even know the time? I have no idea where he is."

"Fuck you!" Cornelius yelled out. He slammed the phone receiver down, peered out the window again and thought about his missing semi-automatic Beretta. Cornelius became enraged and quickly suspected Shawna of stabbing him in the back. He seized the phone and threw it against the wall. There was a loud noise as the phone shattered on impact and fell in pieces to the floor. Shawna came running down the hallway from the laundry room upon hearing the noise and found Cornelius raving mad. "This is all your fuckn' fault!" he yelled out.

"Me? What are you talkin' about?" Shawna asked.

"Don't play games with me. First, my Beretta goes missing and now this. It was you! You wanted that money for yourself and wanted me out of the picture!"

"I didn't take your damn gun! Why don't you ask that little tramp, Lisa! When was the last time you even heard from her?! Don't think I didn't know about the two of you!" Shawna shouted.

Cornelius did not know what to think anymore and aggressively shoved Shawna aside causing her to fall to the floor on her backside. He grabbed Shawna's shotgun from the nearby closet and headed down the hallway towards the backdoor of the house.

In the front yard of the property, Yates motioned to Bonnie and Peter to get closer to the house. The two deputies quickly ran towards the gazebo, taking positions behind it. Cornelius exited the backdoor and came around to the side of the house. He ran towards his pickup truck, parked under the carport and crouched down alongside it. He quickly assessed the situation and decided to make a run for it as John had suggested. Cornelius threw his shotgun through the open window of his truck and jumped inside.

"Come out with your hands up, Cornelius Bennett. We've got the place surrounded!" Yates yelled out from behind his sheriff's cruiser.

Cornelius started his truck and floored it, tearing up the dirt and grass. He headed straight for the picket fence to the right of the blocked laneway. Bonnie let out two shots from her revolver and missed. Peter did the same and also missed. Yates stood up from behind the sheriff's cruiser and took aim. Cornelius drove right through the picket fence and easily crossed the small ditch. Yates fired and shattered the rear window of the pickup truck. The truck made it onto the road, nearly running into an oncoming car. The car blasted its horn at Cornelius as it went skidding into the ditch in an effort to avoid the truck. Yates jumped into his police cruiser and gave chase.

Upon seeing Yates tear away in the sheriff's cruiser, Bonnie and Peter ran across the front lawn, jumped into the deputy's police car and drove down the road in the direction the two men had taken. "We're way behind y'all, Sheriff," Peter said into the radio.

"You'd better floor it!" Yates said.

Cornelius turned onto the interstate and began to

weave in and out of the morning traffic that was heading into town from the outlying areas. The sirens of the police cruiser screamed. The traffic tried to pull over to let the speeding vehicles through but not all of the cars were able to move out of the way. Instead, Cornelius muscled the cars off the road. He caught up to a tractor trailer and got into the opposite lane to go around the transport. Yates floored his police cruiser, passed the big rig and pulled alongside Cornelius trying to force him off the interstate to no avail. An exit came up and Cornelius made a right turn. The off-ramp merged onto a county road. Cornelius sent another car spinning into the ditch, but try as he might, he couldn't lose the sheriff.

Yates grabbed the radio receiver while keeping an eye on Cornelius. "Peter, we turned off the interstate at exit two-o-one. We're travelling north on Blackstone Road," Yates said.

"Roger that, Sheriff. We're still a few minutes behind, following the trail of cars in the ditch," Peter said.

Yates put the radio receiver down and continued to chase Cornelius. They drove for a few more miles at high speed, when suddenly Cornelius began to slow down. Yates had to back off to avoid a collision as Cornelius drove onto the shoulder of the road and came to a complete and sudden stop. He lay down on the truck's bench seat and took his revolver out from the glove compartment. Yates turned the sound of the police siren off, opened his car door and knelt down behind it, pointing his shotgun at the pickup truck in front of him.

"Come out with your hands up, Cornelius Bennett!" Yates yelled out.

Cornelius fired two rounds at Yates through the blown

out back window. Yates ducked behind the car door to avoid the wild shots. Cornelius slid across the front seat, jumped out of his truck and ran into the bush as he fired at Yates again. The sheriff took cover, then ran after Cornelius. Bonnie and Peter pulled up behind the sheriff's cruiser and saw Yates disappear into the trees.

Cornelius knew the lay of the land around Reeves County, and he knew that just up ahead, there was an old abandoned mine. Yates was further back, but could see Cornelius in the distance and fired a shot in his direction. Cornelius ducked while running, turned around, and let out a shot of his own towards Yates. Cornelius jumped over rocks, plowed through bushes and shrubs, and then jumped and splashed through a stream of knee-deep water. He then stopped, turned around and fired at Yates again. Yates dove down into the water to avoid the shot while Cornelius ran off into the bush. Yates stood up soaking wet and grabbed his hat that was floating on top of the water. He stepped out of the stream and onto the rocks on the other side. He put his hat back on and continued the pursuit. Cornelius turned around, but could still see Yates although he was much further in the distance. Cornelius came up to a rock formation and knew right away where he was. He followed the rock wall to the right until he came to a boarded-up tunnel. He removed the boards covering the entrance and quietly slipped into the darkness of the abandoned mine.

Yates reached the rock formation and stopped. Dripping wet, he looked left, right, then up the rock wall, then down and saw tracks on the ground. He turned right and followed the tracks around the rock face until he arrived at the abandoned mine entrance. He saw wooden boards on the ground and peered into the mine. He turned around, looked behind, but did not see his two deputies. He knew that Bonnie and Peter were on their way, but Yates couldn't afford to wait for them. He decided to take his chances and entered the void of the abandoned mine tunnel alone.

# 35

CORNELIUS HAD BEEN using the abandoned mine for months as a hideout and a place to get away from Shawna. Yates entered the mine tunnel and immediately noticed the lights dangling from the rock ceiling illuminating the path ahead. "Looks like Cornelius rolled out the red carpet for me," Yates said under his breath. He heard the sound of a generator up ahead. He glanced down and saw fresh tracks in the dirt heading into the depths of the mine. Yates began to walk, following the path of light and tracks, knowing full well that it was most likely a trap.

Outside, Bonnie had arrived at the mine entrance. She stepped into the tunnel, but did not see the two men anywhere. Instead, she saw the light bulbs hanging from the rock ceiling, and a trail of tracks in the dirt. A look of worry crossed her face. Bonnie took a step back and turned around. She saw that Peter was still in the distance and waved at him, motioning him to hurry as she waited by the tunnel entrance.

Yates reached a large opening where the ceiling shot straight up and the walls expanded out in all directions. It looked as if he had arrived at a focal point in the mine where various tunnels converged. He quickly scanned the area for Cornelius when suddenly a shot rang out that narrowly missed Yates' head. He dove for cover behind a minecart nearby. "Hey, Bob, why don't you come out with your hands up!" Cornelius yelled out with a psychotic laugh.

Yates was pinned down behind the minecart. He carefully poked his head out and fired a few shots from his revolver that gave him enough time to notice a shack and two more minecarts. The light inside the shack was on and he saw Cornelius in the window. Cornelius let out a blast from his shotgun. Yates quickly ducked back behind the minecart and formulated a plan. He reloaded his revolver and looked up at the rock ceiling, counted the lights and took aim. He shot out the first light nearest to him and then the second light further ahead. He then courageously rose, shot wildly at the shack and ran towards a second minecart nearby. Cornelius shot at Yates, but missed.

Back outside, Peter arrived at the entrance of the abandoned mine tunnel. "You got out of the car and took off on me so dang fast. I didn't even have a chance to turn the car off! Which way did they go?" he complained.

"They must've gone deep inside. I don't hear anything. We'd better go in after 'em," Bonnie replied. "Stay close, and be ready for anything."

Peter nodded and the two drew their weapons and entered the abandoned mine tunnel. They followed the path and soon heard gunfire.

"Sounds like he needs us. Come on!" Bonnie said.

Yates was now closer to the shack, but not close enough and there was still too much light. Cornelius fired at the sheriff again and Yates returned the shots until he ran out of bullets. "You can't win Bob! Give up!" Cornelius yelled out.

"You first!" Yates yelled back as he reloaded his revolver and shot out two more lights.

Bonnie and Peter entered the theater. Neither of the men noticed the two deputies until Bonnie took aim and fired at Cornelius. The bullet missed and dug deep into the side of the shack wall startling Cornelius for a brief moment. Cornelius turned his attention to the two deputies. "Maybe I can bag me a deputy or two. What do y'all think Bob!?" Cornelius yelled as he fired his weapon at the deputies.

Bonnie and Peter both ducked for cover behind the first minecart. "Did he just call him Bob?" Bonnie commented.

Peter shook his head. "Yup!"

"Uh-oh!"

Cornelius concentrated his attention on the deputies which gave Yates the opening he needed. He made a dash for the shack and hid. He waved at Bonne and Peter and pointed at the two remaining ceiling lights. The deputies both understood. "You shoot the lights and I'll shoot at Cornelius," Bonnie whispered to Peter. Peter nodded. Bonnie shot at the shack while Peter did his task and shot the lights out. The only lights left now came from a bulb on the outside wall of the shack and another bulb hanging inside the shack.

Cornelius poked his head out of the window once more and saw all the cavern lights were out. "I know you're out there, you son of a bitch! You can't hide from me!" Cornelius yelled out.

"We need to help Robert and draw Cornelius out," Bonnie whispered to Peter.

"How are we supposed to do that?"

"I've got an idea. Follow me." Bonnie rose from behind the minecart and ran towards the next buggy. Peter quickly followed. Cornelius heard noises and fired again, but he could barely tell where the sounds were coming from. Bonnie stood up and shot out the external light on the far side of the shack near the window. Cornelius couldn't see anything outside the shack now. He stuck his shotgun out the window and began to shoot randomly.

"He's not coming out," Peter said. "What'd we do now?"

"Let me think. What's Robert up to?" Bonnie whispered.

Cornelius fired another round. Yates slowly came out from behind the shack, knelt down and crawled underneath the open window as quietly as possible in the dark and waited. Cornelius reloaded his shotgun and stuck the barrel out the window once more. Yates reached up from under the open window, snatched the barrel of the shotgun from Cornelius and flung the weapon in the dirt. Cornelius stood in the open window looking at his hands in disbelief. Yates rose to his feet. The two men drew their revolvers simultaneously, but Cornelius wasn't fast enough and Yates shot him in the heart, point-blank. Bonnie and Peter ran towards the men. Yates looked at Cornelius through the open window, lying on the floor of the shack and said, "Don't call me Bob."

"Are you okay?" Bonnie asked.

"I'm fine. Let's see what Cornelius was doing in there?"

The three officers entered the shack and saw Cornelius in a bloody mess on the floor. Peter bent down and placed two fingers on Cornelius' neck, but did not find a pulse. "He's dead alright!"

The officers looked around. Yates immediately spotted

a large trunk underneath the open window. He bent down and opened the lid. Bonnie and Peter both gasped as in front of them rested the lost heist money.

"Holy shit!" Bonnie and Peter both exclaimed.

"I wonder how much is there," Yates said. "Look around. See what else turns up."

Bonnie and Peter began to search and saw a cot in the corner with a table beside it, while Yates found several rifles, shotguns, machine-guns, semi-automatic handguns, revolvers, grenades and boxes upon boxes of ammunition on the floor near the wall underneath a tarp.

Peter's eyes widened as he turned to look and raised an eyebrow. "That's a lot of hardware."

"Did you two find anything?" Yates asked.

Bonnie put her gloves on, bent down and looked under the cot. She pulled out a cardboard box and looked inside. "We've got some bags of drugs here."

"You two stay put. I'm going back to the car to radio for help. Look for more evidence while I'm gone and stay alert. I won't be long," Yates said.

Yates walked through the tunnel and back outside. He traversed the forest the same way he came until he made it to the roadside where the three vehicles were parked. He sat inside the sheriff's cruiser and grabbed the radio. "Beth, you read me? Beth?" he said but only heard static. Yates tried again. "This is Sheriff Yates." Static.

"I read you Robert. What's your situation?" Beth asked.

"I need a tow truck. I'm five miles up from exit two-o-one on Blackstone Road, heading north and tell Paul to bring the meat wagon," Yates said.

"We'll do. I'll make the calls. Hang in there, it won't be long," Beth replied.

"Thank you. Roger, and out," Yates said.

# 36

Later that same day, John arrived at Shawna's property in search of Cornelius. John parked his truck near the car-port, exited the vehicle and walked to the front porch. He knocked on the door, took a drag from his cigarette and tapped his foot as he waited. Shawna opened the door. She was dressed provocatively and singing along with the radio, happy as a tick on a fat hound. "Well, well, well, look what the cat dragged in," she grinned.

John stepped into Shawna's home. "I'm looking for Cornelius. Is he here?"

Shawna smiled as she lit a cigarette. "Oh, he left early this mornin' with the sheriff and two deputies hot on his tail!"

"I don't suppose you had anything to do with that?"

"Who, lil' ol' me? Why shoot, no suga'."

"Just let me know when he turns up," John said suspiciously as he turned around, walked out onto the front porch and tossed his cigarette on the ground. Shawna closed the door and went back to her singing. John got into his truck and decided to go talk to Charlie at the Rusty Mule.

Before long, John arrived at the Rusty Mule. He entered the establishment, headed over to the bar and sat down on a stool. He whistled at Charlie to get his attention. Charlie glanced at John, immediately poured him a beer from the keg and brought it to him. John grabbed the beer and the two men left the bar and walked into the back hallway to Charlie's office. John took a drink from his beer mug and sat down on the leather couch. He lit a cigarette, while Charlie walked over to his office chair and sat down behind his desk.

"I think the sheriff did us a favor," John said.

"What do you mean?" Charlie asked.

"Shawna told me the sheriff and his deputies chased Cornelius away from her house early this morning," John replied.

"Is he dead or arrested?!" Charlie asked inquisitively.

"I don't know. I'm going to assume the worst and say he's dead because I can't find him anywhere and haven't heard from him. If he was arrested, I would have head something from Peter."

"Good riddance to the guy. Let me call Florida."

"Wait, there's one more thing."

"What's that?"

"The last time I talked to Cornelius, he said that a mine worker named Dylan Sanders handed Jack a key at the bar. Then Jack left, and Cornelius followed Jack."

"Do you think Jack has the key?"

"No, I'm assuming Cornelius killed Jack as instructed and the sheriff has evidence to prove it, which would explain why the cops chased Cornelius away from Shawna's house this morning and why he's suddenly missing," John said.

"So, where's the damn key?"

"Well, that's the tricky part. Either the sheriff's got it now or Dylan Sanders had it all along," John replied. "If Yates has it, he won't know what it's for, but if Dylan has it," John paused for a moment. "Call Nickels. Tell him to follow Dylan and see what he's up to."

"Damn, you think Dylan might have the key that could lead us to the money? I'll tell Nickels to follow Dylan right away."

John rose from the couch with his beer mug and cigarette. "It's a chance we can't afford to waste. I'm gonna go back to the bar and have something to eat while you make the call. Let me know when you're done," he said.

# 37

Dylan arrived late for work that day. After punching his time card, he walked over to the foreman's work shack and knocked on the door. "Come in," Doug said from inside.

Dylan opened the door and found Doug sitting at his office desk going over reports. "Did y'all just get in?" Doug asked sarcastically.

"As a matter of fact."

Doug's eyes narrowed. "That's what I thought. You're already over an hour late and pay isn't 'til next week, so what're y'all doin' in my office? No, no, don't tell me. Lemme guess. You're sick, right?"

Dylan sat on the old wooden chair in front of the office desk. "No. I wanted to ask for a transfer over to the River View Mine for a few days seein' how Scott's laid up for a while."

Doug put his paperwork down, grabbed his coffee mug and took a sip. "Why?" he asked. "I got plenty of work for y'all to do 'round here."

"No reason. Just wanted to help," Dylan replied.

"Since when are y'all so keen on workin' extra?" Doug asked suspiciously.

Dylan rose from the chair. He knew right away that this was going to turn into an argument. "I don't wanna work extra. I just wanna help out over there."

"I don't see any reason for y'all to go there. They'll survive without Scotty for a while. Besides, he does 'bout as much work as y'all do."

"What are you implyin'? That I can't do the job."

"No, that y'all got no will to do the job. Now get out there and do your job here"

"No! I wanna transfer away from the likes of you!" Dylan said emphatically.

Doug's eyes widened. "Son of a bitch! Now it comes out!" Doug rose from his chair, grabbed Dylan by the arm and forcefully ejected him out the door. "Now get to work or I'll suspend y'all 'til Monday without pay!"

"No way, man!" Dylan yelled back.

"Then get off the dang property! You're suspended 'til Monday mornin'! Now git!" he barked out at Dylan and pointed to the front gate.

Dylan spat on the ground and stomped away as Doug continued, "And don't forget to punch your dang punch card out!"

Doug walked back into the shack. Dylan punched his card and got in his car, dejected that he couldn't get to the River View Mine, but instead, got himself suspended until Monday with no pay.

Doug sat back down at his desk, took a drink from his coffee mug and dialed John's number. John answered the phone only to hear Doug's irritated voice on the other end. "John, I may have a problem, but I'm not sure," Doug said into the phone receiver.

"What seems to be the issue?"

"It's that young feller, Dylan Sanders."

"What does he want?"

"It's like this. He came in out of the blue lookin' to be transferred to the River View Mine. I told him no. Then we got into an argument and I sent him home and suspended him 'til Monday with no pay."

"It doesn't sound like much, but considering what's at stake, I'll get Nickels to look into it," John said knowing full well that Charlie had already talked to Nickels.

"Sounds good to me," Doug said. He placed the phone receiver down and the two ended their phone conversation.

**38**

A BLACK CHARGER slowly pulled onto the shoulder of the road across from Scott's house. Nickels stepped out of the car smoking a cigarette and walked around to the passenger side. He bent down near the front tire and pretended to have car trouble. Nickels peered up and watched Dylan ring Scott's doorbell.

"I'm ready. Let's go!" Scott said as he opened the door.

"How's the shoulder?" Dylan asked.

"Gettin' better."

The two friends walked over to Dylan's Camaro. Dylan started the engine with a thunderous roar and slowly crept up the driveway. "Well, I got a story to tell," Dylan said.

"What's that?"

"I went to talk to Doug 'bout workin' at the River View Mine."

"What did he say?"

"Well, we got into an argument over me wantin' to transfer and he told me where to go and suspended me 'til Monday without pay."

"Shoot."

"Don't worry 'bout it. I argue with Doug all the time. We've got this thing goin' where I give him a hard time. He'll forget all about it by Monday," Dylan said as he pulled onto the road and noticed a black Charger sitting on the opposite side.

Once Dylan's Camaro was out of sight, Nickels ran around to the driver's side of his Charger, got inside and did a full one-hundred-and-eighty-degree turn, nearly colliding with an oncoming car. His tires squealed and ate up the asphalt as he tore off after Dylan in a cloud of white smoke, leaving an angry driver honking his horn madly. Nickels managed to catch up to Dylan and settled back two cars behind.

Dylan looked in his rearview mirror and saw three cars behind him. "I gotta fill up for gas before we do anything." He continued to drive then took a right and turned into the first filling station they came across. One car drove passed while two others followed Dylan into the gas station, with the last car being driven by Nickels. Dylan stopped at the first gas pump and got out. Nickels parked near the service center window and unfolded a map pretending to be lost while keeping his eye on Dylan. Dylan went about his business and got back into his Camaro. He noticed the black Charger again, but did not pay much attention to it and started to pull away from the filling station. Nickels followed Dylan back onto the road. Dylan and Scott drove down the county road for a good five minutes before Dylan casually glanced into his driver side-view mirror and noticed that same black Dodge Charger. "Is it me or is that Charger behind us the same one that was in front of your place and at the fillin' station?" he observed.

Scott glanced into the rearview mirror. "I did see one on the side of the road when we pulled out of my place. You don't think we're being followed?" he said.

"Let me step on the gas and see if he stays with us. Hold on tight!" Dylan said. The exhaust pipes made a loud growl and the Camaro bolted forward leaving the Charger behind. Nickels was surprised by Dylan's sudden move and floored it. He caught up to Dylan and stuck with him. Dylan made an abrupt turn to the right at the next road. Tires smoked and squealed as the two muscle cars drifted through the right-hand turn. Dylan floored it even harder and started passing cars on the county road, but Nickels kept right with Dylan.

"I don't think we're gonna shake him," Scott said.

Dylan glanced into his driver side-view mirror again. "I think I'm gonna head into town and over to the police station for safety. He won't dare follow us there."

"That's a good idea, man."

Dylan went as fast as the traffic would let him until he arrived in town. Once in town, he slowed down. He made a left turn and then a right a little further up the road and headed for downtown. Nickels kept up with Dylan, but was now three cars behind. Dylan managed to make it to the town square, pulled into the parking lot of the police station and watched the black Charger prowl by.

Nickels circled the square and parked under a tree near a flower shop.

"Come on, let's tell the sheriff what's goin' on," Dylan said.

The two friends exited the Camaro, walked out of the parking lot, up the sidewalk and burst into the front entrance of the police station. Nickels watched from inside his Charger.

"You two look like you're in a hurry!" Beth said.

"Is the sheriff here? We need to see him straight away!" Dylan said.

"I think he just came in a little while ago. Let me go check," Beth replied. She rose from her chair, walked over to Yates' office, rapped her knuckles on the door, opened it and poked her head inside. "Sheriff, there's two young men here to see you."

"I'll be right there."

Beth returned to her desk. Yates followed and saw the two friends standing near the front entrance. "What brings the two of you to my front doorstep?" he asked interestedly.

"I thought we were being followed, so we came here for safety," Dylan replied.

"Oh!?" Yates said curiously.

Dylan walked over to the first window, parted the Venetian blinds, looked out and pointed at the black Dodge Charger sitting across the square underneath a tree. "There, look, that black Charger. He was following us all over the dang place," Dylan said.

Yates looked out the window and then Bonnie, Peter and Beth too came over to see what was going on.

"I can't really get a good look at him. He's wearing a ball cap with sunglasses," Yates said.

"That tree isn't helping any," Beth commented.

"Now, why would he be following you two? Who is he and did either of you manage to identify him or get a license plate number?" Yates asked.

"We don't know who he is, sir. He started tailing us

outside of my place when Dylan came to pick me up," Scott replied.

"We didn't notice him at first, but when we got to the fillin' station, we saw that he was following us. We tried to shake him but he stuck with us and then we came here as fast as we could." Dylan looked at Scott and continued. "Neither of us got a good look at him or got a plate number, sir. He took us by surprise."

Yates and Bonnie both looked at each other.

"What have you two not told us? The both of you were involved in a gunfight at the auto body shop. Scott here was almost suffocated at the hospital and now Jack's dead. I think you two know more than you're letting on," Yates said as he took a pull from his cigar.

Dylan and Scott's eyes widened as they looked at each other. "We know about the bank heist money, sir. Jack made us promise not to tell anyone. We were gonna split it with him when we found it." Dylan pulled the brass key from his pocket and handed it to Yates. "I found this at the mine where I work. It was around the neck of a skeleton buried in an abandoned tunnel. We told Jack about the key."

"Jack's dead?" Scott asked sadly.

"Yes, he was killed in his auto body shop," Bonnie replied.

"Dylan, I'm going to have to take this key as evidence and I want you to show me exactly where you found the skeleton that you said you pulled this off of. Can you do that?" Yates asked.

"I sure can, sir," Dylan replied.

"Good. For starters, where did you find the skeleton?" Yates asked.

"Miller Hill Mine, sir. Doug Ramsey is the foreman there. It's where I work."

"You two boys wait here for a minute while I talk to my two deputies. Peter and Bonnie, come with me to my office."

Leaving Scott and Dylan sitting on the bench near Beth's desk, the three officers entered the sheriff's office and closed the door. Yates tapped his cigar ashes into the ashtray and sat in his chair. "I have a hunch about the stalker and the key Dylan found, but first I want to see that skeleton for myself. Bonnie, you come with me to the mine while Peter you stay here and get me three search warrants. One for the Thomas estate, one for the Rusty Mule and one for Shawna Ray's home."

"What do you think we'll find at the mine?" Bonnie asked.

"Do you two remember the letter I found in that old cabin out in the bushes where we came across Raymond Moore's body parts? If I remember right, the letter read that *he didn't trust him anymore,*" Yates said as he took a pull from his cigar and continued. "Now we know that the robberies were orchestrated by John and Charlie's grandfathers. It stands to reason that that skeleton is the remains of one of those two men. I'm betting they fought over the money and the one killed the other. The only question is who killed who."

"They're both dead, but if that skeleton reveals the truth about this whole thing, then I'm right behind you," Peter said.

"With this case being a family affair for you, Peter, I'm glad you've been cooperative and levelheaded throughout this whole ordeal. It has been a conflict of interest for you and normally, I would've asked you to step aside, but you have shown good judgment," Yates said. "Let's not keep those two boys waiting any longer. Bonnie, you're with me."

The three officers rose from their chairs and exited the office.

"Just a minute. I want to pick up a few things in the supply room before we go," Yates said. He headed downstairs to the basement for a brief moment and returned with a couple of paintbrushes in a paper bag.

"What're the brushes for?" Bonnie asked curiously.

"To brush the dirt away from the skeleton," Yates replied as the three walked over to where Beth, Scott and Dylan were waiting. "Any news on our mysterious stalker?" Yates asked.

"He's over at the pay phone booth," Dylan replied.

Yates walked over to the window and peered through the Venetian blinds. "He's probably calling John or Charlie. Bonnie, Dylan, you two come with me. Scott, stay here with Peter and Beth until we get back and watch our mystery man. Come on. Let's go find out what the dead have to say," Yates said.

Across from the police station, Nickels was still on the phone talking to John. Nickels quickly turned his back when the sheriff, Bonnie and Dylan emerged from the building. "The sheriff and that hussy deputy of his just left the station with one of the two boys. Looks like they're in a hurry."

"You were supposed to be careful when you followed them. The police might be after you now," John said annoyingly.

Nickels turned around and saw a car pulling out of the parking lot. "Nah, they're stupid," he said and took a drag from his cigarette. "One of those two squares is still inside the police station. What'd you want me to do now?"

John paused and thought for a moment. "Which one of those two troublemakers was with the sheriff?"

"Uh, the taller one with dirty blonde hair and a goatee."

"That's Dylan Sanders. I wonder where those three are headed too."

"Should I follow 'em?"

"No, stay put for now. It's too late to follow them anyway. Wait maybe an hour and see if anything else happens, then go see Charlie. Nothing more we can do now but wait."

Nickels threw his smoked cigarette on the ground and stomped it out with his boot heel. "Sounds good to me. Getting hungry anyway." He hung up the phone, returned to his car, leaned up against the fender, lit a fresh cigarette and patiently waited an hour as he was instructed.

**39**

THE SHERIFF PULLED off the road and followed the signs to Miller Hill Mine. Yates parked the police cruiser near the front entrance and the three exited the vehicle.

"By the way, before we go any further, I should tell y'all that I was suspended from work," Dylan said.

"How did that happen?" Bonnie asked.

"I was askin' the foreman if he could transfer me to a different mine. We argued about it and the next thing I knew, I was goin' home," Dylan replied.

"Your mine foreman is more than likely searching for the heist money for John and thought you knew something about it," Yates said.

"Well, he was right about that. I do!" Dylan said and continued, "watch your step, miss. Mud holes everywhere. This way, this way."

The three walked past the check-in point and approached Doug's shack. Doug was standing outside, smoking a cigarette and chewing out one of the workers.

Dylan smiled at Doug. "Hey man, give the guy a break. He's new 'round here."

"I thought I suspended you," Doug barked out.

Yates approached Doug and stared him down: "I reinstated him. Suspension revoked."

Doug's eyes narrowed. "What're you doin' here?" he demanded angrily.

"We're here on an official investigation. I have reason to believe there's a dead body in the mine," Yates replied.

Doug paused for a moment, not really believing what he was being told. "Alright, but no funny business," he said.

Yates tipped his hat to Doug and the three walked off past the shack and continued until they reached the mine entrance. Dylan snatched three spare hardhats from a wooden crate and handed one to each officer. Dylan turned his head and saw Doug spit on the ground and walk back inside his work shack. "Follow me," Dylan said with a smile.

Back inside the foreman's shack, Doug grabbed the phone receiver and dialed John's number. "John, it's me, Doug Ramsey. We've got a problem."

"What is it now? Did Dylan come back to haunt you?" John said sarcastically.

"He sure did and he has the sheriff and deputy with him!"

"Is that where they went off to. What in the hell are they doing there!?"

"Sheriff said there's a dead body in the mine so I let them pass."

"You did what?!"

"I let them pass. He said there's a dead body."

"You numbskull! He's tricking you for some reason."

"What can he possibly know?!"

"For starters, he has Dylan with him," John huffed. "Look, go and follow them and see what they're up to."

"I can do that," Doug said. He hung up the phone and exited the shack.

Meanwhile, Dylan was leading the two officers deeper into the mine. "If I remember right, it should be just up ahead," Dylan said.

"How did you come across this skeleton?" Yates asked.

"It was by accident. I was looking for anything that would point me to the money and came up empty-handed. I started walking back to the rest of the workers down a different passageway and came across a tunnel that had been boarded up."

"These tunnels all look alike to me," Bonnie said.

"I know my way around. It should be just up ahead."

"How long have you been working here?" Bonnie asked.

"Long enough," Dylan said. "They were the first job openings we found when Scott and I came back from the war. We snatched them up right away."

"It's too bad you two didn't go into law enforcement. You got a good nose. How good of a shot are you?" Yates asked.

"Good enough to save my ass when it was needed in Vietnam."

"The three of us should go to the firing range sometime," Yates said.

"That sounds like a great time, Sheriff!" Dylan grinned as he stopped in front of the abandoned tunnel. "We're here, Sheriff. The tunnel is behind these boards. Give me a hand in pulling them down."

Dylan and Yates began to pull down the old boards, one

by one, until the entire opening was clear. "Watch your step and follow me. It's just up ahead, but be careful. The tunnel will start to shrink the further we go."

Dylan led the way through the tunnel as the passage began to get tighter. Dirt and pebbles fell from the ceiling onto their hardhats and the dry ground became softer. Dylan pointed up ahead with his flashlight. "There's that mound of dirt I made. The remains are under it," he said.

The three approached the mound and knelt down beside it. They began to carefully unearth the skeleton piece by piece. Yates handed each of them a paintbrush and between the three, they swept away the dirt until the skeleton was revealed. Yates examined the bones, starting with the skull and working down. His eyes caught a glimpse of a ring on the left hand. He leaned over, carefully plucked the ring off the finger bone and brushed the dirt off. Yates examined the ring closely and saw an etching on the inside. "There's an inscription, but I can't make it out," he said as he reached into his pocket and pulled out a magnifying glass.

"I thought you didn't need glasses?" Bonnie smiled.

Yates looked at her, smiled and read: "*James J. Thomas and Elizabeth B. Thomas bound forever, July 1892.*"

"Peter's great grandpa," Bonnie and Dylan both said together.

Yates placed the ring into a plastic bag and stuffed it into his coat pocket. "Keep looking for more clues."

"I think I see something," Bonnie said. She carefully picked up a bullet lying on the ground underneath the rib cage.

"Looks like a .45 caliber slug," Dylan said.

"Sure is," Bonnie said. She handed the bullet to Yates

who placed it into another plastic bag and stuffed it into his pocket.

Suddenly, out of nowhere Doug appeared out of the darkness shining a light into Yates' face. Doug looked at the three crouched on the ground with paintbrushes in their hands. "Is this what you were talkin' about," he said.

"Yes. We're done for now," Yates replied. "I'll need to have the remains removed from here. It shouldn't take long."

Doug kicked dirt onto the skeleton. "It better not," he complained.

Bonnie rose to her feet. "Hey! Show a little respect for the dead!"

"He's been dead a long time. Who cares! Now, shut up and move it," Doug barked angrily. "I got a mine to run."

Not wanting any trouble, the officers and Dylan rose to their feet and walked away from the skeleton. They exited the abandoned tunnel and continued through the mine until they reached the entrance where they tossed there hardhats back into the wooden crate.

Sheriff Yates, Bonnie and Dylan returned to the police car where Yates radioed Beth requesting assistance for the remains of James J. Thomas. Doug slipped into his office and dialed John's number, informing him that the officers had actually found a dead body in the mine, but little did either John or Doug know who the remains belonged to.

# 40

Sheriff Yates and Bonnie arrived at the Rusty Mule, casually dressed, off duty and late at night. Yates parked his '72 Cadillac Eldorado along the side of the building. The two officers exited the car, entered the bar and looked around. Yates pointed to their usual place in the corner. "Quiet evening tonight," he said.

Over at the bar, Shawna was having drinks with another lady. The two had just met that night. Shawna saw the officers out of the corner of her eye and nudged her new friend. "I need to see the sheriff for a minute. He just walked in."

The lady friend took a sip from her vodka, turned her head and noticed the sheriff. Her eyes lit up like a Christmas tree. "That's my ex-husband," she said with a smile.

Shawna's eyes bulged from her face. "Oh, my!" she said as she grabbed Melanie's hand. The two ladies rose from their bar stools with their drinks and sauntered over to greet the officers. Melanie approached Yates, tapped him on the shoulder and sat down beside him. Shawna grabbed a chair and sat next to Bonnie as Samantha arrived at their table. "What will it be folks?" she asked.

"Just a whiskey for me," Yates replied.

"Make it two," Bonnie said.

"Tequila Sunrise for me, suga'," Shawna said.

"Harvey Wallbanger for me," Melanie said.

Sam wrote the drinks on her notepad and drifted back to the bar.

"What brings you two ladies here tonight?" Yates asked.

"We just met and were having drinks together," Shawna replied.

Melanie nudged Yates with her elbow. "Aren't you going to introduce me?"

"Where are my manners? This is Melanie, my ex-wife. Melanie, this is Bonnie James, my deputy and you already met Miss. Shawna Ray," Yates said.

Bonnie looked at Melanie and reached over to shake her hand. "Pleased to meet you."

Sam came back and gave everyone their drinks. "Enjoy y'all," she said and glided back to the bar.

Shawna struck a match and lit a cigarette. "Sheriff, thanks for takin' care of my problem," she said casually.

The two officers looked at each other and remained silent.

"So, Shawna, what shade of lipstick are you wearing tonight? I love that color," Melanie said in an attempt to keep the conversation going after an awkward silence.

"It's not my usual lipstick. Just something I threw on tonight. Usually, I wear Scarlett Cherry Red," Shawna said.

Bonnie's eyes widened as she sipped her drink. "I usually wear that too," she commented.

"Well, all this girl talk must be making Robert bored. He hasn't said a word," Melanie observed.

"Let's leave him to his drink and use the ladies' room. You two care to join me?" Shawna asked.

Bonnie and Melanie both nodded and the three ladies rose from their chairs and headed for the washrooms.

Yates took a fresh cigar from his coat pocket and struck a match. A cloud of smoke began to hover over the table. He took a drink from his whiskey glass and started to scan the bar for Charlie and anyone else of interest. Yates sat there watching people going back and forth, entering and exiting the bar, until he finally saw someone come out from the back with a box tucked under his arm. The man went straight to Charlie behind the bar and started talking to him. Then the two men left the bar and vanished into the kitchen. Yates sat there and wondered who the man was, what was in the box and what were they discussing. He whistled over to Sam to get her attention and she quickly scurried over. Yates handed Sam his empty glass. "Can I get a refill?" he asked.

"Sure, anything for the sheriff!" she replied.

"Wait a minute, Sam. Who was that man that disappeared into the kitchen with Charlie? I've never seen him before," Yates said.

"Oh, that's just Nickels. Well, Jacoby Nicholas is his real name," Sam replied. "You haven't seen him around?"

"No, first time."

"Well, he's always in here doing deliveries and pick-ups for Charlie. Kinda like an errand boy, I guess."

"Thank you, Sam. You've been a big help."

"Anytime, Sheriff!"

Sam went back to the bar. Bonnie, Shawna, and Melanie returned to the table and plunked themselves down on the empty chairs. Sam quickly returned with another glass of whiskey.

"Thank you," Yates said.

"Anytime," Sam replied and left the table.

"Did you three tell each other secrets? You were gone an awfully long time," Yates said jokingly.

Melanie looked at her watch. "Uh-huh! Shoot, I better get going. It's getting late. I only have one day left in Lancaster Falls."

"Did you get a chance to go on the riverboat tour?" Yates asked.

"Oh, yes. You have a very quaint town here. The river is gorgeous and it's so much warmer than back home," Melanie replied with a smile. "But I really must be going. Take care of him, Bonnie."

"I will," Bonnie said.

"I'd better get going too. I have to drive to Georgia tomorrow for a weekend of shows," Shawna said. "Y'all know I'm the headline!"

The two ladies finished their drinks and rose from their chairs. Melanie leaned over and kissed Yates on the forehead. "Maybe we'll see each other again," she said.

"You never know," Yates replied.

Shawna leaned over and kissed Yates on the left cheek. "I know we'll see each other again, suga'," she whispered breathlessly and winked.

"I suppose," Yates replied.

"It was nice meeting you, Melanie," Bonnie said.

"Likewise," Melanie replied. "Hopefully, we'll see each other again."

Yates and Bonnie waved goodbye to the two ladies as

they vanished out the front door of the bar. Bonnie moved her chair closer to Yates. Yates smiled at Bonnie and took a pull from his cigar. "I saw something interesting while you three were in the washroom."

"What's that?"

"Nickels came out from the back with a box tucked under his arm. He stopped to talk to Charlie and then the two disappeared into the kitchen."

"How did you know it was him?"

"I asked Sam. Apparently, he's in here all the time making drop offs and pick-ups for Charlie. She described him as an errand boy of some sort."

"Errand boy my ass."

"That's exactly what I thought."

"What does he look like?"

"He's tall, middle-aged with short black hair, a mustache with stubble and sideburns."

"That shouldn't be too hard to spot."

Yates nodded his head. "It's been an interesting night."

"The comment about Shawna's lipstick took the cake."

"Well, it's no surprise. We should probably get going, though," Yates said as he polished off his drink and rose from his chair. He approached the counter to pay the bill and offered Sam a hefty tip.

"Oh, you don't have to do that, Sheriff," Sam said.

"Yes, yes, I do. You may have helped more than you realize," Yates said.

"Okay then. Thank you," Sam replied as she accepted the tip.

Yates walked away from the counter and observed that Charlie and Nickels had not returned. Yates approached

Bonnie sitting at the table and took a pull from his cigar. "You ready to go?" he asked.

"Yup, it's been a long day," Bonnie replied with a yawn.

The two officers waved to Sam and exited the Rusty Mule. The parking lot was almost empty. Yates thought about his chance spotting of Nickels and was satisfied to finally know Nickels' real name and what he looked like. Yates also had a bad feeling in the pit of his stomach as his mind began to speculate what Nickels may or might not do when the two men finally meet.

# 41

CHARLIE PULLED INTO the Rusty Mule earlier than usual the next morning in anticipation of the shipment from Florida. He parked in the back of the building, walked over to the rear exit door and unlocked it just as Nickels arrived in his Dodge Charger with a medium-sized transport truck on his tail. Nickels came to a stop, giving the transport truck plenty of room to park near the back door. Charlie had already gone into the building to turn on the lights and unlock the stockroom. He returned through the kitchen and propped open the heavy steel exit door with a two-by-four. Nickels approached Charlie. "The boys pulled through for us this week. Got a full load in the truck."

"Good, good. I smell profit in the wind!" Charlie said with a grin.

Two large men unlocked the back latch, swung the rear trailer doors open, climbed inside and began unloading the drugs, stacking boxes on the ground. Charlie and Nickels carried the boxes one by one through the kitchen, down the hall and into the stockroom where they plunked the boxes near the cabinet. The two men moved the cabinet out of the way, revealing the secret storage room. Charlie unlocked the door and the two began stacking the boxes onto the shelves.

"Is Fernando sending a replacement for Cornelius?" Nickels asked.

"Yeah, in a day or so," Charlie replied.

"Well, that's no good."

"You can handle things. I've seen you with a gun before."

"Yeah well, I'm no Cornelius."

"I don't think anyone is," Charlie replied with a grin, "except his brother, and who knows where he is these days."

"Fernando couldn't get ahold of him?"

"No, and I couldn't either. The Bulldog does his own thing, remember."

Charlie and Nickels finished stacking the boxes. Charlie locked the secret storage room and the two men moved the cabinet back into place, covering the door. They left the stockroom and walked back down the hall into the kitchen. Charlie approached the rear exit door and saw the two large delivery men swinging the transport truck doors closed. "Give my regards to Fernando," Charlie said.

"See you next time," the truck driver replied.

Charlie removed the two-by-four and slammed the heavy steel door shut. Charlie and Nickels left the kitchen and walked into Charlie's office. Nickels sat down on the couch while Charlie propped his feet on his desk, leaned back in his leather chair and stared into space. "What do you suppose happened to Cornelius anyway?" he asked.

"No one knows for sure," Nickels replied.

"Shawna was the last one to see him, right? The sheriff was hot on his tail. That's what John told me," Charlie said.

Nickels took a long drag from his cigarette, rose from

the couch and paced around the office. "You don't mind if I stay here in the bar and mingle. See if I can figure out what's goin' on."

Charlie rose from his chair. "Just be careful what you say and who you say it to," he said. He exited the office and began opening the bar for another day of sales.

Nickels left the office shortly after Charlie, walked down the hall into the kitchen and ran into Freddie. "Freddie, you got a minute?"

Freddie was taking ingredients and condiments from the pantry. "You got five, brother."

"Cookin' the usual today?"

"I got the special this mornin." Freddie tied his grease-stained cooking apron and began preparing hash browns, bacon and eggs and the special breakfast biscuits for the morning crowd. The aroma began to fill the kitchen as the meat sizzled and hissed. He thought to himself for a moment and spoke. "Today's a bit of a drag though."

"How come?"

"Sheriff hasn't let my friend out of jail. I'm starting to get worried."

"Do you know why?" Nickels asked curiously.

"No, I don't know but I'm guessing it had somethin' to do with the guy she was seein'," Freddie whispered.

Nickels shrugged his shoulders.

"Someone named Jeb, man."

"Thanks man," Nickels said.

"Anytime, brother."

Nickels turned around, walked into the bar, sat down at a window booth and ordered something to eat and drink from Sam. After a few minutes, Sam returned with a plate of food for Nickels and a drink. Charlie approached Nickels and sat down across from him. "Did you find anything out?" Charlie asked.

"Yeah, your cook said his friend is in jail. Sheriff arrested her," Nickels replied as he wolfed down a piece of bacon.

"Who fuckin' cares!"

"Well, your cook said she was seein' a guy named Jeb."

Charlie let out a boisterous laugh and rose from his chair. "Man, Nickels. You're useless!"

"What?"

"Jeb is Cornelius, you fool and there isn't anyone else by that name around these parts so it has to be him," Charlie leaned over and whispered. "It's his alias, remember, his brother's name. Ring any bells?!"

Nickels took a drink ignoring Charlie's snide remark and said: "Sit down. I just thought of somethin'."

Charlie sat back down. "What?" he said rudely.

"If your cook has a friend in jail and this friend is there because of Jeb and Jeb is Cornelius then Cornelius is mixed up with a young doctor from the hospital named Lisa LeBlanc. I know who she is. I've been to her apartment and I sold to her roommate, just yesterday as a matter of fact, among other things." Nickels paused for a moment to eat and continued. "You know what that means, right. If Cornelius was seein' this Lisa Leblanc behind Shawna's back and Shawna somehow found out, then it would explain why he is suddenly missing."

Charlie shook his head in disbelief. "I can't believe that. Those two have been together a damn long time."

"Yeah, well, you know how Shawna is. If she found out

about it, it would explain things. Hell, she may have ratted him out."

"Eat your damn food," Charlie said disgustedly as he rose from his seat once more and left the table.

# 42

Bonnie and Beth returned to the police station after lunch. The two ladies walked across the hardwood floor and approached the sheriff's office. Beth knocked on the sheriff's door. "Come in," Yates said from inside. Beth opened the door and found Yates sitting at his desk talking with Dylan and Scott.

"Ah, you two are back. I was just chatting with the boys, swapping war stories," Yates said.

"What's going on?" Bonnie asked.

"The boys have been deputized for the day. Use them as you see fit. I'll be heading out to the Thomas estate now," Yates replied.

Beth and Bonnie were concerned. "Why and where's Peter?" Beth asked.

"He hasn't arrived. I'm sure I'll see him at his home," Yates replied as he approached the two ladies. "I'm going to confront John and tell him that we have the heist money."

"I don't think I like the sound of that," Bonnie said.

"I'm going to get him to incriminate himself," Yates said.

"I'm coming with you," Bonnie insisted.

Yates took a pull from his cigar. "No, you're my backup. Even with Cornelius dead, I know it's dangerous that's why Scott and Dylan have been deputized. They both have the experience and we could use the extra man power just in case things go south,"

Bonnie and Beth both agreed.

"Are they any good with a gun?" Bonnie asked.

"They both served two tours in Vietnam with the Marines. Dylan was Scott's commanding officer. They more than qualify to assist," Yates said.

"Don't worry ma'am. Scott and I know how to handle ourselves," Dylan said.

"Well, Peter will be there too, but I still don't like that you're going to confront John," Bonnie said with apprehension in her voice.

Beth placed her arm around Bonnie's shoulders.

Yates patted his gun holster. "I'll be fine."

Everyone left the office and walked over to Beth's desk. Yates grabbed his hat off the coat rack. "If you don't hear back from me or Peter in one hour, grab the boys and come on by," Yates said.

# 43

THE SUN STARTED to break through the overcast sky. Slivers of yellow and gold shone onto the sheriff's cruiser and the road ahead. Yates approached the Thomas residence and swung a right, turning onto the estate. John was standing at his office window, staring into the distance when he noticed the sheriff's police cruiser roll up to the water fountain and stop. "Shit!" John said under his breath. He quickly pulled the large curtain back, walked to his desk and dialed Charlie's number at the Rusty Mule.

"Rusty Mule, Charlie, speakin'."

"Charlie, it's me John. Is Nickels with you?"

"He's in the bar somewhere."

"Tell him to haul his ass over here! The sheriff just showed up."

"I'll tell him. What's going on?"

"Never mind that. Just get him the hell over here on the double!" John demanded and hung up the phone.

Yates exited his police car and began walking towards the house. John opened the front door, stepped outside and approached Yates. The two men met face to face as the sun shone brightly down on them, casting their shadows onto the ground. John extended his hand to Yates, but Yates did not take it.

"What do I owe the pleasure of seeing you again at my estate, Robert?" John asked smugly.

Yates rubbed the dimple on his chin and crossed his arms. He surveyed the area scanning for any possible surprises and finally looked at John. "John, I believe I may have something that belongs to you," Yates said.

"Whatever could that be, Robert?"

"You see, when I shot Cornelius dead yesterday, my deputies and I found a trunk full of bank notes. Apparently, Cornelius had what you were looking for all this time."

John's eyes widened. His brow contorted. His complexion turned purple and his eyes grew red, but he maintained his composure. "I don't know what you're talking about, Robert. Now, please, I'd appreciate it if you left my property. Now!" John demanded.

Just as John finished his sentence, Nickels arrived at the estate and started the long drive up the laneway towards the main house.

John stepped back, turned around and began to walk to his front door. Yates pushed the issue. "I guess I'll go bother Charlie and see what he has to say about the heist money," Yates said.

John stopped in his tracks and spun around upon hearing Charlie's name. "I'd imagine he'd say the same damn thing I just did."

Yates took a step forward. "The way I see it, between the murders, drugs and heist money, the two of you are gonna go away for a very long time."

John advanced towards Yates, stopped one foot in front of him and looked him in the eyes. "Careful Robert, you don't want to be throwing wild accusations around, and besides, you have nothing on me and you know it."

"I wouldn't be too sure about that. I have Lisa Leblanc in custody. Cornelius dead and a trunk full of money. It seems to me I have all the cards," Yates said.

Nickels coasted his car to a stop on the opposite side of the large water fountain and quietly exited his vehicle, unnoticed by the two men. Dressed in black, wearing a long black duster, Nickels resembled the grim reaper. He quietly and quickly snuck behind the sheriff. Yates did not hear Nickels approaching over the loud sound of the water fountain. However, John did see Nickels sneaking up behind Yates. "It's true. You do seem to have all the cards Sheriff, but you missed one," John said arrogantly.

Yates put his hands on his hips. "And what card would that be?"

At that exact moment, Nickels stood behind Yates with a slapjack. Yates saw the shadow of another man on the ground and reached for his revolver. He quickly pulled it out from its holster and spun around, but it was too late. With his right arm high in the air, Nickels crashed the slapjack down onto the collarbone of Yates. Yates let out one single shot that ripped through the air, scaring the birds out of the nearby trees. He dropped down to one knee in pain. The gun fell from his hand and John punched Yates in the head from behind. Yates crumpled to the ground.

Peter was by the front entrance door of his home putting his boots on and getting ready to leave for work when he heard the gunshot. He opened the front door, stepped outside and saw his father and Nickels standing over Yates' motionless body. Peter drew his revolver and fired one single shot into the air. John and Nickels hit the ground.

"Stop right there!" Peter cried out nervously.

John and Nickels both rose to their feet. "Get behind me and let me handle this," John whispered to Nickels. Nickels nodded.

"Peter, my boy, there's nothing going on here. Go back inside the house!" John shouted.

Peter pointed the revolver at his father. "Stop treating me like a child. I know very well what's going on here!" he yelled.

John and Nickels slowly walked closer. John put his hands out. Peter saw his father had no weapon, but Peter was not paying attention to what Nickels was doing behind his father's back.

"Peter, son, we can work this out. Now put the gun down and we'll go inside and talk," John said.

Peter took one step back. "Don't come any closer, I mean it pa!"

At that moment, Nickels pulled out a handgun from his backside and shot Peter in the shoulder. Peter fell backward and hit his head hard. He lay on the ground, knocked out, bleeding from the wound.

"What the hell are you fucking doing!? That's my kid! Go get the damn sheriff. I'll bring Peter," John said angrily.

Nickels turned around and came face to face with Yates. Blood trickling from his nose, Yates swung at Nickels. Nickels caught Yates' wild swing and grabbed his damaged collarbone, squeezing it hard. Yates writhed in pain and Nickels punched Yates' head again, this time knocking him out. The two criminals dragged the bodies of the offi-cers over to the side of the house, stopping beside the cellar doors. John unlocked the cellar and swung the two doors open. They grabbed the two bodies, carried them down into the cellar and bound the officer's hands and feet with duct tape to two separate chairs in the middle of the cellar. Peter suddenly began to regain consciousness. "You'll never get away with this!" he cried out.

"You can yell all you want son, but no one's gonna hear."

"I'm only glad ma isn't alive to see this," Peter said.

John showed no emotion, even though it stung him to think about his dead wife. He said nothing in return and instead, he and Nickels turned around, went back up the steps and locked the cellar doors behind them. "Glad Nina isn't working today or we'd have another problem," John said. "Let's go inside and wash up."

"What should we do with the sheriff's car?" Nickels asked.

"We'll take care of it after," John replied.

The two men walked around to the front of the home. Nickels opened the door for John, and they walked inside.

<h1 style="text-align:center">44</h1>

An hour had passed. Bonnie was pacing around the police station waiting for Yates to return. Beth had just received the three search warrants from the county clerk. She walked into the sheriff's office, placed the three search warrants on his desk, exited his office, approached Bonnie and looked at her still pacing back and forth. "I know. I'm worried too," Beth said.

"I'll give him a little more time. Then I'm going out there," Bonnie said.

"We haven't seen Peter yet either," Beth said, "and it's been an hour now."

Bonnie returned to the bench in front of Beth's desk and sat next to Dylan and Scott. She crossed her legs, tapped her fingers nervously on her knee and turned to Scott. "You two served in Vietnam together, right?" she asked.

"Yes, ma'am, Dylan was my CO," Scott replied.

"May I speak freely, Miss?" Dylan asked.

"Yes."

"I think we should go out there now," Dylan said. "Like the lady said. it's been an hour and the sheriff did say…"

"Just a minute!" Bonnie jumped from her chair, ran down the basement stairs, retrieved two revolvers and ammunition from the weapons locker and ran back upstairs to Dylan and Scott. "One revolver with extra bullets for each of you. Now, let's roll!" She grabbed Dylan's hand and yanked him with her out the front door. Scott followed behind. They jumped inside the police car and tore out of the parking lot as if the asphalt was on fire and headed in the direction of the Thomas estate.

# 45

YATES REGAINED HIS senses. He shook his head and tried to raise his arms, but couldn't. It took a moment before Yates realized he was bound to a chair. He turned his head and saw Peter close by bound with duct tape to another chair.

"You awake, Robert?" Peter asked.

"I'm here, wherever here is?" Yates replied.

"We're down in my cellar. They tied us up about ten minutes ago, by my guess, and left."

Yates began to look around in the dark but his vision was blurry. "Is there anything down here we can use to cut ourselves free?" he asked.

"There should be some tools and supplies on the shelves," Peter replied.

Yates shook his head again in an attempt to clear the cobwebs and quickly scanned the room. Shinning in the light coming through the cracks of the cellar door, a pair of scissors on a lower shelf caught his eye. If he could only get to them. With his legs also duct taped to the chair, Yates slowly crept and scraped across the concrete floor dragging the chair with him.

"Did you find something?" Peter asked.

"Pair of scissors, if I can only reach 'em," Yates replied. With his back to the shelf, Yates grabbed the scissors with his fingers and cut his hands free. He reached down and cut his feet free from the chair.

"Hurry, now me," Peter said.

Yates quickly approached Peter and cut his hands and feet free. Peter rose to his feet and cringed at his shoulder.

"We need to get you to the hospital, but first we have to deal with your father and Nickels," Yates said. "Think you can make it?"

"I can do it," Peter said bravely as he switched on the cellar light.

"Good. We'll need a gun for starters. They took mine," Yates said.

"Mine too. We'll have to go into the house. Follow me," Peter said.

The two officers started up the staircase and entered the house. They walked down the hall, took a left and entered the study. Peter approached a desk and opened a drawer pulling out a key. He walked to his father's gun cabinet across the room and unlocked the glass door, sliding it open. Peter took his father's Colt. "This good enough?"

"That'll do it. Load it up and grab one for yourself," Yates said.

Peter opened the drawer underneath the gun cabinet, took out ammunition and began to load the handgun. He reached back into the cabinet and took another handgun for himself and loaded the magazine. "Okay, follow me back the way we came," he said.

Meanwhile, Nickels and John were on their way out the

front door to dispose of the sheriff's police car when Bonnie, Dylan, and Scott pulled onto the property and began the long drive up the laneway. Bonnie had both worry and determination in her eyes. She knew something had gone horribly wrong and was resolved to make the culprit pay. "Be ready for anything," she said.

"Look out!" Scott suddenly shouted from the rear seat.

Just up ahead, Nickels and John were standing side by side. Nickels pointed a handgun directly at the police car and fired four rounds. The first two shots hit the front grill and damaged the radiator. The third shot bounced off the hood and the last shot hit the windshield. Bonnie rolled to a stop. The two men slowly approached the police car as Bonnie motioned to Dylan and Scott to get out. Dylan hid behind his open car door, and Bonnie and Scott hid behind their respective doors. Bonnie fired a single warning shot into the air and pointed her gun at the two felons. "Stay right where you are!" she yelled out.

Nickels had a handgun, but John had no gun.

John looked at Nickels and said: "Don't make a move until I tell you."

Nickels nodded.

"I suggest you put your guns down if you want to see your sheriff and deputy alive," John yelled out.

"Where are they!?" Bonnie yelled back.

"We have them safely tucked away. Put your guns down and come out from behind there. Right now!" John demanded.

"Do what he says," Bonnie said to Dylan and Scott.

Dylan and Scott both put their guns down and stood with their hands in the air.

"You too, Missy. Let's see those big brown eyes," John said.

Bonnie shook her head, put her revolver down and slowly raised her hands in the air.

"That's more like it," John said. "Now come over here, all three of you. Come on now."

Yates and Peter had now returned to the cellar. They pushed the cellar door open and the two men walked up and out into the yard. Yates put a finger to his lips motioning to Peter to stay quiet. The two made their way across the lawn to the front of the house and saw the situation with Bonnie, Dylan and Scott.

Bonnie looked past John and saw Yates and Peter quietly moving forward. "Pick up your guns when I tell you," she whispered to Dylan and Scott.

"Come on you three. We don't have all day. Quit your stalling and get over here now!" John yelled out, but the three refused to move. "Fire a round into the air," John ordered Nickels.

Yates and Peter quietly approached the fountain. "Stay here," Yates said. Peter nodded and ducked behind the fountain. Yates drew his Colt, pointed it directly at Nickels, silently walked closer to him and stopped twenty feet behind him. "Some people just never learn," Yates said.

Nickels and John heard Yates' voice. The two criminals spun around at the same time to face Yates as Bonnie motioned to Dylan and Scott to grab their guns. Nickels' eyes narrowed as he looked at Yates with a sneer and aggressively pushed John to one side. John landed on the grass on his backside. Yates and Nickels faced each other. Nickels pointed his gun at Yates. Yates looked at Nickels with a glimmer and watched his finger movement on the trigger. The two men fired their weapons simultaneously. In the commotion, John fled into a nearby bush unnoticed. The slug from Nickels nicked Yates' arm, but Yates' round found its target and dug into Nickels' chest. Nickels fell backward and hit the gravel laneway on his backside. Everyone approached Yates as he ran up to Nickels and kicked the handgun away from his lifeless body. Dylan checked Nickels for a pulse but found none. Bonnie disapprovingly looked at Yates. "What am I going to do with you," she said.

"Wait, where's my pa gone off to?" Peter asked.

"Spread out everyone. We need to find John now!" Yates shouted.

Everyone scattered in opposite directions in search of John, but John had stealthily slipped away and entered the cellar. He proceeded up the stairs and into the main house. John ran through his home while the others were outside looking for him. He entered the garage through the utility room, opened one of the garage doors, jumped into his truck, started the engine and floored it. Everyone turned around as John's vehicle roared past them. John fired two shots at the sheriff's police cruiser, shooting the rear tire flat, and headed straight for Yates who was standing on the gravel laneway away from the others. Yates jumped out of the way as John tore past. Yates rose to his feet and let out one shot after another at John's truck, but only managed to shatter the driver's side-view mirror and damage the tailgate. John roared down the gravel laneway. Yates ran to his police car to give chase.

"Damn it! My rear tire is flat!" Yates yelled out.

"My car is dead too!" Bonnie yelled back from across the driveway.

Peter ran into the garage to retrieve his Thunderbird. He placed his hand in his pant pocket and realized his keys were missing. Peter patted his other pockets, but they were empty as well. "My keys are gone!" he yelled out.

John had made a clean getaway leaving Nickels dead on the ground.

Peter held his arm and ran into his home in search of his spare keys. Yates and Bonnie walked over to the sheriff's cruiser and Yates put his head in the open police car window, grabbed the radio receiver and radioed Beth back at the station. "Beth, come in. Need assistance. Beth… Beth."

Yates heard static and then Beth's voice. "I hear you Robert, what's the situation."

"We need an ambulance for a gunshot wound, body pick up and a tow truck at the Thomas estate."

"Hang in there, help is on its way."

Yates put the radio receiver back in the car and the two officers walked over to Dylan and Scott standing near the garage door. "Pete, back?" Yates asked.

"Here he comes now," Dylan replied.

Peter handed the spare keys to Yates. "Take care of my car, sir," Peter said. "She's, my baby!"

"I will. Stay here and go to the hospital. I sent for an ambulance. Bonnie, stay here and wait for the tow truck," Yates said as he climbed into the Thunderbird. He started the engine and drove off in search of John.

# 46

John stopped ten miles away from his home at a filling station. He parked his truck alongside the building, walked over to the pay phone booth and dialed Charlie at the Rusty Mule. Charlie was tending bar when the phone rang. He placed a bottle of gin down and ran to the end of the bar to answer the phone. "Rusty Mule, how may I help you," he said into the phone receiver.

"Charlie, I need to see you. We've got a big problem. Nickels and Cornelius are both dead."

"What? How? What happened?"

"Meet me at Shawna's place tonight after you close up. I'll tell you everything."

"Why there?"

"Shawna's out of town. I'll explain later. Just meet me there tonight after closing."

"Alright, I'll see you there."

They both hung up the phone receiver at the same time. Charlie went back to the bar counter while John got into his truck and sped off in the direction of Shawna's home on the outskirts of town.

John parked his truck near the carport. He stepped onto the porch of Shawna's home. "I can't believe that dumb sheriff has the money. I just can't believe it. I bet Cornelius was hiding it here," John muttered to himself.

John twisted the doorknob, but it was locked. He thought for a moment and remembered what Cornelius had said when he moved here: that the spare key was hiding in plain sight. He scanned the porch and spotted wind chimes dangling near a plant. The wind chimes were made of keys of every sort. John ripped all of the keys from the apparatus and began to try each key in the door until he found the right one. He tossed the remaining keys onto the lawn and opened the front door. He turned the lights on and began looking around the home for the money. From one room to the next John went, opening drawers and closets, tearing the premises apart, but found nothing, and gave up after an hour of searching, leaving the house in a disastrous mess. "Damn it!" He said to himself begrudgingly. He entered the kitchen, grabbed two beers from the refrigerator, and a bag of chips from the cupboard. He took his snack and beers over to the couch, sat down on the sofa, turned on the TV and waited for Charlie.

# 47

At the Thomas Estate, Bonnie finished documenting the crime scene while Dylan and Scott looked on with interest. "Do you always have to take pictures and record what happened?" Scott asked.

"Yes, we do. If it goes to court, they'll need to know what took place. Even you as a police officer might be asked to testify if required," Bonnie said.

"I think I'd like doing that," Dylan said.

"What about you, Scott?" Bonnie asked.

"I think so," Scott replied.

"Maybe you two should have a talk with Yates or Callaghan. They could tell you all sorts of stories," Bonnie said.

Dylan and Scott both looked at each other and nodded in agreement.

The service vehicles came rolling down the laneway of the Thomas estate and stopped near the fountain, behind the sheriff's police car. Two men retrieved the body of Nickels, two others helped Peter into the back of the ambulance and lastly, Marty Maverick approached Bonnie, Dylan and Scott. "What y'all need towin'?" he asked.

"My car has a shot radiator and a bullet hole in the windshield," Bonnie said.

"I'll bring the car over to the garage for repairs."

"Which garage?"

"Bryan and Ted's."

"Alright, get to it then."

Marty proceeded to latch the deputy's car to the tow truck with Dylan and Scott's assistance. When they finished, the three changed the shot tire on the sheriff's car.

One by one, the service vehicles left the estate.

Yates returned and parked the Thunderbird inside the garage and got out. He closed the garage bay door and turned around.

"Did you find John?" Bonnie asked.

"No. I searched the back roads and filling stations but didn't see his truck anywhere."

"He had a good head start on you. Who knows where he got off to?" Dylan said.

"I'll figure it out. Come on, we'll take you two back to the station," Yates said.

"Will Pete be, okay?" Scott asked.

"Yeah, he may not look it, but he's a tough SOB," Yates replied.

"I think we'll go see him at the hospital in the mornin'," Dylan said.

"Pete would like that," Bonnie said as she looked at the Thomas home.

The sun began to set on the horizon. The four climbed into the sheriff's car, headed away from the estate and back onto the road, returning to the police station. Dylan retrieved his car from the parking lot and took Scott home.

# 48

Yates and Bonnie pulled into the visitors parking lot of the hospital. "What're we going to do about John?" Bonnie asked.

"I think I know where John is. We'll check my hunch after we check in on Peter," Yates replied.

"Where do you think he went?"

"He might be hiding at Shawna's house, seeing how Cornelius was living there, and Shawna said she was going out of town."

"That's a good idea. It's worth a look," Bonnie said.

The two officers entered the hospital and approached the nurses' station.

"We're here to see my deputy, Peter Thomas. They should've brought him in with a bullet wound a little while ago," Yates said.

The nurse looked up at Yates and Bonnie with a smile as she pointed down the hallway with her pencil. "Y'all need to go down this hall, turn right and follow the blue line to the end of the hallway," she said.

The two officers thanked the nurse, walked down the

hallway and turned right at the blue line. Yates and Bonnie stopped at the end of the hall and sat down in the waiting area.

"I need a cigar," Yates said.

"You can wait," Bonnie replied.

Yates grabbed a magazine and began to thumb through the pages. Bonnie did the same and glanced at him. "You look pretty beaten up. Maybe you should get checked out while we wait," she said.

Yates stretched his neck and cracked his shoulder and arm. "I'll be okay. It's nothing a bottle of whiskey and a good cigar can't fix," he said.

Bonnie smiled. The two watched patients and doctors going up and down the hallway until a doctor came out to greet them. "Are you here for Peter Thomas?" the doctor asked.

"Yes, sir," Yates replied.

"Follow me, please."

The three walked into a room and found Peter lying on a bed with his shoulder bandaged. Peter wanted to sit up and greet his fellow officers but could not. He smiled at them instead. "Did you get my pa?" he asked.

"No, I looked for him but couldn't find him. I have a hunch where he may have gotten off to though. Bonnie and I will check it out," Yates replied.

"How's the shoulder?" Bonnie asked.

"Doc took the bullet out," Peter replied.

"How is he, Doc?" Yates asked.

"It'll take a few weeks for recovery, but he's young and healthy and should be able to go home in a couple days," the doctor replied.

"Thank you, Doc. We'll see you soon, Peter," Yates said.

"Find my pa and be careful," Peter said.

"We will," Bonnie replied.

The two officers left the room, walked down the hallway and exited the hospital. Yates took a cigar and a guillotine cutter from his coat pocket, cut one end and struck a match. He took a pull and blew out plumes of smoke. Bonnie looked at him and tried to hide a smile. They climbed into the sheriff's car and left the parking lot.

## 49

AFTER LEAVING THE hospital, the two officers headed back to the police station to retrieve the search warrant for Shawna's home.

It was close to midnight, and the air was cool. Yates pulled over to the shoulder of the road in front of Shawna's home and shut the engine off. He stepped out of the vehicle, stomped his spent cigar out and drew his revolver. Bonnie approached Yates. "Do you think John's there?" she asked curiously not really believing that he would be there, but trusting Yates' judgment.

"Follow me and stay quiet."

Bonnie nodded and the two officers crossed the road and jumped the ditch. The cloudy sky made for perfect cover that night and helped to conceal their assault on the home.

"There's John's truck. I can see it near the carport, under the tree. What's the plan?" Bonnie whispered.

"I want you to sneak around the back of Shawna's home and look for a way inside. I'll take the front. I'm hoping we can cut John off if he's inside and tries to escape," Yates said quietly. "Now go."

Bonnie carefully made her way around the side of the house and headed towards the back. Yates silently proceeded to the front. He stepped onto the porch and the wood creaked under his weight. "Shit," he muttered under his breath as he quickly ducked under the window. Inside the house, John did not hear anything and was too busy watching television and getting drunk. Yates peeked into the front window and saw John sprawled on the couch. Yates crouched back down and waited for John to make a move.

Meanwhile, Bonnie had found the rear door. She turned the old doorknob, but it was locked. "Shit," she said to herself. She turned on her flashlight and began to look around for something to break the doorknob. It was hard to see anything in the dark with a flashlight that made as much light as a candle, but Bonnie was persistent and shown the light around. She saw an extinguished campfire surrounded by rocks in the backyard and walked over to it. She fumbled around and found a loose fist-sized rock and grabbed it. She backed away from the extinguished campfire and bumped into something she hadn't seen under a tree. The object was hard and poked her in the back. She turned around and saw something large covered with a tarp. She bent down, lifted the cover, shone the light and saw the orange Honda dirt bike with the broken fender. "Gotcha!" Bonnie said under her breath. She looked at the dirt bike for a brief moment and everything came flooding into her head. The lipstick on Ben's shirt, Peter being assaulted by the roadside, the second person with Cornelius shooting at Yates at the cabin, Peter following the dirt bike to the Rusty Mule and lastly the handgun given to them by the river, it was all Shawna. Bonnie quickly took out a pencil and notepad, jotted down the license plate and covered the dirt bike back up with the tarp. She returned to the backdoor of the house and smashed the rock on the doorknob. The old rusted doorknob broke off and Bonnie quickly snuck inside the home.

John heard a noise over the sound of the TV. He sat up straight on the couch, looked around and quietly placed his beer bottle down on the coffee table. He turned down the volume of the television and began to listen for more noises.

Bonnie's heart pounded as she stood silently in the laundry room looking around for a place to hide. She saw a door on her left and moved towards it. She passed the washing machine and opened the door. The door creaked and she immediately ducked into an empty storage room, closing the door behind her.

John heard a noise again. He quietly rose to his feet and began to move in the direction he thought the sound was coming from.

Outside, Yates peered into the window and saw that John was no longer sitting on the couch watching TV. Yates realized that Bonnie must have found a way inside and now was the time to make his move. He approached the front door and found it open. He quietly entered and walked over to the TV. He noticed the sound had been turned down to low, but the television was still running. He saw bottles of beer on the coffee table and remembered the same brand of beer was found at the cabin. He did not see John anywhere. John had moved towards the back of the house in search of the source of the sound he had heard. He flipped on the lights at the end of the hallway and entered the laundry room. Yates saw a light suddenly come on and started walking towards it. John looked around but did not see anything or anyone. He couldn't figure out what was going on, but recalled that the only person who knew where he was, was Charlie. "Charlie is that you? This isn't funny," John complained as he slowly opened the door to the storage room and was met with the sound of a gun being cocked. John saw Bonnie standing in front of him pointing a gun at his face. John's eyes narrowed. "I know you," he sneered. John raised his hand in the air and was about to strike Bonnie, almost daring her to shoot him, when he heard another gun being cocked and pointed right at the back of his head. John stood there frozen with one arm high in the air.

"Don't even breathe," Yates said.

Yates grabbed John's arms and handcuffed his hands together in back, while Bonnie continued to point her gun at him. Yates shoved John by his back out of the laundry room and down the hallway. Bonnie followed, continuing to point her gun at John. The three exited Shawna's home and walked up the laneway.

"What did you think you were gonna get away with?" Yates asked.

"A whole lotta money," John replied.

"Don't you care about what happens to your son?" Bonnie asked.

"He's big enough to take care of himself," John snorted.

The three approached the police car sitting on the shoulder of the road. Yates informed John of his rights and opened the back door. Yates wrangled a belligerent John into the rear seat. John kicked the car door as Yates struggled to shut it. "Cut that out!" Yates yelled. John kicked the rear seat of the police car, taunted the two officers from inside and spat on the inside car window.

"You don't know who you're dealing with, Robert. Hell will rain down on this town if I go down!" John yelled.

"Shut up!" Bonnie shouted.

"You heard the lady. Stop acting like a jackass," Yates said.

John kicked at the car door again.

Bonnie pulled out her gun and pointed it at John.

"Control that hotheaded, trigger-happy Texan, Robert, or I'll do it for you!" John yelled.

"The only thing that's keeping me from putting a hole in your head is Peter!" Bonnie shouted.

Yates placed his hand on Bonnie's extended arm. "Don't play his game. It's what he wants."

Bonnie looked into Yates' eyes, then back at John, eased her arm and placed her gun in its holster.

"We need to go, Bonnie," Yates said.

John laughed from inside the car.

The two officers entered the vehicle and drove off with a petulant John sitting handcuffed in the rear seat.

# 50

At the Rusty Mule, Charlie was ending another day and closing the bar. Sam was the last employee out the back door and waved goodbye to him as she left. Charlie waved back to her and headed to the cash register. He grabbed the receipts and money from the till, stuffed them into his bar apron pocket and headed over to his office. He dumped the receipts on his desk and put the money into an envelope. *I'd better go see what John wants*, Charlie thought to himself. He grabbed his coat off the rack and locked the office door. He went into the kitchen, flung his apron onto the counter and exited through the back door.

Charlie stood outside under the security light and quickly scanned the parking lot, thinking he had heard the sound of a car door closing. He stepped away from the security light into the dark and began walking to his vehicle when he heard someone calling his name. "Charlie!"

Charlie spun around and saw the shadow of a large man approaching. The large man was dressed in black. Charlie did not recognize who it was. He strained his eyes to see, reached into his back pants for his handgun and pulled it out. The large man came closer to Charlie and called his name again. "Charlie?!"

Charlie pointed his gun at the unknown man. "Stop right there!"

The large man stopped in his tracks. He struck a match and lit a cigarette. The flame briefly illuminated his face. "Charlie, don't you recognize me?" the large man said.

Charlie's eyes widened. "Shit! You son of a bitch!" Charlie exclaimed. "I could've shot you!"

The large man stood beside Charlie. "You're still a little high strung, aren't ya!" The man laughed and swatted Charlie on the back.

"What're you doing here, Marcus? Last time I saw you was in Florida."

"Nickels told me you were in need of help so I drove up here as fast as I could. Walk with me to my car."

"I have to go see John at Shawna's house. He called me a few hours ago and asked me to meet him there."

"I'll drive ya."

The two men approached a '69 black Pontiac GTO and got inside. Marcus fired the engine and a loud rumble came from the exhaust. He turned on the headlights and the two rolled out of the parking lot and pulled onto the main road heading to Shawna's place. Marcus lit another cigarette and handed the pack to Charlie. "Come on. You used to smoke these all the time, man," Marcus said.

"Not anymore," Charlie replied.

"Fine," Marcus said as he slipped the pack back into his pocket. "Shawna workin' the clubs here?"

"Yeah, but she left town for the weekend."

"Ah Shawna, what a gal," Marcus said as he started to

laugh. "Do you remember when we all met her at Fernando's club over on Eighth Street back in San Martino? Cornelius nearly lost his head the first time he saw her on stage. Those were the good ol' days."

"How has The Lucky Dollar been doin' since I left?"

"Pretty good. Place keeps gettin' busier all the time. Fernando is thinkin' of opening up another club soon," Marcus said and continued, "Hey! Do you remember when we used to take those milk runs up to the Keys."

"Cornelius would get wasted on those runs. He'd start singing at the top of his lungs at three in the morning, with no one anywhere on the road for miles. We made a lot of money back then. Hard to believe it's been ten years now," Charlie said with a smile.

"Well, you've been here for quite a while now. How's it been?" Marcus asked.

Charlie made a gesture with his hand. "It could be better, but I'm not complaining any."

"This isn't exactly San Martino."

"Oh, hell no!"

Marcus rolled down the window, threw his spent cigarette out and lit a fresh one. "Mind me askin' but where the hell is Cornelius? I thought he'd be with you?"

"He and Nickels are both dead."

"What?!"

"I don't know. John told me they're both dead.'

"Shit! What happened to 'em?"

"I don't know what happened to Nickels, but I think I know what happened to Cornelius."

"What?"

"Nickels had a theory that Cornelius was seein' another

gal and Shawna got jealous and ratted him out to the local sheriff, but I wouldn't put too much stock in what Nickels says."

"That fuckin' burns, man!" Marcus said as he rolled the window back up. "What the hell has been goin' on up here?"

"There's a new sheriff in town. He's a real piece of work."

"Shit! We'd better do somethin'."

The two arrived at Shawna's property after Yates and Bonnie had left with John.

"Here's John's truck. He must be inside," Charlie said as he got out and shut the car door.

"So, this is the place Shawna bought, huh," Marcus said as he joined Charlie.

"Yeah, she fixed it up pretty good. It was a dump when she bought it. Got it real cheap too."

"Wait, look at the ground." Marcus said. "Fresh tracks. Someone else has been here. When did you say Shawna left?"

"A couple of days ago. Why?"

"Did anyone else know John would be here?"

"Just me. Since when did you become a detective?"

"Since I like to stay alive. Come on, we'd better go inside and take a look around."

The two men approached the porch steps. Charlie reached for the screen door and saw that the inside door was open. They entered the house and began to look in the dark.

"Hit the lights. I can't see shit in here," Charlie said.

Marcus took a drag from his cigarette, reached over and slapped the light switch on the wall with his catcher's mitt-sized hand. The lights came on, and the two men saw the house was a disaster. There were papers and drawers scattered about the floor, cupboards were opened and the television was on with the volume turned down. They walked over to the couch and Marcus leaned over and grabbed an unopened bottle of beer sitting on the coffee table.

"What do you suppose happened here?" Charlie asked.

"I don't know, but I don't like the looks of this," Marcus replied as he took a gulp of beer and yelled out, "John!"

"Shut up! What if someone's still here!" Charlie exclaimed.

Marcus placed the beer bottle down on the coffee table and pulled his handgun out. "If there is, he's gonna be dead!"

The two men exited the living room and walked down the hallway to the back of the house. Marcus took lead and Charlie followed. They passed two locked doors and entered the laundry room at the end of the hallway. They looked around in the dark. Charlie went over to the back door of the house. "The doorknob is busted off," he said.

Marcus looked over Charlie's shoulder and pushed the back door open, "And still no John!"

Charlie flicked on the backyard light and the two walked outside. The lawn hadn't been mowed in weeks.

"Here's Shawna's dirt bike and I see foot tracks around it," Marcus observed.

"Someone has definitely been here," Charlie said.

The two turned around, walked back inside and turned off the outside light. They walked back up the hallway and into the living room.

"Stay here. I'll go check upstairs," Marcus said.

Charlie agreed. Marcus walked up the staircase. He checked each room and saw the same disorder as before. After a few minutes of searching, he returned down the stairs.

"I found nothing. It's been all torn up upstairs too. I don't like the looks of this at all," Marcus said.

"Looks like a struggle took place, but nobody anywhere. No blood. No John. No nothing!" Charlie exclaimed.

"Only his truck sitting outside," Marcus added as he lit another cigarette and flicked the lights off. The two men exited the house. They stood on the front porch staring out into the dead of night with only the crickets and lightening bugs to keep them company, wondering what had happened to John.

Marcus stepped off the porch and looked at John's truck. "What should we do now?"

"I think we should head back to the bar and wait 'til morning for him to call. If we don't hear from him by then, we'll go over to his place," Charlie replied.

"What about his truck?" Marcus asked.

"Start it up. I'll drive it back to the bar."

Marcus opened the door of John's truck and hopped inside. He began to fiddle with the wires and the truck sprung to life. Marcus jumped back out. "She's all yours."

"Just a minute. I want to grab Shawna's dirt bike before we go," Charlie said.

"What the fuck for?"

"Because whoever was here was snoopin' around it," Charlie said.

The two men walked to the back of the house. Charlie flung the tarp off the bike and Marcus rolled it to the front of the house. Charlie took the tailgate down and Marcus hopped onto the bed of John's truck and grabbed the handlebars as the two men lifted the dirt bike onto the bed of the truck and secured the bike.

Marcus jumped down and put the tailgate back up. "Now get in and let's go," he said.

"I'll be right behind you."

Marcus started his GTO and the two backed their vehicles out of the laneway and onto the road. Marcus took the lead and Charlie followed. The two drove back to the Rusty Mule where they spent the night in Charlie's office waiting for John's call.

# 51

YATES AND BONNIE entered the police station with John handcuffed. Bonnie unlocked the second jail cell door and Yates uncuffed John, shoved him inside the jail cell and slammed the door shut. "Welcome to your new home. I know it's not what you're used to, but you'll have to make due for the time being," Yates said.

John's eyes narrowed as he approached the jail cell bars and looked at Yates. "You know you can't keep me here for long. I'll get out and when I do, I'll have your head!" he shouted.

"Oh, I don't think so. I've got search warrants galore. I'm sure I'll find enough evidence to put the whole lot of you away for a very long time," Yates said calmly.

Lisa suddenly awoke from the commotion and approached the jail cell bars while rubbing the sleep from her eyes. She looked across the cell, saw John behind bars and began laughing uncontrollably. "Am I still dreaming? That can't be you, John?"

John's eyes darted towards Lisa. "What the hell are you in for?!" he shouted.

"I tried to kill that young boy like Cornelius told me."

"You obviously fucked that up or you wouldn't be here."

"Speak for yourself," Lisa said as she went back to her bench.

"Charlie will be joining you in there soon," Yates said.

"You think you can arrest Charlie?" John said with a boisterous laugh.

Bonnie approached John's cell. "You're damn right we can and we'll do it too! You son of a bitch!" she shouted.

"Call off your wench, Yates!" John yelled.

Bonnie looked crossly at John and said: "You really do have a big mouth, don't you!"

"Why don't you go do some needlepoint," John replied smugly.

"Sit down and shut up, you son of a bitch!" Yates shouted.

Yates placed his hand on Bonnie's shoulder and led her to his office closing the door behind them, leaving John yelling obscenities. The two officers sat down. Yates took a cigar from his desk and struck a match.

"There's something I need to tell you," Bonnie said as she leaned up closer to the desk. "I found that orange Honda dirt bike in the back of Shawna's place hiding under a tarp. You know, the bike with the broken fender that we've been looking for."

"We all had a feeling she was involved, but there was never any proof until now," Yates said.

"I took down the license plate number."

"Good! We can now prove Shawna is involved and that she probably knocked Peter out, shot at me, gave us Cornelius' handgun and who knows how she was involved in

Ben Steven's death. I'm betting she also has part of that heist money with her. We were what, three hundred thousand dollars short from the official number?"

"Something like that, yes. Do you think Shawna will ever come back from her trip to Georgia?"

"Probably not for a while, if that's even where she went off to."

# 52

AFTER PROCESSING JOHN at the police station, Yates and Bonnie returned to Shawna's house where Marty was waiting.

"I don't see no truck or bike, Sheriff!" Marty scratched his head. "Are you sure you got the right place? It's pretty late, man."

"Stay here a minute while we look around," Yates said.

Marty nodded and lit a cigarette.

The two officers proceeded to the back of the house and found nothing. Bonnie pointed her flashlight at the tree next to the extinguished campfire and the grey tarp lying on the ground. "That's where the bike was," she said.

Yates pointed his flashlight on the ground and saw tire tracks in the uncut grass and imprints of heavy boots. He followed the tracks back to where they had parked. "The vehicles are gone, Marty. There's no sign of them around back. You may as well go home," Yates said.

"Thanks, Sheriff," Marty said and left.

Yates wondered, *who had come by and taken the truck and dirt bike.* He stared at the road and thought to himself, *something like this would have happened, but the situation with John called for two officers, and with Peter in the hospital, there was no one left to guard the house.*

Bonnie approached Yates and stood beside him. "Who do you think took the bike and truck?" she asked.

"Charlie, Joshua, Doug. Could've been any of those three. John had to have contacted someone. But what concerns me are the large tracks that appear to be from a heavier and bigger male, which is not any of those three," Yates said.

"There are a lot of large men who work at the mines. It could've been one of them," Bonnie suggested.

"Maybe, but I'm thinking it's someone else. Maybe one of the Romanos," Yates said.

"We should go back to the station and take another look at the papers that Peter got over the telex. Their physical stats should be included," Bonnie said.

The two officers turned around. Yates spotted in the dirt the impression of where another vehicle had been parked. "Grab the camera and take some pictures of these tire tracks," he said.

Bonnie returned to the police car, grabbed the camera and began clicking pictures of the area. The flash from the bulb illuminated the ground as Yates looked on and said: "They came in one vehicle and left in two."

"Probably placed the dirt bike on the bed of John's truck and left with it," Bonnie added. "I just hate that we don't have any evidence on Shawna, now."

"Don't worry. She'll slip up sooner or later and when she does, we'll nab her," Yates said. "One by one, we'll get 'em all."

"Since we're here, we should make use of that search

warrant and process Shawna's house," Bonnie said. "Hopefully we'll find something inside."

"She probably removed any evidence implicating herself before she left."

"Damn!"

The two officers processed Shawna's home, found nothing and left.

**53**

EARLY THE NEXT morning, Yates and Bonnie were quietly working when they suddenly heard John bellowing from his jail cell. The two officers exited their respective offices. Yates approached John's cell and glanced at him sitting on the bench. John sneered at Yates and was mad as hell. "Did you two get lost or something. It must be hard for half-wits to find their way out of an office," John said sarcastically.

"What do you want?" Yates asked.

"I want my one phone call," John demanded.

"Come over here, and I'll bring you to the pay phone," Yates said.

John rose from his bench and approached the cell door. He stopped and looked at Yates and Bonnie. "Rough night?!" Neither officer spoke. Yates unlocked the cell door and swung it open with a loud creak that awoke Lisa from her sleep. Lisa, groggy-eyed, glanced at the officers and John, then rolled over on her shoulder.

"Your phone call awaits, Mr. Thomas," Yates said.

"Follow me please to the pay phone," Bonnie said.

John stood there not moving, looking at Yates dead in

the eyes. Yates took a cigar and a guillotine cutter from his coat pocket, cut one end and struck a match. The two men stood and stared at each other until John stepped forward and Yates gave John a shove from behind. "Move it," Yates said through cigar smoke.

"Easy Robert, you don't want me to sue you," John said.

Yates continued to puff on his cigar and did not say a word or bat an eye. The three arrived at the pay phone on the wall near the basement steps. John grabbed the receiver and looked at the two officers. "Got a dime?" he asked.

Yates rolled his eyes, reached into his pant pocket, fished out some loose change and handed John a dime. "Better make it a good call," Yates said.

John took the dime. "Please, a little privacy," he said smugly.

Yates and Bonnie glanced at each other and walked to the middle of the room.

"Watch and see who he's dialing, if you can," Yates whispered.

John put his dime into the pay phone and dialed the Rusty Mule. Charlie was sitting in his office, counting his money with Marcus when the phone rang.

"Rusty Mule, how may I help you?" Charlie said into the phone receiver.

"Charlie, It's me.""

"John, you had me worried. Where are you? What's going on? Me and Marcus found Shawna's home in a mess," Charlie exclaimed.

John looked over his shoulder and saw Yates and Bonnie watching him. John turned back around to face the wall and covered his mouth with his hand. "Marcus is there? Good, he can help. Now listen. Yates has me in jail. I want you and Marcus to get everything you can together and get the hell out of the state," John ordered.

"Shit John! We're gonna bust you out!" Charlie exclaimed.

"No, don't you do that. Get out of the state. You're better off helping me back down in Florida. Do you understand?" John whispered.

Yates and Bonnie looked at each other and began to approach John. John turned around, saw the two officers, then turned back to the wall again. "Get out of the state now! Do what I tell you!" John ordered again as he slammed the phone receiver down just as Yates came to him.

Yates leaned up against the wall and looked at John. "Everything okay?"

"Yeah, yeah," John replied.

The two officers escorted John back to his jail cell. John entered his cage and Yates closed and locked the cell door.

"Have you ever heard that old saying?" John asked.

"What old saying?" Yates inquired.

"He who laughs last laughs the loudest," John said.

"I'm not laughing," Yates replied as he shook his head in disgust and walked away from the cells with Bonnie, leaving John to ponder his fate.

# 54

Yates and Bonnie arrived at the Thomas estate at the beginning of a rainstorm. Yates took a pull on his cigar as he drove up to the fountain and parked beside it. The two officers jumped out of the police cruiser and ran to the front door of the main house. Yates rang the doorbell. The maid opened the door and smiled at the two officers. "Sheriff, Bonnie, please come in. Peter informed me that you were coming with a search warrant," she said.

Yates showed the search warrant. "We won't be long. Can you take us to John's office?" he asked.

"Of course. Follow me."

The two officers followed the maid into the house. She escorted them down the long hallway, finally stopping at John's office. The maid opened the door. Yates tipped his hat to her and thanked her.

"If y'all need anything else. Let me know. I'll be in the kitchen," the maid said and drifted away.

Yates and Bonnie entered John's office. Bonnie preceded to the filing cabinets first. She began rifling through the drawers, while Yates started looking through the bar on the opposite end of the room. He pulled out the ledger that Peter had found, still in the same place he had said it would be. Yates flipped open the ledger and began reading through the pages of figures until he came to the payment entries that Peter had described. He marked the page with a dog-ear and continued carefully reading the ledger until he saw what was going on. Bonnie approached Yates and looked at him.

"Did you find anything in the filing cabinets?" Yates asked.

"No, everything in the filing cabinets is from the mining operation. Employees and such," Bonnie replied.

Yates continued to read the ledger. "There it is," he said.

"What?"

Yates pointed at a page. He moved his finger from line to line. "Here. See these numbers. He's moving money from one place to another."

"Money laundering," Bonnie commented.

"And I'm thinking tax evasion, but I'm no accountant."

"I wonder what the books for the Rusty Mule would show?"

"Same song and dance, I'd imagine," Yates said. He handed the ledger to Bonnie who slipped it into a plastic bag.

Next, they turned their attention to John's desk in the middle of the room. Bonnie opened the center top drawer of the desk and searched its contents but found nothing. Yates tugged at the two right side drawers but they were both locked.

"Give me a minute with the lock," Bonnie said. She took a hairpin from under her hat and began working the two locks.

"Got any other surprises under that hat?" Yates asked jokingly.

"Hush! I'm a little rusty," Bonnie said.

Yates leaned against the desk and took a pull from his cigar while watching Bonnie pick the locks.

"Voila!" Bonnie said. She rose to her feet and slid the right top drawer open.

"Next time I lock my keys in the car, I'll know who to call," Yates said with a smile.

The two officers peered inside the drawer and found stacks of cash. Yates reached into the drawer, pulled out a stack of bills and flipped through the bills with his fingers. He looked at the serial numbers on the hundred-dollar bills and noticed the numbers were all identical. He then pulled one bill out, held it to the light and felt it with his fingers. "I believe John has been up to some counterfeiting," Yates said.

Bonnie pulled out the remaining stacks of bills, placed them on the desk and spotted something else underneath. She reached back in and yanked out counterfeiting plates and placed the plates down on the desk next to the money.

"Let's see what's inside drawer number two," Yates said as he took a pull from his cigar, leaned down and opened the right bottom drawer. Inside, he found a stack of files, a strong box and some dirty magazines. He took the files out and dropped them onto the desk. Bonnie reached inside and grabbed the strong box. She placed it down on the desk and opened it. Inside the metal box, she found small bags of white powder and several pills.

"What should we do with the dirty magazines?" Bonnie asked jokingly.

"Leave 'em for Pete," Yates laughed.

"Look, there's something else at the bottom of the drawer," Bonnie said as she reached down and picked up a crystal ring.

"Looks like the same skull ring that Cornelius wore," Yates said. "Bag that too."

Yates grabbed a file from the desk and began to flip through it, while Bonnie did the same.

"See anything?" Yates asked.

"Not yet. You?"

Yates did not reply at first and continued to read the file. "Interesting," he said.

Bonnie placed her file down. "What?" she asked curiously.

"John has been keeping a record of his gambling out of state."

"Sounds like Lisa was right!" Bonnie said.

"Yup," Yates said as he took a pull on his cigar. He placed the file down, opened the ledger from before and began skimming over it again.

"What?" Bonnie asked.

"Some of the numbers and dates from this ledger match up with the ones in the file," Yates said.

"We'd better head over to the Rusty Mule," Bonnie said.

"Grab everything and put the evidence in the trunk of the car," Yates said. "We'll drop the evidence off at the station first."

The two officers gathered all of the evidence and placed it into plastic bags. They walked down the hallway, stopped in the kitchen to thank the maid and left the premise.

# 55

Charlie was pacing back and forth in his office while Marcus was sitting on the couch, drinking a glass of scotch and smoking a cigarette. Charlie let out a huff and stopped in front of the wall safe. He swung the painting to one side and proceeded to unlock the safe. Marcus gulped down the remainder of his drink, rose from the couch and approached Charlie. "You haven't said one word since you got off the phone. What did John say?" Marcus asked curiously.

Charlie began taking the money out of the wall safe, stack by stack, placing it down on the desk. "John wants us to get out of the state and head back to Florida. The sheriff has him in jail."

"First, Cornelius and Nickels! Now, John! I'm gonna tear that sheriff apart!" Marcus yelled angrily as he pounded his fist down on Charlie's desk.

"Save your energy. We gotta get everything outta here fast!" Charlie ordered.

"This is gonna be a long haul back to San Martino," Marcus said. He took another drag from his cigarette and walked out of Charlie's office.

Marcus entered the stockroom, slapped the light switch on the wall and walked over to the secret storage room. He carried box after box of drugs down the hall and outside, loading the boxes onto the bed of John's pickup truck, placing them under the tarp beside Shawna's dirt bike.

While Marcus was busy outside, Charlie boxed the cash from the wall safe. He grabbed the Rolex and donned it on his wrist. He clutched the old Schofield revolver, looked at it and thought to himself, *maybe it was time to destroy it.* He was tired of totting it around. Instead, he shoved it under his rear belt behind his back. Lastly, he grabbed the cash that he had boxed and left the office heading outside.

"Got everything?" Marcus asked.

"Yeah, that about does it. I'll put the money in the rear seat of your car," Charlie said as he opened the passenger door and slipped the box inside. In his hurry, he hit his head on the door frame as he backed out and bumped into the open door behind him. Charlie spun around, straightened his back and rubbed his head. He brushed his backside against the door again and unwittingly dislodged his revolver. The old Schofield fell to the ground as he slammed the passenger door shut. Charlie carelessly kicked the old revolver under the car with the toe of his boot as he leaned against the fender facing Marcus. "Did you manage to get everything out of the storage room?"

"Yeah, as much as John's pickup truck can carry. I tied it all down next to Shawna's dirt bike and covered everything. I'd suggest burning the place down before we leave," Marcus said.

"It's gonna be sad to see the bar go, but not much we can do about it," Charlie said.

"We gotta finish fast before people start showing for work. Got any gas cans?" Marcus asked.

"Should be some in the stockroom where the generator is," Charlie replied.

The two men re-entered the building and retrieved four gas cans from the stockroom. They doused the stockroom and secret storage room with gasoline. They went into the bar and began dousing the area with gasoline, splashing the counter and throwing gasoline over the wood floor. Marcus made a trail leading into the kitchen, emptied his last can, threw it on the kitchen cutting table and walked out the back door. Charlie approached the stage at the far end of the bar and showered it with gasoline. He dumped the remaining gasoline on the tables, threw the can on the floor with a loud empty thud and looked out the front window. Through the rain covered glass, under a dark overcast morning sky, Charlie saw the headlights of a police car rolling into the parking lot of the Rusty Mule. "Fuck!" he said. Charlie turned around, walked into the kitchen and out the rear exit door. "The fuzz arrived up front. Are you ready to go?" he asked.

"Yeah, I'm ready. You take John's truck," Marcus said.

"Give me a minute to start the fire," Charlie said. He returned inside and went to the front windows. He peered outside and saw Yates had parked the sheriff's cruiser in front of one of the entrances, blocking the way to the road. Charlie watched the sheriff and Bonnie exit the vehicle. Charlie turned around and dropped a match on the gasoline covered floor near the front entrance doors. The fire began to spread quickly across the floor. He ran out of the bar, through the kitchen and turned on all of the gas stoves. He opened the exit door and went outside where Marcus was waiting in his car.

"She's gonna blow!" Charlie shouted.

"Let's roll!" Marcus yelled.

Suddenly from the rear parking lot of the bar, Charlie and Marcus came tearing out, with Charlie in the lead in John's truck. Yates and Bonnie turned around only to see Charlie and Marcus leave through the second entrance of the property. The officers ran towards the speeding vehicles and fired their weapons, but only hit the side of the pickup truck.

At that moment, an explosion erupted from inside the building. Glass from the front windows blew through the air as the officers' dove face down onto the ground. Debris from the building littered the area. Flames shot straight into the rain clouds above. The fire burned loud and strong. The old Rusty Mule that had been on the roof top of the building came crashing down in front of Yates as he picked himself up from the ground.

"Come on! Before they get away!" Yates yelled out.

Yates helped Bonnie to her feet and the two ran towards the sheriff's cruiser. Yates started the engine and tore off onto the main road. He steered in the direction that Marcus and Charlie had taken, while Bonnie radioed the fire department. Yates turned on the police sirens and lights.

"They got a pretty good head start on us," Bonnie said.

"Yup, but I know where they're heading," Yates replied calmly.

"Want to enlighten me?"

"If I were them, I'd be trying to get the hell out of the state as fast as I could. Which means they should be taking the interstate into North Carolina," Yates said.

"That makes sense. Let's catch 'em!"

Marcus and Charlie had built a good lead. They had already left Reeves County and were on the interstate. Marcus pulled out in front of Charlie, honked twice and took point. A few miles back, Yates passed the county line, but did not care. He was determined to get the two men. Yates grabbed the police radio and kept his eyes on the traffic ahead. "This is Sheriff Robert Yates from Reeves County. I just crossed the county line and I'm pursuing two armed men travelling east on the interstate. Armed and dangerous. One is driving a two-tone beige and white Chevy K20 pickup truck; the other, a black Pontiac GTO. Looking for assistance, over," Yates said into the police radio.

Static. "I read you loud and clear, Sheriff. We got you covered. Scrambling a deputy to assist the chase," a voice said over the radio.

Static. "Sheriff, we'll set up a roadblock here at the state line. We'll make sure they don't leave," a second voice said over the radio.

Static. "Roger and much obliged," Yates replied. He placed the radio receiver back and stepped on the gas pedal until it touched the floor of the car.

It wasn't long before a deputy from the neighboring county pulled onto the interstate about a mile ahead of Yates. The deputy slowed down, and in a few moments, Yates caught up. With sirens wailing like banshees, the officers drove as fast as they could in the rain. As they approached the felons, the overzealous deputy acted first. He pulled out from behind Charlie and drove alongside the pickup truck. The deputy tried to signal Charlie to pull over, but Charlie refused. Instead, he began banging into the squad car, trying to knock the deputy off the interstate. The deputy swerved, became frustrated and slammed his police car into the pickup truck, but that big Chevy did not give an inch. The deputy tried to signal Charlie again and honked the horn several times with no luck. Now livid at the young deputy, Charlie grabbed his gun from the passenger seat and rolled down the window. He took aim and shot at the police car. The first bullet shattered a window. The impulsive deputy slowed down and moved in behind the truck and in front of Yates. The deputy began tailgating Charlie. Charlie saw in his rearview mirror what was going on and slammed on the brakes. Charlie's truck slid and the tires squealed on the wet asphalt. The deputy quickly braked and swerved to avoid a collision. Yates following behind did the same, narrowly missing a collision with the deputy. Yates fell a few car lengths back.

Marcus saw what was going on in his rearview mirror and slowed down. He drove beside the deputy's car slamming the GTO into the squad car. The deputy returned the favor. Marcus dropped back behind the deputy and pushed the squad car, sending it careening off the road. Marcus smiled to himself and settled behind Charlie. Next, Yates drove up to Marcus and smacked the police cruiser into the back of the GTO. Marcus bounced in his seat and grabbed a handgun. Yates banged his car into the GTO again. Marcus rolled down the window, stuck out his arm and began shooting wildly behind at Yates. The slugs missed their target. Yates pulled alongside the GTO. "Pull over!" Bonnie shouted from the passenger window.

Marcus looked at the police car. "Ladies first!" he shouted as he fired at the front passenger tire of the police car. Yates muscled the steering wheel but it was too much and the car spun off the interstate into the grass. "Shit!" Yates said as he slapped the steering wheel with his hands. "Are you okay?" he asked.

"I'm fine," Bonnie replied.

"There's not much we can do now. It's all up to the boys at the roadblock," Yates said.

Charlie and Marcus advanced towards the state line. Marcus was driving point again and saw the roadblock ahead. He started to slow down and drove alongside Charlie. Marcus honked his horn and yelled out the open passenger window. "Roadblock ahead!"

Charlie strained his eyes, saw red lights in the distance and two police cars sitting at the state line. "Get out your gun! Fire a few rounds at 'em. Then get behind me. I'm gonna ram 'em down the middle!" Charlie yelled out.

"You sure that'll work?" Marcus yelled back

"It better or we're fucked!" Charlie shouted.

Marcus pressed down on the gas pedal and floored it. He grabbed a handgun from the passenger seat and stuck the barrel out the window. Even though he was still out of range he began shooting randomly at the officers standing in front of their squad cars. The two officers ducked for cover behind their vehicles. Marcus took his foot off the gas and let Charlie take the lead. Charlie floored it like a runaway freight train and slammed the pickup truck in the gap between the two parked police cars sitting on the road. The two officers jumped out of the way in the nick of time and began shooting at the felons, but it was too late. Marcus and Charlie had made it out of state.

The two criminals took the first exit off the interstate and travelled onto a main road before taking a side road. Marcus passed Charlie to survey the damage and saw that the front of the pickup truck had been smashed. He motioned to Charlie to slow down and pull over. The two men came to a stop on the shoulder of the road and exited their vehicles.

"Front end is smashed to hell," Marcus observed.

"It's still drivable," Charlie said.

"We should stick to the side roads from now on," Marcus said.

"This is gonna be a long, long haul back to Florida," Charlie complained.

"Better than gettin' nabbed by the cops," Marcus replied.

# 56

BACK IN LANCASTER Falls, Yates and Bonnie returned to the police station and found Peter conversing with Beth near the entrance. "Sheriff, I need to talk to you," he said.

"They let you out of the hospital?" Yates asked.

"I let myself out. I wanted to help and research the case," Peter replied. "Can we sit in your office?"

Yates and Bonnie followed Peter into the sheriff's office. The three officers sat down around the sheriff's desk.

"First, I have some information about Shawna Ray. I ran a check on the license plate number Bonnie took down. The bike is registered to a Miss Grace Noel. I then ran her name through the system and found out she was arrested in San Martino, Florida numerous times for shoplifting and solicitation. They wired me her prints with a picture," Peter said as he gave the file to Bonnie.

"It's her alright," Bonnie said.

"First rule in her line of work, never use your real name," Yates said.

"Makes sense," Bonnie said. "But I wish we had something on her."

"All we have is a lot of speculation with no evidence," Peter said.

Yates took a cigar from his desk and struck a match. He rose from his leather chair, walked over to the window and looked out across the town square. "We should go back to what's left of the Rusty Mule and look for evidence," he said.

"Think we'll find anything?" Bonnie asked.

"We might. It's all we got left to nail 'em," Yates said.

# 57

Smoke rose from the debris of the Rusty Mule. Charred pieces of wood littered the ground. A pack of dogs circled around the rubble like buzzards circling the dead. Yates pulled into the parking lot, honked his horn and flashed his high beams several times at the animals. The dogs stared at the lights and ran off as if they had seen an apparition.

Yates parked the car near the debris and the three officers exited the sheriff's cruiser. "Fan out and keep your eyes open for anything out of the ordinary," Yates said.

"Looks like a bomb went off," Peter said.

"The fire chief said they started the fire with gasoline in the bar, turned on the gas stoves in the kitchen and left," Yates said.

Yates approached what remained of the front entrance of the bar. He kicked pieces of charred wood with the toe of his boot and stepped onto a blackened floor. Yates walked around looking at the debris, trying to determine where the kitchen would have been. He knew there was a hallway of some sort that led to Charlie's office, but everything looked the same now, only burnt pieces remained. He walked further into the wreckage and saw bits of food on the ground beside what was left of the freezer and thought to himself, *that must have been what lured the stray dogs here*. Yates turned around and walked again. He passed through the broken frame of a wall, bent down and saw a scorched safe on the ground. The door was open, but there was nothing inside. Yates walked further and saw pieces of metal and what was left of what looked like a generator. He diligently looked over the remains, but found nothing, only a skeleton of what used to be. Yates walked away from the wreckage and found dirt under his boots again. He saw tire tracks on the ground and more debris. He shoved another piece of charred wood aside with the toe of his boot and uncovered an old revolver lying on the ground. He reached into his pocket and pulled out a rag. Yates picked up the gun and placed it in a plastic bag. He looked at the gun sitting inside the bag, dangling it in his hand under the sunlight.

"That looks like an old slug thrower. Smith & Wesson, Schofield, I believe. Something like my grandpa used to have," Bonnie said.

"Find anything?" Yates asked.

"No, but come over here. Peter is in the dumpster," Bonnie said as she began to walk.

"How did he get in there?"

"I gave him a boost."

The two officers approached the dumpster sitting near the tree line on the edge of the property. Yates took a cigar from his inside coat pocket and struck a match. "Find anything useful?" he asked.

"Not yet. But I will," Peter replied.

"Ah, good. You put your rubber gloves on," Bonnie said. "Watch your shoulder. You got shot, remember."

"Yeah. Yeah," Peter said while not really paying attention. He sifted through the garbage, piece by piece, looking for any kind of clue. He tore apart garbage bags and rifled through two weeks' worth of junk and food scraps. He was waist deep in rubbish when he spotted a grubby men's dress shirt under one of the bags of garbage. Peter grabbed the shirt and looked at it. It was stained and torn, but something caught his eye. "Sheriff, look at this."

Yates looked at the dress shirt. "What am I looking at?"

"Here," Peter said as he pointed to a stain on the upper chest of the shirt.

Yates took the shirt from Peter's hand and looked at it closely. "That might be blood."

"Give me a hand out of here," Peter said.

Yates handed the dress shirt to Bonnie and helped Peter out of the dumpster. Peter brushed the garbage off his pants and shoes and smelled himself. "Wow, I stink," he said.

"Good job, Pete. Let's head back to the station and send the shirt and revolver off to the lab," Yates said.

The three began walking back to the sheriff's cruiser as Yates thought about the old gun he had found.

**58**

THE LUCKY DOLLAR, located on the strip near the beaches and hotels of San Martino, Florida, was erected in the 1950's. It was originally a gambling den that was converted into a strip club in the late 1960's. When Fernando Romano bought the property, he kept the original name and renovated the interior. Outside the joint, you could read "GIRLS, GIRLS, GIRLS," in flashing neon and when you entered, you could smell cheap perfume, sweat, alcohol, and cigarettes. The club had two center stages, one for main acts and one for local girls. Each stage had chairs seated around it. The staff referred to those particular seats as *perverts' row*. To the left, there were over a dozen champagne rooms where the girls would bare it all for their customers. On the right, there were pool tables where the patrons could unwind with a game. Towards the back of the club, there was a large bar where half naked all female waitresses and bartenders served and mixed drinks, and collected big tips, especially the *body shot girls*. The dressing rooms for the girls were located near the bar, behind a door marked "Staff." The dressing rooms led onto the stages. Lastly, there was a hallway that branched out from the kitchen leading to Fernando Romano's private office and his manager's office. The manager used the office to book the shows and girls on a daily basis, while Fernando used his office for private business.

Shawna turned into the parking lot of The Lucky Dollar at the end of Eighth Street and parked her red Corvette towards the back of the lot. Her long feathered yellow hair shone in the sun and her sunglasses gave her a mysterious look as she seemed to glide across the baked white concrete parking lot in her yellow stilettos. She approached the white steel rear door of the building and knocked twice, paused five seconds and knocked rapidly three more times. The lock made a clattering noise and the latch turned. Shawna stepped back two paces, the door swung open and there stood Fernando Romano, with two bodyguards. Fernando looked at Shawna and smiled. "There's my girl," he said. Shawna smiled back and entered the strip club with a walk that commanded every kind of attention.

Fernando Romano was an arrogant and intelligent man. He was fluent in four languages, giving him an edge in his dealings with other syndicate bosses. He was head of the Romano crime family and would kill anyone that stood in his way. Unlike Marcus Romano, Fernando was much shorter in stature. He sported yellow tinted glasses at all times and smoked hand rolled Cuban cigars. Fernando wore various gold rings on three fingers on his right hand, including the same crystal skull ring as Cornelius, John and Charlie. However, Fernando was missing his pinky finger that had been cut off years ago. He dressed impeccably at all times in a three-piece suit and proclaimed himself the king of San Martino.

"Where's my money?" Fernando asked as he followed Shawna.

"One thing at a time, suga'," Shawna replied.

First, Shawna stopped at the bar and picked up a martini. She waved hello to her friends and sauntered to the back dressing rooms. Shawna had her own room. It was the very last door on the right, the one with the big yellow star. She entered and threw her leather bag on the couch. She sat down and took off her high heels. Fernando sat down beside her and crossed his arms. "I'm still waiting for my money," he said.

"You certainly are, suga'."

"Do we have to play these games every time?"

"Only when there's money involved, suga'."

"Where is it?"

"Where's what?

"The money that Cornelius promised me?"

"What money is that, suga'?"

"You know what I'm talking about. I want my portion of John and Charlie's heist money that Cornelius promised me."

Shawna finished her martini and rose from the couch with her leather bag. She walked behind the three-panel room divider and started to undress. "Oh, that lil' ol' money," she said.

Fernando rose from the couch and crossed his arms. "Yeah, that money. Where is it?" he asked again impatiently.

Shawna finished dressing and came out from behind the privacy divider wearing a long red see through robe trimmed with ostrich feathers. Underneath she had slipped on a red bra studded in jewels and a red miniskirt over a red garter belt and white fence net hosiery. Shawna approached Fernando in her red stilettos and pressed her large chest up against him as she reached over, opened her leather bag and gave him a manila envelope. "That's it," she said.

"That's it? Cornelius, he promised me three hundred thousand," Fernando said. He tore open the envelope, thumbing through the money and quickly added up the amount. "There's only fifty thousand dollars here. Where's the rest?"

Shawna placed her fingers under Fernando's chin and gently nudged his head upwards: "My eyes are up here and that's all there was, suga'!"

"What do you mean that's all there was, suga'?"

"That's all Cornelius left me after the sheriff killed him and took the money."

"Fuck! Shawna, you wouldn't be lying to me, would you?"

Shawna, scratched the back of Fernando's neck with her fingernails and kissed him on the lips. "Who me? I wouldn't lie to you, suga'," she whispered breathlessly.

Fernando sat on the couch and dragged Shawna down with him sitting her on his lap. "Now wait just a minute. You're telling me that this is all Cornelius he left before he died?"

Shawna wriggled around on Fernando's lap. "Are you getting old or somethin'? Hard of hearing? Definitely hard!" she said.

Fernando suddenly rose from the couch, nearly knocking Shawna over. "What am I gonna do with you?" He said as he adjusted his pants.

"Suga', you know I'm your best girl. Now, let me go out there and make you some money."

Shawna fixed her outfit and kissed Fernando aggressively on the lips leaving him speechless. She exited her dressing room and took the door that led to the main stage. The disc jockey started the music and called her name. The audience of male watchers clapped and hooted. Shawna seductively walked out onto the stage, grabbed the pole and started her act.

Fernando sat at the bar and a half naked female bartender handed him a beer. He began to watch the show. A bouncer with an attitude approached him and tapped him on the shoulder. Fernando turned his head. "What? *Cosa vuoi?*" He asked.

The large bouncer leaned over and whispered into Fernando's ear. "Charlie and Marcus are here."

Fernando put his beer down on the counter and followed the bouncer out of the bar area, through the kitchen, down the hall to the offices where Charlie and Marcus were waiting. Fernando greeted the two men and the three sat down around the big office desk. Fernando waved the bouncer off and said: "It's about time you two showed up. What news do you bring me?"

"I want to spring John," Charlie said.

"Before we go anywhere, where's my money?" Fernando asked.

"It's in my car," Marcus replied.

"Marcus, I knew I could trust family," Fernando said. "How much?"

"There's around a hundred thousand in a box, plus all of the merchandise we brought back in John's truck, before blowing the joint sky-high," Charlie said.

"Speaking of which, you'll have to destroy the truck and dirt bike," Marcus said.

Fernando leaned back in his leather chair, took a deep pull from his Cuban cigar and began tallying up numbers in his head. He leaned forward over the desk and said: "We'll take care of the vehicles later. You know, we didn't make much with this little venture in Lancaster Falls and now you want me to invest more money and time in getting John back. Let him rot."

"We need him," Charlie said. "The mining company is the perfect front for our operation and expansion."

Fernando shook his head and mashed his cigar in the crystal ashtray. "You're asking a lot, Charlie. I know he's your friend, but this has gotten out of hand. However, I do agree. We need Tennessee. It's the perfect launching point to go north. Tell me what you have in mind."

"The feds are shipping him out with Lisa Leblanc, a local who became romantically involved with Cornelius. I'll have to check with my sources for the exact time and day."

"When the feds transport him is when we'll make our move," Marcus interjected.

Fernando rose from his chair and stuck a match. He inhaled the smoke from his hand rolled Cuban cigar and grinned. "You can go, Charlie. Marcus, stay here. I want to talk to you."

Charlie rose from his chair and left. Marcus looked at Fernando.

"Marcus, I want you to go with Charlie and keep an eye on him and John. They screwed up looking for the heist money. Cornelius, he told me everything that was going on."

Marcus rose from the chair. "I know," he said.

"And I'm going to give you some of my best men for this job."

"What about the Bulldog?"

"I'll see if I can't get a hold of him. Last time I heard he was in Nevada."

"Sounds fine with me."

The two men shook hands.

"Now go out there and say hello to Shawna," Fernando said.

Marcus smiled and left the office.

When the strip club closed, Shawna left for her condominium in downtown San Martino. She parked her Corvette in the underground parking lot and popped the trunk. She removed a large suitcase, locked her car, boarded the elevator and rode it to her apartment on the tenth floor. Shawna unlocked the door and entered her two-bedroom suite. Her condo was oversized and sat on the top floor directly across her neighbor's. Those were the only two apartments on the floor. She flung her suitcase onto the bed and sat down. Shawna reached over and unlocked the latches and smiled to herself. "Fifty thousand went to David for helping me find the money, fifty thousand for Fernando to get him off my back and two hundred thousand for me," she said. She closed the suitcase and shoved it under her bed. She exited her bedroom and went straight for the liquor cabinet. She poured herself a whiskey and cola, sat down on the couch and put her feet up. She began to sip her drink when a knock came on the front door. Shawna rose from the couch, placed her drink down on the coffee table and approached the door. She peered through the peephole but saw no one. She opened the door and looked both ways. There was no one in either direction. She was about to close the door when she noticed a folded piece of paper on the floor. She bent down and grabbed the paper. She unfolded it and read: *I want my diamonds back.*

Shawna closed the door and locked it. She returned to her couch, struck a match and lit the paper on fire. She lit a cigarette with the burning paper. Pieces of ash floated away and she dropped the remains of the paper into the crystal ashtray. Shawna grabbed her glass and stared at the burning paper as she drank her troubles away.

# 59

Sheriff Yates walked into the police station and hung his hat on the coatrack near the door. He greeted Beth and walked across the hardwood floor to his office where he found Bonnie and Peter waiting for him. The two deputies greeted the sheriff. Yates struck a match and lit a cigar. "I see you two have files. What do you have for me?" he asked.

Peter handed a file to Yates and began: "The bloodstain on the dress shirt from the garbage dumpster at the Rusty Mule matches foreman Nathaniel Thompson's blood type."

Yates looked over the file. "Finally, a break," he said.

"It's too bad we can't confirm that it's actually Charlie's dress shirt though," Peter said.

"Finding the dress shirt stained with Thompson's blood type in Charlie's garbage dumpster at the bar he owns is something at least," Yates said.

"There's one more thing, sir," Peter said.

Bonnie handed another file to Yates. "The gun that you found amongst the debris of the Rusty Mule parking lot matches the bullet that we found on the remains of James J. Thomas at the mine," she said.

"You know what that means, sir," Peter said.

"It means my hunch was right. Dwight Rhodes killed James J. Thomas all those years ago in the mine over the heist money. But when Dwight killed James, Dwight couldn't find the heist money anywhere and wound up leaving the state empty-handed and started a new life in Florida.," Yates said.

"It's hard to believe the Rhodes family didn't dispose of the gun," Bonnie said.

"You can never tell what people may do," Yates said. "What remains a mystery is how Cornelius found the money."

"Shawna," Bonnie said. "It had to have been her."

"Those two were a regular Bonnie & Clyde," Peter said. "No offense."

"None taken," Bonnie said.

Yates took a pull from his cigar and leaned forward in his leather chair. "But how did she come across the information. You can't tell me she went digging for it herself. She doesn't strike me as someone who does manual labor."

"Maybe she seduced someone to help?" Bonnie said.

"Or paid someone?" Peter added.

"Either scenario wouldn't surprise me in the least, but I think Bonnie is on the right track," Yates said. "Do you have the information on the Romanos?"

"Yes, sir. The largest male is Marcus Romano," Peter said. "All the others are six feet and under."

"So, he must've been the one who helped Charlie at Shawna's house and the one who helped Charlie to escape," Bonnie said.

"The one driving the black GTO," Yates said.

"We still haven't found the remains of Raymond Moore's body," Bonnie said.

"And who killed Ben Stevens?" Peter added.

"Those two questions are left unanswered, but as far as Ben Stevens goes, I'm sure it was Cornelius with Shawna's help, which would explain Shawna's favorite lipstick brand being smudged on his shirt," Yates said.

"She could've picked him up at the Rusty Mule, gotten him drunk and brought him out to the cabin where Cornelius was waiting for him," Bonnie said.

"That's a very good observation and you're probably right on the money with it," Yates said.

"Do you think we'll ever find Raymond Moore's body parts?" Peter asked.

"I'm sure the body parts of Raymond Moore will turn up," Yates said as he tapped the cigar ash into the crystal ashtray. "Well, with John and Lisa being shipped out soon, its case closed for now. The heist money has been found and the drug operation has been closed."

"Do you know when they'll be leaving us?" Peter asked.

"No, not yet," Yates said even though he already knew when the prisoner transfer would take place. He was keeping the day and time a secret over concerns that the prisoner vehicle carrying John would be ambushed and John would be set free. It's not that he did not trust his deputies, he only wanted as few people to know as possible.

"You'll let us know then?" Peter asked.

"I will, yes," Yate said and then changed the subject. "Peter, I want you to know that you've been a great help to us despite the conflict of interest. Can you keep a level head and continue?" Yates asked.

"I think he can. Pete's good people," Bonnie said.

"Okay, we'll keep you in the loop," Yates said.

"How's the business going now that your pa is not there?" Bonnie asked.

"It's going well. I have a good man running things for now. After that, I'm not sure what I'll do. Take it one day at a time, I guess," Peter replied.

"I don't have to tell you, Peter, if you hear anything about your father, you have to let me or Bonnie know," Yates said.

"I know, sir, and I promise I will," Peter said.

Yates rose from his leather chair. "That will be all for now," he said. He walked over to the window puffing on his cigar and stared at the statue of the Confederate soldier directly across from the police station in the town's square. Yates watched the children with their mothers under the statue and thought about the events that had unfolded over the past week.

Peter left the office while Bonnie approached Yates and stood beside him. "What're we looking at?" she asked.

"You know this isn't over," Yates said.

"I had a feeling it wouldn't be, otherwise you wouldn't have said what you did to Peter."

"Charlie and the Romanos will be back. You can bet your life on it. I didn't say that to Peter, though. I don't want to worry him. He's been through enough already."

"What about John?"

"John's the wildcard. There's enough evidence to convict him, but it's what Charlie and the Romanos may do that worries me," Yates said.

"And Shawna. Don't forget her," Bonnie said.

"Like I said before, I'm sure she's involved in Ben Stevens' death and she still has her house here, so I know she'll be back," Yates said.

"We'll get her!" Bonnie exclaimed.

"She's a slippery one."

"And Joshua and Doug?" Bonnie asked.

"We'll watch those two as well," Yates said as he took a pull on his cigar. "In the meantime, keep your ear to the ground."

*Here ends the first part of our story. Join Sheriff Yates, Bonnie and Peter as they thwart John, Charlie, Shawna, the Bulldog and the Romanos in the second and concluding part to our yarn.*

www.ingramcontent.com/pod-product-compliance
Lightning Source LLC
Chambersburg PA
CBHW060247100726

47907CB00003B/796